WINDOW
SHOPPING

Also by Tessa Bailey

Big Shots
Fangirl Down
The Au Pair Affair

Vine Mess
Secretly Yours
Unfortunately Yours

Bellinger Sisters
It Happened One Summer
Hook, Line, and Sinker

Hot & Hammered
Fix Her Up
Love Her or Lose Her
Tools of Engagement

The Academy
Disorderly Conduct
Indecent Exposure
Disturbing His Peace

Broke and Beautiful
Chase Me
Need Me
Make Me

Romancing the Clarksons
Too Hot to Handle
Too Wild to Tame
Too Hard to Forget
Too Beautiful to Break

Made in Jersey
Crashed Out
Rough Rhythm
Thrown Down
Worked Up
Wound Tight

Crossing the Line
Risking It All
Up in Smoke
Boiling Point
Raw Redemption

The Girl Series
Getaway Girl
Runaway Girl

Line of Duty
Protecting What's His
Protecting What's Theirs (novella)
His Risk to Take
Officer Off Limits
Asking for Trouble
Staking His Claim

Serve
Owned by Fate
Exposed by Fate
Driven by Fate

Beach Kingdom
Mouth to Mouth
Heat Stroke
Sink or Swim

Standalone Books
Unfixable
Baiting the Maid of Honor
Off Base
Captivated
My Killer Vacation
Happenstance
Wreck the Halls

WINDOW SHOPPING

A Novel

TESSA BAILEY

AVON

An Imprint of HarperCollinsPublishers

WINDOW SHOPPING. Copyright © 2021 by Tessa Bailey. All rights reserved. Printed in the United States of America. No part of this book may be used or reproduced in any manner whatsoever without written permission except in the case of brief quotations embodied in critical articles and reviews. For information, address HarperCollins Publishers, 195 Broadway, New York, NY 10007.

HarperCollins books may be purchased for educational, business, or sales promotional use. For information, please email the Special Markets Department at SPsales@harpercollins.com.

Originally published as *Window Shopping* in the United States in 2021 by Tessa Bailey.

FIRST AVON TRADE EDITION PUBLISHED 2024.

Interior text design by Diahann Sturge-Campbell

Christmas city street © gyoganjin/Shutterstock
Bow tie © Bogdan/Stock.Adobe.com

Library of Congress Cataloging-in-Publication Data has been applied for.

ISBN 978-0-06-333008-5
ISBN 978-0-06-333005-4 (library hardcover)

24 25 26 27 28 LBC 5 4 3 2 1

For Patricia
Since this is your favorite.

WINDOW SHOPPING

Chapter 1
Stella

Normally, I avoid Fifth Avenue. But not today. I'll never be able to explain why I deviated from my route and veered down the bustling thoroughfare of high-end shopping.

If I were a girl who believed in magic, I would say there was a tingle of Christmas magic in the air that propelled me east, carrying me through the shopper's paradise on a wintery gust of wind. Or I would say Santa's elves were nipping at my heels, urging me to this exact spot where I'm now standing transfixed by the giant display window outside Vivant. But magic is for suckers and children, so that can't be it. Maybe I was just ready to look again.

A pedestrian tries to overtake the slow walker in front of them and doesn't quite make it in time before reaching where I stand, a roadblock dressed in black and severely lacking in anything resembling holiday spirit, thus knocking into me at full speed with his shoulder.

I bite down on my tongue to quell the words *NEEDLE DICK* that want to come flying out of my mouth like darts toward a bull's-eye. What would Dr. Skinner tell me? *Don't trade emotional currency with strangers. You will never get a refund.* Skinner might have smelled like moldy granola, but she did have some good advice from time to time. Following that counsel is how—in the twist of the century—I got released from Bedford Hills Correctional early for exemplary behavior.

If I was in one of my many mandatory counseling sessions right now, my former beatnik shrink would tell me to take myself out of this situation that has potential to irritate me.

Galled to find out therapy actually worked, I step out of the flow of foot traffic, bringing myself inches away from the display window. As I look up at it, my nose wrinkles of its own accord and not because the combined scents of hot roasted nuts and boiling hot dog water are so prevalent on this block. But because I can't for the life of me figure out what the window dresser was going for here.

On the other side of the glass, an assembly line has been re-created. Penguins are dressed in little red, white-fur-trimmed jumpsuits and they are putting toys together as they come down the trundling rubber belt. Of course, the penguins are mechanical, so they only complete one awkward swivel, then revert to their original position, their expressions frozen in a sort of maniacal glee. It's a scene straight out of a child's nightmare. The only way it could be worse would involve penguins getting maimed by machinery. A little sign would unfurl above the crime scene reading IT HAS BEEN ZERO DAYS SINCE OUR LAST ACCIDENT.

My mouth twitches, reflecting back at me from the smudge-proof glass.

"Uh-oh," says a resonant timbre to my left. "See, I was going to mind my business and keep moving, but you went ahead and smiled. Now I have to know what you're thinking."

"That wasn't a smile," I blurt automatically, outraged that someone thinks they caught me—*me?*—engaging in anything but hostile judgy-ness. Not likely. But my words trail off when I lay eyes on my accuser.

What in the fresh living hell?

I'm not rendered speechless by many things, but this giant man in a candy-cane bow tie and a beaming smile makes me wonder if I'm hallucinating. No one is shoulder bumping this dude. They couldn't reach that high. Not to mention, he has completely shifted the flow of foot traffic—and when he realizes he's making himself an obstacle, this very tall, very broad-chested stranger *hops* out of the sidewalk intersection with a few *sorry, ma'ams* and *apologies, sirs.*

In his hand, he's holding a blue-and-white paper coffee cup, his long, thick fingers stretching the entire distance around. Deep brown hair with a slight curl to it waves in the wind. I'd put his age at thirty-two, give or take a year. He's drenched in a practiced kind of success and that takes time to acquire. His suit is impeccable. Navy blue, complete with a crisp white pocket square. Nary a wrinkle. But the most remarkable thing about him is those smile lines. They bracket his mouth, they fan out from the corners of his eyes. They are deep and worn-in like a pair of jeans that have been washed seven hundred times.

This man smiles constantly.

I hate him.

"If that wasn't a smile, what was it?" Somehow he takes a sip of his coffee without dimming the wattage of his smile. "A twitch or something? My uncle Hank had one of those. Used to spill beer all over Aunt Edna's carpet, thanks to that tic. One day she got so mad about it, she walloped him over the head with a colander and the damn twitch went away." He gestures with his cup. "Like flipping off a light switch. After that, he just spilled beer for the tradition of it." He pauses. "Aunt Edna eventually remarried."

Okay. *Am* I hallucinating?

I scan the immediate area for maimed penguins or some other sign that I've gone around the bend. All is well. As normal as New York City can be, which is to say there are three people fighting over one cab, the strains of a saxophone emanate mysteriously from the ether and a sparkly pink wig lies forgotten in the gutter. Nothing that would be considered unusual, though. If I'm not hallucinating, why has this man stopped to tell me a story about his relatives? I'm not what one would refer to as *approachable*. In fact, I'm fluent in Fuck Off. Hopefully he speaks it, too. Or at least knows how to read body language.

Looking him square in the eye, I shove my knockoff AirPods into my ears and go back to staring up at the would-be penguin crime scene.

There. Done.

I'm not really seeing the penguins, though. I can't help but marvel over the man's and my reflections standing side by side. He's easily six foot four, robust, in a ten-thousand-dollar suit. I'm a full foot shorter, dressed in a black puffer jacket and thick, matching tights, second- or third-hand boots of which the sole is rapidly coming loose from the rest of the shoe. My busted fuchsia messenger bag is the only pop of color on my entire person and that's because it was the cheapest I could find at Goodwill. My thick black hair has been chopped unprofessionally just below my shoulders and cloaks a pale face, its expression reading Do Not Disturb.

We are the most opposite of opposites. Thank *God*.

Why is he still standing there, smiling into his coffee like he doesn't have a single care in the world? My rudeness hasn't even registered. Has my talent for avoidance faded while in the slammer? Losing my superpower would just be the icing on the shit cake of the past few years.

Another full minute passes and he's still there, standing a couple feet away, facing the window like me. Tilting his head to the right in consideration of the penguins. I could just leave. Continue on my way downtown until I reach the rent-controlled apartment in Chelsea I'm subletting from my uncle while he's shacked up in Queens with girlfriend du jour. There is nothing keeping me in front of this artistic monstrosity. But my feet won't seem to move. And why should they? I was here first.

I pop out my left earbud. "Is there something I can help you with?"

"Oh, me?" A dimple appears on his cheek. "I was just waiting for your song to be over."

There is no music playing, but I'm obviously not going to tell him that.

"Why?" I ask, jerkily removing the second bud and shoving both of them back into my jacket pocket. "Do you have another pointless story to tell me?"

"Aw, hell." His eyes are green. And they twinkle in a way that reminds me of fairy lights. "I've got *thousands* of pointless stories to tell you."

My smile is saccharine. "One was more than enough."

"All right," he draws out, tossing back the remainder of his coffee. "But after the beer-spilling era, Aunt Edna eloped with a rodeo clown named Tonto. Guess you'll never know about it."

"Devastating."

"Sure was. Let's just say the bull took *him* by the horns, instead of the other way around." He gives a full body shiver. "All he left behind for Edna was a half-used face-painting kit and some floppy shoes. She patched things up with Uncle Hank about a year later. Now they go yard-sale hopping on Sunday mornings."

I'm pretty sure my jaw is hanging down at my knees. "Is this like a strange kink? Instead of flashing people, you just go around accosting people with bizarre tales?"

"Well, it's too cold to flash people in December. My options are limited."

He grins at me. Doesn't temper it at all. He's all smile lines and warm eyes.

Woefully handsome. Maybe even dapper.

And the most disturbing thing happens. Something I couldn't have predicted in a hundred million years. The flip-flop in my stomach must be a sign of the apocalypse. The end of days is nigh. It has never flipped nor flopped for anything but Kraft macaroni and cheese. I can't be having a reaction to this man. An *attraction* reaction.

"I'm going to go now," I say, my tone a little off.

For the first time since he appeared, that smile is gone. A hint of panic gusts through the green of his eyes just momentarily, before he bows his head. He looks down at the ground for a second, as if trying to regroup, then lifts his head to pin me with a fresh grin. "I did have a purpose for stopping, if you don't mind humoring me just a while longer." He dips his chin in the direction of the window. "I'm curious what you make of all this."

"You're referring to Penguin Chernobyl?"

His laugh booms down the block, stopping shoppers and looky-loos in their tracks. The sound of it reminds me of hot chocolate in front of a fire in Bruce Wayne's mansion. It's rich and hearty and thick with quality. "Yes, I suppose that's what I'm referring to."

I raise an eyebrow. "You want to know what *I* think about it?"

My skepticism gives him pause, one corner of his mouth turning down. "Yes. I do."

"Do you work at Vivant?"

He shrugs one of those strapping shoulders. "In a manner of speaking."

I narrow my gaze and give him another once-over. He definitely works in management. Maybe one of the upper offices. His gratingly jovial disposition makes me think he works in PR. Perhaps this entire conversation is his way of testing a new *meet the consumers* initiative. There is a part of me that really wants to ask, but I refuse to seem interested just because of that cataclysmic flop in my stomach earlier.

"Fine, whatever," I mutter, wrapping my gloved hands around the cross strap of my messenger bag, stomping my feet for warmth as I turn to face the window again. "I think it's more likely to drive shoppers away from the store than bring them in. No one wants to think of their Christmas gifts being put together on an assembly line. It's too impersonal. It's a reminder that we're all just trapped in a pattern of consumerism and we'll never escape it. The pattern will just keep rolling and rolling like that conveyor belt. People want to pick out something for their loved ones that they believe is unique. One of a kind. Not something produced in a factory."

Oh, now I'm on a roll. A few passersby have even stopped to listen to my spiel and normally that would derail me, clam me up, but window dressing was my dream job once upon a time. Before my life was placed on hold, I took three years of online college courses that focused primarily on fashion merchandising and marketing. I'd hoped to one day style window displays. It's one of the only things I've ever been passionate about. It's why I usually find it too painful to walk down Fifth Avenue, reminded of how badly I messed up.

Pedestrians are still paused around us, waiting to hear what I'm going to say. And, hey. I'm never going to see any of these people again, especially Bow Tie, so why not give my opinion? It's been a really long time since someone besides Dr. Skinner asked for it and she was only doing her job.

"That brings me to the penguins." I make the mistake of glancing over at Bow Tie and almost lose my train of thought. He can't be half as interested in my opinion as he looks. Can he? The man doesn't even look like he's breathing. "And . . . you know. The average life span of a penguin is like, thirteen years, so technically this is child labor. Not a good look."

He studies the window as if seeing it for the first time. "You're right. It's awful." He shakes his head. "One of those penguins is seconds from losing a flipper."

I jolt a little at the way he mimics my thoughts, but hide it well by clearing my throat.

And tucking hair behind my ear, over and over again. Unnecessarily.

"Are you an artist?" he asks. "Have you window-dressed before?"

I wish. God, I wish. I never got that far.

"No, I'm just critical."

He huffs a small laugh, his eyes somehow shrewd and thoughtful and welcoming at the same time. In that moment, I am absolutely certain there is something unique about this man. A distinctiveness. Layers. And I really wish I would have just walked away when I had the chance. He's maneuvered me to a place where I have a voice and don't feel invisible. I didn't see it coming. Did he do it purposely? If so, why would he take the time to do that? What did he sense about me that made him stop? What is even happening?

"How would you dress the window instead?"

Dammit.

Dammit.

I'm letting him pull me out of my anonymous solitude and it's so rude and presumptuous of him to do so, but I'm already halfway sunk into the quicksand. Plus, I have to answer. It's too tempting not to. Saying the words out loud is the closest I'll ever come to the real thing. A girl with a prison record is never going to decorate a store window at Vivant.

A line appears between his brows as if he's reading my thoughts. *Rude.*

"I wouldn't remind them they've come to the store to spend their money. I would remind them that buying presents is about . . . surprise. Surprise is priceless." I blow out a breath, white condensation billowing in the air in front of me. "That moment when a loved one takes the lid off a box and gasps. That's what we're in it for. There's a whole corner of TikTok dedicated to it."

Since being released from Bedford Hills, I've been finding comfort in watching people on the internet hear famous songs for the first time. Or their first time watching *Star Wars* or *Twilight*. I watch those videos and wonder if I'll ever be able to express emotions like that again. Just pow. No hesitating. Without toning the feelings down or worrying that if I get too emotional, my dam will break and everything will just come pouring out.

"We go out looking for a magical item, no idea what it is. If we see it, we'll know, but we rarely find it. So show them. Show shoppers the item that will shock their lover or sibling or mother and make them feel not only loved, but exciting as a human being. The keys to a moped, the perfect nude lipstick, a designer martini shaker. If this was my window, I'd . . . display the dress a woman would never buy for themself, but secretly wished they owned. And I'd make that dress a new lifestyle. A new start. Their desired result is on the other side of the window."

He nods for a moment, chewing on the inside of his cheek.

Then he turns slightly to look down the side of the building, which takes up an entire city block. "And what would you do with the other three windows?"

I blink up at him, not sure if he's calling me out for being an armchair expert or if he's genuinely curious. Somehow . . . I sense it's the latter. Sarcasm isn't his personality. Wait. How has he impressed his personality on me in the space of five? Ten minutes? How long have I been standing here talking to this man? "I should go—"

"You should apply," he says at the same time, chuckling over our verbal collision. "I have it on good authority that Vivant is looking for a new window dresser."

"Oh." I choke on the word, unable to keep the longing off my face when looking back at the window, imagining myself on the other side with a Vivant-sized budget. Four windows to design. All manner of materials and fabrics and baubles at my fingertips. And that is never, *ever* going to happen. My résumé has a giant employment gap between age twenty-one and twenty-five when I was serving time in Westchester. For a crime I do *not* deny committing. I can't even get hired at a diner, let alone at this upscale department store. "No. I . . . I'm not interested."

Bow Tie studies me closely. "Sure about that?"

"How is this your concern again?"

He tucks his tongue into the side of his cheek and winks at me—and *oh my God*, it happens again. That weightless turnover beneath my rib cage. Maybe I've contracted some kind of disease.

It has been a really long time since I dated or had a boyfriend, but I remember my type. This guy is not it. There is a *pleat* in his dress pants. He's wearing a bow tie and a grin and a piece of hair is now curling down the center of his forehead. The pads of my fingers definitely shouldn't be rubbing together, wondering what kind of texture that lock of hair would be. Or what his reaction would be if I curled it around my knuckle slowly.

I look down quickly before whatever is happening inside me plays out on my face. "All right, I think we're done here." With a restless scratch to the back of my neck, I skirt around him, reentering the flow of sidewalk traffic.

Just before I'm completely out of earshot, he calls, "There's an application on the website. Can't hurt to give it a look-see."

I don't stop walking until I'm inside my apartment. Pacing to the very corner of the room, I toe off my boots, then I doff my jacket, bundle the garment up and place it on top of the boots. Next, my earbuds. Out of the way. Neat. A memory catches me off guard from just about a month ago—my parents watching me perform this habit from across the dining room, exchanging a nervous glance with each other. Like they weren't sure who exactly they'd allowed into their home.

I bounce on the sore soles of my feet to clear my thoughts, moving to the radiator to make sure heat is coming out. During the long walk to Chelsea, I told myself my heart was pounding because of the brisk pace I set, but it still hasn't stopped. The organ continues to drum unsteadily as I sit down on the edge of my bed. Gradually, my gaze meanders over to the ancient laptop left behind by my uncle. I shake my head, refusing to entertain the notion of filling out an application for a job I am not qualified for. Or even if I am *slightly* eligible to dress windows, three years of online courses with a focus on fashion merchandising will be wildly eclipsed by four years in lockup.

My right leg bounces up and down.

Why am I so itchy?

I last another five minutes before lunging to my feet with a curse of Bow Tie's existence, and I start hunting through drawers for the laptop charger. What's the worst that can happen? I submit the application and they never respond?

No, that's what *will* happen. I'm an ex-convict.

But for some crazy reason, I send it anyway.

I'll never hear back.

Chapter 2
Aiden

I sit down at my desk and clap my hands. "It's going to be a good day."

On the other side of the office, my assistant's fingers pause in the act of typing out God knows what at two hundred miles an hour. "And what exactly is your basis for that theory?" asks Leland over the top of his wire-rim glasses. "It's a Monday and it's *snowing*."

"Both of those things are the sign of a clean slate. It's like we've got a fresh spiral notebook from the drugstore and this time we're going to use good handwriting the whole way through. Not just on the first page."

Leland stares through the floor-to-ceiling window at the big, chunky flakes falling from the sky down onto Fifth. "The extra-wintery vibe is a reminder that I haven't done any shopping and there's only twelve days until Christmas. I'm never going to make it in time."

"You always make it in time," I reassure him.

He picks up a ballpoint pen and uses his forehead to click it open. Closed. Open. "I bet you have all of your shopping done. Wrapped. Thoughtfully written cards attached."

"Everyone knows you don't wrap presents until the twenty-third of December."

"I don't know that." Curious, he stops clicking and arches a cautious ginger eyebrow. "Why do you wait?"

Realizing I forgot to take off my overcoat, I stand up and cross to the rack by the door, draping it over the top hook so the hem won't brush the floor. Snow falls from the collar and melts onto the gray carpet, leaving little wet spots behind. "Let's say you bought your aunt a green scarf. You bought it assuming she didn't already have one. But you have to leave yourself a cushion in case she shows up wearing one three days before Christmas. Or out of the blue she might say, 'I hate green scarves. I hope no one ever buys me one.'"

Leland sputters. "Now, what are the odds of that?"

I hold up my hands. "You want to wrap presents pre-twenty-third and gamble with Scotch tape, that's up to you. You just better hope my theory doesn't *stick*."

Slowly, my assistant turns back to his computer, muttering, "You asked. You know better than to ask," to himself.

I chuckle under my breath and tap a key to wake up my computer. Leland is twenty-nine—three years younger than me—but he has the disposition of a cranky senior citizen and the pessimism of Eeyore. That's one of the reasons I hired him five years ago. Hell, someone needs to balance me out. He also brings a mean homemade peach habanero salsa to company parties and that is a quality that cannot be underestimated.

My calendar alerts pop up on the screen, causing an odd pinch in my chest.

Same odd pinch I had in my chest on Friday during that impromptu conversation outside the store. How . . . odd. Rubbing at the spot with a knuckle, I hide the calendar alert that reads NOON INTERVIEWS WITH WINDOW DRESSER APPLICANTS and open the drive file I share with Leland. There are sixteen applications inside. Is one of them her?

"Before you ask, all the applicants have been vetted," Leland says without looking up from his computer. "In the interest of saving time, I weeded it down to the ones that have potential. Excluded anyone who used all caps or used the word *thrive* in their cover letter. That word is *literally* draining in and of itself. My personal pick is Vivian Blake, former Bergdorf's window dresser. She was responsible for the elf runway show design of 2019. Iconic."

Leland is right. That window beat the band.

Santa's little helpers in bustiers and wigs? Tends to stick out in one's memory.

I definitely never have nightmares about one of them breaking through the glass and chasing me down the avenue waving an ice pick heel.

"Did anyone else stand out?"

I'm not even sure why I ask. There's nothing Leland could say that would make me positive one of these applications belongs to her. Like a bozo, I didn't get her name. I didn't get any information about her whatsoever, except for the fact that she's a little standoffish and a whole lot of pretty. Insightful about window design, too, and that's what counts. That's why I encouraged her to apply.

Not because I want to see her again.

Ignoring the twist south of my throat, I click through the applications, positive that I'll somehow know which one belongs to her. I just will. There's going to be some defining characteristic. Past work experience in an edgy coffee shop/gamer lounge or college spent abroad somewhere like Bruges or Berlin.

Nothing doing. All of these applications are too straightforward. Impressive in a way that I'm used to seeing as general manager of Vivant. Some of these hopefuls are even overqualified. None of them are her, though. I would just . . . know.

I lean back in my chair, calling myself nine kinds of ridiculous for panicking. This is a girl I met and spoke with once and she didn't even like me. I lost count of the times she rolled her eyes up into those thick black bangs or tried to end our conversation prematurely.

But before I ever stopped to engage her, I saw that half smile reflected in the window and I couldn't seem to quit trying to get it back on her face. To make her lips tick up again.

Her half smile was beautiful. It stopped me dead in my tracks.

And at the end of it all, I didn't even ask her name.

Now I have to rely on the far-off chance that she applied to dress windows at Vivant. That's a riskier gamble than wrapping presents before December twenty-third. For all I know, she has a job. Or she's just visiting New York City. I had a few bourbons too many over the weekend coming up with possibilities. Which, again, is ridiculous. I met her one time.

Yet her face is clear as day in my head.

I can remember it in finer detail than my childhood bedroom in Tennessee.

The big, blue walnut-shaped eyes rimmed in black makeup. The gentle slope of her brows, the deep crease running down between her nose and her upper lip. That series of freckles along her lower right jawline. The *go away* vibrations coming off of her in waves.

And the certainty she inspired in me that . . . she didn't really want me to go. That she was feeling kind of lonely and wistful and just needed someone to stand beside her for a spell.

I've been there. I recognize the signs in a person.

Those signs in someone else don't usually make my stomach trade places with my lungs, however. Or inspire me to miss a meeting so I can try and help. Try and figure her out.

"I mean, there were a couple of standouts in the terrible department. Like the first round of an *American Idol* competition?" He pauses for drama. "This one girl had an honest-to-God *prison* record."

A jolt goes through me, snapping my spine straight.

Prison?

No.

But the hair on my arms is standing up and that's usually an indication that the universe is about to send me a challenge. Usually I get pumped when that electricity races up my skin, like a nerd before a pop quiz, but if this application connects to Go Away Girl, what am I going to do about it?

"What is her name?"

Leland rears back a little, his fingers continuing to fly over the wireless keyboard. "Uh, I don't recall. Why do you ask?"

I'm already rolling my chair closer to my desk, hand on the mouse. It's not my first flicker of optimism that I might get to see her again—good thoughts equal good things—but this time I have an actual lead. "What did you do with the applications that didn't make the cut?"

My assistant doesn't answer right away, and when I glance over, he's got a slight wince on his face. "Uh, well . . . they're in a sub-folder marked Utter Rejects."

I give a low whistle. "How someone so cold can craft such a spicy salsa is a mystery."

"It's the habanero juice and pickled—"

"I don't want to know, man, I just want to eat it."

Leland is shifting in his chair, as if still feeling guilty for giving the file such a harsh name. While I would like to alleviate that guilt, I find I'm a little protective over the blue-eyed girl who doesn't even like me and her information might be in this folder, so unfortunately Leland will have to stew a spell. "I'm bringing some of my salsa to the Christmas party next week," he ventures. "A whole jumbo Tupperware container of the stuff."

"I sure hope so. It's a requirement of your employment." I flash him a quick grin to let him know I'm joking (mostly), but my smile drops when I locate the folder and click. Because I see the name Stella Schmidt and somehow I just know that's her.

She's a Stella.

Before I go any further, I remind myself of something very important. I'm not going to get her phone number off this application and use it. That's creepier than a daddy longlegs spider and I already made her talk to me longer than she wanted to outside the store.

Now that I've assured myself that this situation will remain ethical, I have the Main Dilemma. If Stella Schmidt is, in fact, the applicant with the prison record, I can't hire her. I can't even bring her in for an interview. Can I?

I might be the general manager of Vivant but I answer to a board of tough buzzards, one of whom is my father. Another of whom is my grandmother. And they aren't even in good moods on the Friday before a three-day weekend.

If I don't bring Stella in for an interview, I'll never see her again.

But I can't call her in here *just* to ask her out.

That would elevate me from a daddy longlegs to a hairy tarantula.

"You look conflicted, Mr. Cook."

Leland never calls me anything but Aiden. "You can drop the formalities. I'm not going to lecture you about the file name."

"Oh, thank God." He lets out a hoot and deflates, sending his chair back into the file cabinet with a rattle. "I was having flashbacks to my job interview where you said the one thing you'll never tolerate is unkindness. And I really shouldn't have labeled the file that way. No one is a reject. Everyone has ups and downs. That's all. We're all at different phases of our lives . . ."

Leland is still rambling, but my thoughts drown him out.

Everyone has ups and downs.

That's damn well right.

God knows I have.

When I took over as general manager of Vivant five years ago, I promised myself I would be fair in all things, no matter what it cost me. Before I arrived, decisions were based solely on the bottom line—and I'm not so idealistic that I believe profit margins aren't important in business. But there has to be a balance. *Everything* is a balance. For instance, Leland's pessimism balances out my optimism and keeps our office running somewhere in between.

If Stella is the one with the prison record and I *don't* interview her based solely on that, I'm not listening to my gut, which is telling me she deserves a shot at the position. I'm dismissing her because of the board of directors and their preconceived standards.

Not mine.

Lastly and perhaps selfishly, I want to see her again, and then there's only one way to do so the right way—and that's to give her a real shot at the job. Interview her with the same open mind

I interview everyone else. Being in prison shouldn't preclude her from a chance if she's served her time, right?

I'll worry about the fact that I'm not allowed to have romantic relationships with employees without filing documents with human resources another time.

Finally, I allow myself to scroll down.

Stella Schmidt. Based on her birthdate, she's twenty-five. Sheesh, that's young. I'm one and a half presidencies older than her, but okay. Moving on. Three years' worth of online courses in fashion merchandising and product marketing. All right. That's definitely something, even if she didn't graduate.

I stop when I reach the box asking if she's been convicted of a felony.

The answer is yes.

Under "more information," it simply says Bedford Hills Correctional from 2017-2021.

No further explanation. And I can almost see her stubbornly tight-lipped expression.

I spear my fingers through my hair. Jesus, she *just* got out. What the hell could she have done to get herself four years behind bars? The girl barely reached my shoulder. Not that height has anything to do with committing crimes. Unless she's one of those spies who has to carefully climb over a complicated series of green lasers protecting a giant diamond. Being small in stature might give someone an advantage in a situation like that.

I keep scrolling.

She didn't even put down a single reference.

Work with me, Stella.

Based on the application alone, it's a real stretch to call her in for an interview, but if I don't, it's going to be a pinwheel under my skin for a long time. *Balance. Find the balance.*

If Stella gets a second shot, so does everyone else.

"All right, Leland, here's what we're going to do. Call *everyone* in the no pile and set them up for interviews, too."

His jaw dangles down in the vicinity of his knees. "What? Even the musicians?"

"Even them."

It's much later when I start to regret this decision.

Past five o'clock. Everyone, including Leland, has gone home for the day. I'm on my thirty-first interview and I haven't had lunch, so my groaning stomach is drowning out the answers of the woman sitting across from me. Kimberly. She's one of the overqualified applicants. NYU graduate. Top of her class. Impeccably dressed, a gold cuff wrapped around her deep brown bicep. She answers everything correctly, but I don't get the same kick in my gut when we're discussing concepts for the window. Nor do I get it with the next hopeful—Jonathan from Minnesota, who is only in town for two weeks with his death metal band and thought maybe they could perform in one of the windows, like, "a conceptual thing or whatever." Or Lonnie, a former contestant on *Project Runway* who got voted off in one of the early rounds and insisted on me watching his highlight reel.

None of them make me *see* what they're describing. Especially Minnesota Jonathan.

And that's a problem.

Because Lonnie is my last meeting, besides Stella, and she's nowhere to be found. The row of chairs outside my office is empty for the first time since I started interviewing at noon, and I'm beginning to lose hope that she'll show.

I finish the interview with Lonnie, letting him know we'll be in touch, either way. Now I sit, drumming my fingers on the solid pine of my desk. Restlessly, I pull her application back up and look for hidden messages, of which there are obviously none. It would be ethical to call her and ask if she's coming, but it's not something I would do for any of the other applicants, so I force my hand away from the phone.

With a sigh loud enough to wake the dead, I roll away from my desk and stand, taking about ten times longer than usual to pack everything into my leather briefcase, just in case she's running late. I drop my phone and stoop down to get it—and that's when I see a flash of something in the gap between my desk and the floor.

Am I crazy or did something just move outside my office?

Quickly, I straighten to my full height, but find my doorway empty.

"Stella?" I call, grateful Leland isn't here to make a *Streetcar Named Desire* joke, because he's definitely the type.

Getting no response, I come around my desk and walk out onto the empty main floor just in time to hear the stairwell door open and close. Who is taking the stairs down from the tenth floor when there's a perfectly good elevator?

The universe sends me another one of those here-comes-a-challenge skin prickles and I start to jog in the direction that the person (or possible ghost) just disappeared. I yank open the door to the stairwell and listen for footsteps, hearing a quick patter of them below.

"Stella," I say again, my voice echoing off the concrete.

The footsteps stop abruptly. Several seconds pass.

"I changed my mind," she finally answers. "About doing the interview."

Oh boy. I forgot how much I like her voice. It's got a sweet, smooth tone to it and she probably hates it like hell. "You're allowed to change your mind," I say, weighing my options. I don't want her to leave. But I can't exactly barrel toward her in a stairwell that looks straight out of an M. Night Shyamalan film. "Wow. My office looks like the North Pole. It's lit up within an inch of its life. You'd have no idea we were sitting right on top of a portal to hell."

I hear an intake of breath that sounds suspiciously like a laugh, but I'm not getting my hopes up.

Damn. Too late. They're up.

"You might have mentioned you were the general manager when we met outside," she says with a hint of bite in her tone.

"If I'd done that, you would have been more diplomatic and less refreshingly honest."

"What a nice way of saying judgmental." She releases a slow huff. "No, I would have been exactly the same."

"You're right. You would have," I say to the girl I can't even see. "Can we go somewhere less soul-crushing to talk? I've got peppermint bark in my office with your name on it."

She groans. "I can practically *hear* the bow tie in your voice."

"It's a Mrs. Claus theme today. That woman doesn't get enough credit for holding down the fort." I know it's a risk, but I start to descend the staircase, slowly, like a serial killer. "Maybe we could spitball about a window dedicated to Santa's better half. What do you say?"

"I say you really can't be serious about interviewing me. *Hiring* me." There's a shuffling sound, like those black boots of hers on the concrete landing. Hell, she wore combat boots to a job interview. There's no way not to smile about that. "Look. Is this . . .

some kind of window dresser casting couch situation? If so, I'm going to knee you in the jewels as hard as possible, even if I have to get on a stepping stool to do it."

"And I would deserve that ambulance ride." I continue down another five steps, watching her shadow move on the stairwell below me. "That's not what this is."

"So what is it? You don't seem the type to play a joke this elaborate on someone, but then again, I've been away awhile." A beat passes. "Which you now know. Obviously."

The flutter of nerves in her tone makes me swallow. "Yeah." I round the bottom of the staircase and she comes into view, leaning against the cinder-block wall of the landing six steps lower than me. And there's no mistaking that she's the source of the chest tug I've been experiencing for the last few days. I'm like a metal detector beeping over a silver dollar.

Here it is. X marks the spot.

She might be wearing the same boots, but her clothes are different. Her dress is tight, black, long-sleeved, made of sweater material. Thick gray tights cover her legs. Legs I definitely shouldn't be checking out in a dark stairwell but can't seem to help doing. It's a shortish dress and those tights hug her thighs in a way that a priest couldn't ignore, let alone a man who hasn't had sex since . . . well, let's not put a date on it. Pre-pandemic, at least. No need to remind myself that I hadn't been intimate with anyone for a good while *before* that. Or that I'd taken a break from dating because women seemed to find my personality baffling.

Too unusual. Too *nice*.

And speaking of people who think I'm just a smile and a piece of neckwear—although this time, I can sense her questioning it, wondering if she's wrong—there's a folder in Stella's hand. Which she promptly hides behind her back.

Okay, then. Here we go.

I sit down on the top step, leaving her at the bottom, and her shoulders relax slightly. "Did you know my grandfather named this store Vivant because he wanted to impress a French lady named Camille? It didn't even work. Now here we are fifty years later. Stuck with it."

"Your family owns this store," she states slowly, clearly having no idea. "Wow. I guess it was a mistake to skim the About Us section of the website."

I wave that off. "Ah, it's mostly boring nonsense about tradition and quality."

Her head tilts to the right. "You seem like a guy who would value tradition."

"Oh, I do. It's just . . . my family hasn't always valued it. At least not in the way it's portrayed in their store windows." My fingers fly to my bow tie, adjusting it hastily, the back of my neck gathering like wool in water. I didn't mean to say that out loud. I'm supposed to be making her comfortable enough to do this interview, not bemoaning the pitfalls of being a Cook. Especially when it's clear this girl has had it a lot harder than me. "I'm just telling you about the legendary rejection of Camille and naming of Vivant as a way of saying . . . crazier things have happened than me interviewing someone with great ideas and a background in fashion merchandising. Even if we are conducting said interview in Lucifer's living room."

She scrutinizes me while turning that over in her mind.

"The way you're looking at me reminds me of those lasers that scan thumbprints in a spy movie. You know what I'm talking about?" Scenes from the film I watched last night play in my head and I slap my thigh. "I love a good spy movie. *Enemy of the State* might be my favorite. There's already high stakes and intrigue and espionage. Then they want to throw in Will Smith and Gene Hackman on top of it? Hell, I'll rent it twice."

Stella looks around as if she's just been teleported to the moon. "This might be the weirdest moment of my life and I've been trading corn bread for toothpaste and other assorted toiletries for the last four years."

My heart jumps up into my mouth at that.

I don't like thinking about her being locked up.

But she probably likes thinking about it a lot less, so I force myself to imagine it, what her day-to-day life must have been like, and I can't stop my frown.

The silence is ticking by.

She cocks her head. "Aren't you going to ask me what I did to get sentenced?"

Am I curious? As all get-out. As a prospective employer, I *should* be asking. Perhaps selfishly, I don't want to be predictable to her, though. And I don't want to make her tell me something uncomfortable when we're already standing on fragile ground. "No, I'm not going to ask. I'm just going to cross my fingers and hope you weren't a bow tie thief. My collection is valued at forty, some might say fifty dollars."

A laugh just gets to building in her throat, but she locks it down and visibly searches for something to say. "Okay, don't ask. But you should know . . . I deserved to be there for what I did. A lot more than some of the other prisoners. My crime was serious. Some inmates were given harsher sentences for doing way less. Stealing to feed their families. Or getting caught with weed—and they're still in there while I'm already back out here. I was given more consideration thanks to privilege when I probably deserved my sentence more." She brings the folder out from behind her back, twisting it in her hands. "And now you're going to overlook my record? It's just more special consideration that I don't deserve. I don't know if I can . . . I don't think I should let you do that."

"You're getting ahead of yourself. We haven't even done the interview yet." It's hard for me to say those words, because I sound like a grade A asshole, but she's about to walk. I can feel it. She needs me to be tougher on her than I'd like to be in this moment because my kindness is making her feel guilty. I'm not going to point out what that says about her character, as much as I'd like to. So I reach my hand out for the folder instead. "Why don't you start by showing me what you brought?"

Her fight-or-flight instinct is in high gear.

She shifts in those boots, like a runner waiting for the gun to go off.

My pulse is sprinting but I try not to show it. Try not to show how badly I want to stay in this stairwell with her and keep talking.

Finally, she rolls her eyes, stomps up a few of the stairs and hands over the folder, before clomping back down and resuming her defensive stance. But this time, there is a spark of determination and hope lighting up her expression, thank the lord.

I let out my pent-up breath, flipping the folder open to find a copy of her résumé, which holds all of the same information as the online application form. Beneath it is a series of sketches. They're good enough to make me sit up straight—and my spine is already as vertical as a highway mile marker by default. "Talk me through this one."

I hold up a sketch of a window featuring a red dress in the center surrounded by greenery. Vines with big pops of white. Cutout butterflies hanging from the ceiling. Along the bottom of the window are the words, *Give them a new beginning.*

Stella's eyes are closed, but she takes a deep breath now and starts talking. "Give and take. That's the theme I settled on. Next year is all about renewal, a fresh start after two years of lockdowns and masks. We're looking past the melancholia of Christmas and cold weather. The message is this: Help your loved one find their footing again." She nods at the artwork I'm holding. "A lot of people wouldn't buy themselves a bright red dress like that, but if someone else did, it would be a breath of fresh air. Suddenly they're wondering, am I the kind of person who wears a red dress? The answer is we all *are*, we just need help believing it. A loved one's vote of confidence goes a long way. It can lead to discovering more of your own.

"As far as the 'take' in 'give and take,' studies show that consumers, especially women, do a lot of shopping for *themselves* while buying holiday gifts. They've just gotten their work bonus. Or they're using holiday stress as an excuse to splurge. So why not take this opportunity to draw them into the store and make them want to come back in the New Year?"

She rolls her finger at me, and for a few seconds, I'm confused, because I've gotten completely absorbed by her voice and the way she's just become . . . animated. I can barely glance away long enough to hold up the next sketch, which is a rainbow assortment of shoes arranged in a geometric shape, drawing the eye from the front of the window to the back.

Inviting. Eye-catching.

"That's where 'take' comes in. *Take* a new beginning. Buy the shoes. Wear the lingerie for yourself." She pauses to wet her lips.

"Vivant has always been high-end. My opinion is . . . either lean into that image or don't. Your current window is accessible and that's fine, but it doesn't match what's in the store. They're coming in expecting Macy's prices and finding five-hundred-dollar Hermès scarves. It's important to brand as much as it is to sell products, so the first step is a clear vision before we start executing." She shakes her head a little. "I don't mean to say 'we,' as if it's a foregone conclusion."

I like her saying "we." A lot.

Probably too much.

My instinct was to give her the job the second she started talking. Not only do I agree with everything she's saying, not only are her designs well-defined and vibrant, but I *want* to believe in her. So this is where I have to check myself. I'm an optimist to a fault. I was taught to search for the best in people and—refusing to take my attraction to her into account—I see a lot of good in the person standing at the bottom of the stairs, holding her breath for my response. She wants the position more than anyone I interviewed upstairs. She needs to prove herself . . . to herself, doesn't she? And I want to help her do that. If this were a perfect world of my own design, I would say, "You've got the job!" and we'd cut to a music montage of her working diligently, hair tied up with a pencil while we try not to make eyes at each other in the break lounge. But this isn't a perfect world. She needs a chance, but she's also *averse* to receiving one. I have to do this in a certain way.

"How does a trial period sound?" I clear my throat, trying to make my voice sound more official. "Normally our Christmas window designs would remain for the duration of December and into January, but our board wasn't happy with the penguin design, either. In fact, the words *vomit-inducing* might have been tossed around. They want something new for the week before Christmas when the majority of shopping is done. Essentially, we're reinventing the wheel on a very tight schedule. I can give you three days to complete one window—and we'll go from there. You could start tomorrow and have until Friday."

For long moments, there's only the sound of her breathing.

The quick rise and fall of her chest.

She shoves hair behind her ear in a hasty movement, lowering her eyes to the ground. But not before I catch the sheen of tears and my heart goes sideways. It takes superhero strength to remain seated on the top step when I want to take all six stairs in one lunge and wrap her in a hug, however inappropriate that would be. "Stella—"

"Thank you." She quickly trudges up the stairs and shakes my hand. "I . . . you can keep those." She's already running back down the stairs. "I'll see you tomorrow, Mr. Cook."

"It's Aiden," I call after her.

There's a short hesitation before the door slams down on the lobby floor.

Finally, I let myself drag in the huge breath I haven't been able to take with Stella's presence causing my lungs to crowd up. Straightening my bow tie, I whistle my way back up the stairs, looking forward to tomorrow more than I have in a good long while.

Chapter 3
Stella

This far transcends impostor syndrome.

I'm standing in the front window of Vivant, passersby staring at me like I'm a zoo attraction. Following an email I received last night from Aiden, I've checked in with Mrs. Bunting in human resources, filled out paperwork, taken a picture for my employee identification—which felt eerily similar to a mug shot. With my shiny new badge around my neck, I was given a tour by one of the other HR administrators who definitely knows about my prison record, leading to a lot of curious once-overs that I tried to ignore.

This is a huge chance.

I can't help but feel undeserving, but starting now, I'm going to do everything I can to change that. I'm going to design the shit out of this window. First, I'm going to try not to throw up from nerves. Second, I'm going to draw on the knowledge I've managed to retain from three years of online classes and combine it with the new insight I gained last night while devouring design and marketing strategies on the internet. There have been a lot of changes in technique since I studied the art of showcasing products, but the basics are the same.

Step one: Cover the window for some privacy.

It takes me twenty minutes to tape up the opaque paper with the use of a stepping stool. When I arrived after my tour with HR, my sketches were waiting for me in the tight window display space and Aiden's scent lingered in the air. Zingy peppermint. He even smells cheerful. It's almost fascinating.

Right. I'm blaming the weak knees he gave me yesterday on *fascination*. I can only imagine what my best friend, Nicole, would say if she knew about my left field attraction to Aiden, the polar opposite of the rebellious hell-raisers whose names I used to doodle in the margins of my school notebooks.

The wayward musing about my best friend clips me on the chin, forcing me to pause in the act of tidying up the scraps of discarded paper. Suddenly she's there, with her quick, tight-lipped smile and tan Italian complexion. Nicole is still incarcerated and will be for a while longer. Since the trial, our only communication has been through handwritten letters—and they were few and far between. We grew up together, shared everything, so the total lack of communication hasn't been easy. I had to set a boundary, though. That's what Dr. Skinner called it. I don't blame Nicole for everything that happened. God, no. Ultimately, my decisions are what got me in trouble. But I can't pretend like I didn't get a swift push off the high wire, leaving me without a safety net.

Shaking my head to rid myself of the cobwebs of the past, I leave the window space and travel through a small storage room. And I enter the main floor of Vivant.

Cardamom-and-vanilla scents find me immediately, beckoning me forward with the promise of holiday luxury. Pentatonix sings about the twelve days of Christmas at the ideal volume. Not loud enough to be abrasive, but not too quiet that gossip might be overheard. Big, dramatic, original crown molding draws the eye to the ceiling, then softens the blow with properly worn art deco style wallpaper in cream and mint, offset by big, beautiful garlands made up of pine, holly, red ribbon, twinkling lights and pinecones.

It's early, so there are no customers in the store yet, but the head of every single employee turns in my direction as I cross the thick mauve carpeting that runs between two crystal clear jewelry cases. In a skull and crossbones sweater, bangs halfway into my eyes and a giant rip in the knee of my wool tights, I am not what they were expecting.

My palms start to sweat with the need to explain myself. Or to lead with an apology.

Hi. Sorry, I'm Stella.

But then I think about the designs I spent every waking moment creating over the weekend. My theme is new beginnings. What if this is mine? What if this is really happening and I have miraculously been employed as a window dresser at Vivant? Don't I want to start off the right way, in a manner I won't cringe over later?

Yes. I do.

I reach the center of the floor where several main floor employees are gathered having a murmured conversation that somehow blends in seamlessly with the winsome a cappella soundtrack.

"Hi. Sorry, I'm Stella."

Dammit.

The pack of them, impeccable in black pantsuits and gleaming gold name tags, seem to turn to me in slow motion. Once-overs all around. A few eyebrows rise. And then the most graceful of their ranks steps forward with a deliberate smile and holds out her hand. "Sorry, I'm Jordyn. I manage the main floor." She winks a brown eye. "Welcome to Vivant."

"Thank you," I breathe, shaking her hand, my nausea subsiding ever so slightly. "I know we're about to open and you're busy, but I'm wondering if I could . . ." I gesture to the expanse of carpeted space where we're standing. "This might be unusual, but I'm wondering if you'd be open to having a dress displayed here starting Saturday. I'm going to feature a certain dress in the window, and when people walk inside, I want them to see it immediately along with some . . . direction on where they can find it in the store."

The group of women behind Jordyn duck their heads together, whispering.

I try and keep my chin steady.

"We've never done that before," Jordyn says slowly, but not dismissively. Yet. "Let's walk." I nod, following her to the perfume section where the vanilla-and-cardamom scent is strongest. "Keep talking."

"Thanks." I try to choose my words carefully, searching for a tasteful way to express what I've been reading all weekend in the Yelp reviews about Vivant. "Jordyn, do you have a lot of people walk in here and walk right back out?"

There's a tick in her smooth, bronze cheek. "More than I would care to admit."

"Okay. I think a lot of that might be the fault of the misleading window displays. Hopefully we can change that." I don't even have to call on my fashion merchandising lessons, they're so deeply engraved on my brain. I've been mentally crafting windows for four years without a single tool in hand. Even though I'm nervous, getting to say these words out loud is like unbuttoning jeans after a huge meal. I can finally breathe, but I'm also short on air. "If we are able to bring people into the store with whatever I design, we need to leave a trail of breadcrumbs so they can find what brought them in here in the first place. That's why I'm asking about the dress display."

She seems curious, but a little affronted. "What about this floor? It's not appealing?"

"It is. If I can pull off the first window and Aid— Mr. Cook likes what I do, then I have an idea to draw people into this space, as well."

Her eyebrow goes up when I almost call our boss Aiden. Does that mean he doesn't ask a lot of people to call him by his first name? My stomach probably shouldn't be doing a somersault over that. I shouldn't be glancing over Jordyn's shoulder toward the elevator banks and wondering if I'll see him today, either. He's such a *dork*. He probably says phrases like *hunky dory* and *holy cow*. Why was my first waking thought, *what kind of kisser is that man?*

Because he might be a massive dork, but he's . . . surprising.

I never know what he's going to say. But he always finds a way to nudge me . . . center. Instead of *off*-center. Whether he's telling a story to pull me out of an anxiety spiral or purposefully sitting ten feet away so I'm not uncomfortable, those thoughtful moves have me daydreaming about my boss when no good—or bad—can come of it. *Nothing* can come of my tiny hint of curiosity, so I need to blow out that flicker of interest real quick.

Anyway, even if he wasn't my complete opposite, I read the employee handbook this morning and members of management are "strictly prohibited from fraternizing with employees," so that's that. End of story.

Good. Anything else would be *ridiculous*. I've only been out of Bedford Hills for a month. A lot of that time has been spent simply getting used to being in public again. Ordering coffee from a barista, making small talk with my neighbors, going to the grocery store. Super-basic things. A romantic relationship of any kind, especially with someone so vastly different from me, seems less likely than being abducted by little green men holding stun guns.

Jordyn opens her mouth to respond to my request, but it snaps shut, her eyes narrowing on something over my shoulder. I become aware of the sound of rolling wheels.

"Morning, Miss Jordyn."

"This motherfucker again," sighs Jordyn, raising my eyebrows. Didn't see that coming from the flawlessly coiffed floor manager. She crosses her arms and leans to the side, pinning whoever is approaching with the kind of look a mother gives a toddler tracking mud through their living room. "Seamus. What did I tell you about wheeling your dumpster through my department?"

Turning slightly, I see she's addressing a young man, around my age. A custodian, based on his gray jumpsuit and the fact that he's pushing a big container full of white trash bags. His head is shaved, but coupled with his fair, freckled complexion, it's easy to tell he's a redhead. He's not holding back his admiration for the manager, his expression openly longing.

"Sorry, Miss Jordyn," he singsongs, a heavy dose of Brooklyn drawing out his words. "You know I can't pass up a chance to see your beautiful face."

I stare, transfixed, as the brown of her cheeks turns richer. "You're about to see the back of my hand, Seamus, that's what I know."

His answering laugh is carefree, as if she didn't just threaten to smack him. "Did you have your coffee yet, my queen? I'm doing a run. Cream, no sugar, right?"

"For the last time, I don't need you to get me coffee—"

"I'll leave it in the break room microwave." He stops on his way out the side door to sigh loudly, giving Jordyn one last, long look and shaking his head. "Just . . . *damn.*"

"Out!" she orders, pointing in the direction of the street.

With a final laugh, he goes, the door closing behind him without a sound. I wait for her to stop blustering under her breath, my bottom lip caught between my teeth to subdue a smile. "That was interesting."

"That boy isn't right in the head. Flirting with a woman ten years older than him." She stares after him. "He lives with his parents, for the love of everything holy. If he'd saved the amount of money he spends on my coffee, he'd have a palace by now." She smooths the side of her French twist. "I've done nothing to encourage him, either." A beat passes. "I mean, there was that *one time*—"

"Oh, that one time," I echo, forgetting to hide my smile. "The plot thickens."

"The plot wasn't the only thing thickening," she mutters, tugging on the neck of her blazer. Shaking herself slightly as if to dispel her thoughts. "You can put the dress display on our floor, but I'm going to hold you to featuring us in that second window."

"Mr. Cook will have to officially hire me first."

"Well, then." She inclines her head. "Better get to work, new girl."

* * *

I TAKE A deep breath and let myself plop backward onto my butt, glancing around the storage room where I've spent a lot of my day. My most recent activity included painting an oversized corkboard hunter green and spraying it down with glitter. Then I decided it looked tacky and painted over the glitter. Fanned it dry.

How long have I been at this? What time is it?

After speaking with Jordyn, I went to the women's fashion

department and spoke to the manager there, consulting with her about which red dress to feature in my window. After we made our decision, she placed an order for more stock of that particular dress in anticipation of customers being lured in by the A-line silhouette, plunging neckline and ruffled sleeves (accessible, but adventurous).

Then I hoofed it to the art supply shop and used the company debit card I was assigned to purchase supplies for the first phase of my design: the background. I'm going to offset the vibrant red with deep green jewel tones. My plan tomorrow is to track down silk vines to staple to the corkboards, plus some fake white peonies for pop. It almost feels like a dream to be applying my vision to real-life materials, but I don't have time to savor the surrealness.

Not yet.

My stiff muscles protest as I stand, leaning the boards against the wall of the storage room to dry. Massaging the back of my sore neck, I wander into the window space, surprised to find it dark outside. Is the store closed? I slide my phone out of my back pocket, rearing back a little when I see it's 10:15, meaning Vivant is closed. Time really slipped away from me.

I start to turn in a circle, considering strategic places for the spotlight I plan to use to highlight the dress in the evenings—and that's when the door between the storage room and the window snaps shut. I stare at it kind of numbly, trying to decide if I should be worried. Not because I think there's a ghost walking around opening and closing doors. No, that door just doesn't remain open on its own. I've had it propped open all day with a wedge of wood.

Problem is, I didn't originally plan to come back into the window, so it's not propped this time. And my stuff, including my key to unlock the door, is in the storage room sitting on a metal fold-up chair.

"Shit," I whisper, striding to the door and tugging on the handle. Locked.

It's locked.

"Okay, don't panic." I slide a handful of fingers into my hair and hold on while considering my options. Someone has to be in the store. Will an employee on the main floor be able to hear me from here? Taking a deep breath, I start to knock loudly on the door. "Hello? Hello! Is anyone out there? I'm locked in the window."

Silence.

And then a vacuum starts humming, drowning me out.

My pulse is starting to thrum faster. I can't help but notice how much smaller the window box looks when I can't get out of it. I'm trapped. Locked up. I can't get out.

Cold sweat breaks out underneath my clothes and I can't seem to slow my breathing.

Is this a panic attack? Something to do with claustrophobia?

This has never happened before. I'm living in a four-hundred-square-foot apartment, for God's sake. *You can get out of the apartment, though. You can open the door at any time.* I can't open the door to the storage room. Just like I had no way out of prison.

I'm going to be confined in here all night.

I'm right back in the yard, standing on dead grass and staring up at barbed wire.

"Oh God," I pant, dropping down to my haunches, wrapping my arms around my knees and rocking. "Calm down. Come on, calm down."

The chant does nothing to help. I'm beginning to get dizzy.

Breathing through my nose and counting backward from ten don't stop my teeth from chattering, a thick layer of ice forming on my skin. My hand is shaking as I tug my phone back out of my pocket, managing to pull up my email and get the store's main number off an email from Aiden's assistant.

No one answers the main line. It's a recording.

Then I notice there's an extension included in the signature line of his email. So I dial Vivant again, this time plugging in the extension. It rings. It rings four times. I'm beginning to give up hope when a familiar voice fills my ear.

"Aiden Cook, at your service."

"Aiden," I blurt, my relief toppling me sideways onto my left hip. "I— I'm locked in the window. I'm locked in here." That's what I'm trying to say, but I can't seem to unclench my teeth, so the words come out garbled.

"Stella?" Sharp concern replaces his jovial tone. "What's wrong?"

I take a long breath and relax my jaw as much as possible. "I'm locked in the window. The door closed behind me and my key is outside and I can't get out of here."

His sigh is shaky with relief. "Okay. All right. I'm on the way." In the background, I hear his fast-moving footfalls. "Is there a tiger trapped in there with you or something? I hope you don't mind me saying you sound more nervous than Pete Davidson walking into confession."

"I don't know what's wrong," I say raggedly, using the wall to push up onto my feet. "It's the tight space, I think. It's just . . . I don't know, maybe I just don't want to be locked up anymore."

He's silent a moment. "I didn't think of that. I'm going to go ahead and walk faster."

I press the phone hard to my face, his jaunty optimist voice giving me the only comfort I seem to be able to find in this predicament. "Thank you."

"You got it. I'm taking the stairwell so I don't lose reception. We're going to keep talking. Sound good to you, Stella?"

"Yes. You talk."

"Hot damn. That's the first time anyone's ever said that to me. I'm going to take a few seconds to savor the glory if you don't mind." A second ticks by. "Done. Did I ever tell you about the time my aunt Edna accidentally baked a sock into a pie? A dirty one. She didn't keep the laundry basket in the pantry after that. Moved it back to the bedroom where it belongs. She'd originally hidden it in the kitchen so Uncle Hank would stop digging through it for his favorite shirt and wearing the old thing, whether it was clean or not. Anyway, that's where her saying 'you can't avoid dirty laundry' came from. Craziest part of the story for me, though, is they ate the sock pie. I think about that a lot."

How am I trembling and laughing at the same time?

I sound like a scared Chihuahua at the groomer's.

"Are you almost here?"

"Crossing the main floor now. Hey, Seamus!" Aiden calls out, obviously to the custodian, who is vacuuming, and relief hits when I hear that zippity doo dah voice in my ear *and* through the door. "You probably tried yelling, right? He's got his headphones on."

I nod, pressing my cheek to the cold wall, breathing. Breathing.

"Aunt Edna must have been a sweet lady," I say. Am I trying to prompt him into telling me *more* about Aunt Edna? My soul must be leaving my body. "If she had so much influence on you, I mean."

He chuckles, but the sound is tight. "Edna would tell you herself that she's meaner than a snake. But she taught me different. She taught me what would work for me, not her. Two steps away, Stella."

The door opens and Aiden appears in the doorway, his tall frame taking up every inch of it. And I can see he's not as calm as his voice portrayed. There's a sheen of sweat at his hairline, his chest puffing up and down. And I don't know what I'm thinking. Or if I've gone momentarily insane to have *missed* him? But I throw myself at this big, solid, reassuring man who tells the most ridiculous stories. I throw myself at him and he picks me up, cradling me against his huge chest like a baby.

"Okay, sweetheart." As if he senses that I need to be anchored, he squeezes me tight with his left forearm, stroking his right one down the back of my hair. "You're okay."

Relief. It hits me even harder this time than it did when I finally walked out of Bedford Hills, free to leave. Free to go home. A home that didn't really exist for me anymore, but still. I could walk and walk and no one would stop me. How can this feel even better? Maybe because if we were smack dab in the middle of a tornado right now, he'd shield me. I just know it somehow. And that assurance turns my limbs to jelly, melting me against him.

"I don't know what happened," I say in a gulp, digging my nose into the peppermint scent of his dress shirt lapel. "I just freaked."

Slowly, he turns and carries me out of the window box. "You don't get locked up somewhere for four years and leave without a few soul scrapes."

"I know you're not speaking from experience." My heart rate is steadily coming down but now I'm shivering. "What would be the charge that sent you up the river? Telling too many dad jokes? Over-complimenting while intoxicated?"

"Hey, I took an extra sample of tandoori chicken at the supermarket once. Been looking over my shoulder for eight years since."

The vibration of his rumbling laugh makes me close my eyes, resting my head on his shoulder. When his steps turn muffled, I crack an eyelid and realize we're crossing the main floor toward the elevator bank. Seamus is standing in between two jewelry cases with his mouth hanging open. "You never saw us, Seamus," calls Aiden.

Seamus nods, gives a thumbs-up and goes back to vacuuming.

A moment later, we're about to step into the elevator when Aiden hesitates. "Are you going to be all right in here? It just occurred to me you took the stairs yesterday for the interview and now . . ."

Have I unconsciously been avoiding enclosed spaces?

It's not as if I was in a classic prison cell while locked up. There was a giant room of beds separated by partitions. I was never in a tight room with bars, like in a super max. The fear seems to stem from not being able to leave. Not having an exit. Lacking control. Right now, though, the thought of stepping into an elevator with Aiden doesn't strike me as scary. "No, I'm fine as long as I'm with you." Realizing what I said, I scramble to jog it back. "I mean, you know. You *own* the store. You probably have keys and codes and phone numbers if something goes wrong. You know?"

"Yeah," he says warmly, near my ear. Still holding me close, he steps into the elevator and hits a button. We say nothing as the car begins to move. But his chest is still rising and falling. Only now, I'm noticing that every time his chest puffs up and down, my breasts rasp over the slopes of his pecs. Yeah. Pecs. He's got them. Big ones.

Dammit.

I'm also becoming very, very aware that over the course of Aiden carrying me from the window to the elevator, my legs have crept up around his hips. When? I have no idea. But they're there now, the very tips of my knees brushing the back of the elevator wall when he steps farther inside, his forearm snaking under my bottom to keep me held. I'm slightly too high on his body for anything *private* of ours to touch, but my neglected body is potently aware that I could slide down, just a little, and feel him between my thighs.

Not with your boss, idiot.

I'm now trying to calm my pulse and libido at the same time.

But Aiden blows my progress to smithereens when he turns his head, ever so slightly brushing his lips against the lobe of my ear. "Don't let the bow tie fool you, Stella. I'm not always nice," he says, a deep burr in his voice. "When the situation calls for it, I can be downright rough."

My vagina clenches so tight, the very wind is knocked out of me.

I'm seeing nothing but twinkling stars as the metal door rolls open and Aiden carries me off the elevator onto a floor that is decorated within an inch of its life for Christmas, Hanukkah and Kwanzaa. All of the decorations are intermingled, done without artifice, but lovingly placed and somehow, some way, I know that Aiden is the one who did the decorating. The abundance of flutters that gives me is truly alarming.

We leave the brightly lit reception area and enter his dark office where only a small lamp is on. Over his shoulder, I spot paperwork scattered on the floor, his chair halfway across the room, as if he charged out of here when I called.

Gulp.

Aiden settles my backside on the edge of his huge desk, remaining between my legs just long enough for us both to suck in an unsteady breath, before stepping back. He crosses to the floor-to-ceiling window and stands looking out, hands on hips for a moment. Getting himself under control? "You feeling better?" he asks me, looking back over his shoulder, his smile not quite enough to hide the hunger.

Phew. Okay, we're attracted to each other.

It's not one-sided.

This is going to be a problem.

Maybe what we need right about now is a defining of the lines here. Because they should be thick and easy to spot. Like a fresh, black Expo marker on a whiteboard.

For one, he's my boss and the handbook was clear. Employers are not to have romantic relationships with their employees, of which I am one. Even if it's on a trial basis. I broke a lot of rules in the past and I'm not sure I want to do that anymore. Maybe at heart, I'm still the girl who trespassed with impunity and vandalized the sides of buildings. Do I still have that in me? Or am I capable of permanently changing?

I don't know. I'm still trying on this new identity for size.

Two. Aiden is the real deal. He's . . . genuine. And delightful.

There, I said it. By my third encounter with him, I should be noticing a crack in his aura of kindness, but I'm really thinking there isn't one. And he is not—*not*—a man who sleeps with or dates or *anythings* with an ex-convict.

If he did, it would be another Good Samaritan move.

Show the tragic goth girl she's worthy of love!

No, thanks. Not happening.

As badly as I'd like to find out how he kisses—and just how "rough" he can be—I will not start making major decisions when I've only been out of prison for a single month. I'm not letting *him* make any bad decisions, either. Aiden is the guy who wants to save people. Look at the way he charged downstairs and rescued me, carrying me upstairs like Prince Charming.

But I'm not a princess. Not the kind of girl who ends up with Aiden Cook.

Nor do I want to take advantage of his good nature. Isn't that what I'd be doing if I let this turn into something when I know he'd only be in it for noble reasons?

Get out the Expo marker.

"Armed robbery," I blurt, my fingers curling hard into the edge of the desk. "That's what I was in prison for. My friend Nicole, she . . . no, *we* arranged to rob a restaurant where our friend was closing up. It was going to be easy. We'd make a show for the camera, wave our fake guns around and walk out with the drop before he could put it in the safe. But, uh . . ." I give a jerky shrug, finishing the rest of the story through pinched lips. "It turns out, the guns weren't fake. And our friend's boss came back because he forgot his phone. He took a gun out from beneath the register and fired at Nicole. She panicked and fired back, hitting him in the side. He lived," I say quickly, glancing up for the first time to judge Aiden's reaction. For once, he's stoic.

"What happened after that?" he prompts quietly.

It's on the tip of my tongue to tell Aiden certain details about what happened next. But those facts might absolve me in his eyes. Or make me seem less guilty somehow, when the fact is, I made the decision to steal. I *am* guilty. End of story. And making myself look innocent right now would defeat the purpose of my goal, which is to impress upon Aiden how different we are. He would never, ever take someone's hard-earned money. Never end up in the back of a cop car or an interrogation room. This is how I nip this attraction in the bud before it flourishes.

"The rest is history," I say, hopping off the desk and backing toward the door. "Thanks for coming to let me out, boss. Good night."

"I want the rest, Stella."

With my pulse ticking in my temples, I keep walking.

He wants the rest.

The rest of what? Me or the story?

His gruff tone makes it impossible to tell. But I can't give him either one.

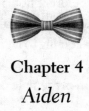

Chapter 4

Aiden

I t's going to be a good day," I mutter to myself, popping two Advil and swallowing them dry. Unfortunately, on board meeting days, my mantra doesn't ring quite as true.

Leland crosses the office and stands in front of my desk with the demeanor of a pallbearer. "Are you ready, boss?"

No. "Of course." I force a decent smile onto my face, though it's a struggle. "They're waiting in the conference room?"

"Yes. According to Linda in reception, they have rejected the muffin tray and are requesting sashimi."

Hold on to that smile. "At ten thirty in the morning?"

"Yes," Leland sniffs, disapprovingly. "I don't know why board meetings can't still be done remotely. They just come here to flex their power and kill our vibe. Linda says they didn't even *comment* on your decorations. They have some nerve—"

"Easy now, buddy." I push back from my desk and stand, reaching out to pat Leland on the shoulder. "You're going to pop a blood vessel in your eye again."

The vein adjacent to my assistant's eye throbs ominously. "Don't you ever want to tell them to just . . . fuck right off?"

I start to deny it, but that would be a lie. I'm a terrible liar, too. He'd see through me easier than a piece of Swiss cheese. "Of course I do." I sigh. "But they own this department store same as I do. They kept it going through some tough times and we all have jobs because of it."

"You're conveniently forgetting the fact that you bailed out Vivant five years ago. *They* conveniently forget, as well. They treat you like they did you a favor, instead of the reverse."

I gather up the necessary paperwork for the meeting. "Leland, if complaining a little makes them feel better about not being hands-on, let them. I don't need a pat on the back."

Ah, geez. The tip of his nose is turning red. "But you deserve one, boss."

"Well, there. Just got one, didn't I?" I come around the desk, grinning. "Let's go eat some raw fish and pretend it's a blueberry muffin."

On the way out of my office, I can't help but glance back at my desk. At the exact spot where Stella sat on Tuesday night after I carried her up here. It's Thursday now and I haven't seen her once since then. It's been killing me to stay away, but Jesus, I have no idea what to do about her. I came dangerously close to kissing her perfect mouth right there in the elevator. Then once again in my office. And after having her thighs hug my waist for nearly five minutes, my body wanted a lot more than kissing. I haven't been that hard in God knows how long. My cock was so stiff, I had to face the opposite direction and think about the time I walked in on Aunt Edna shaving her bikini line with a straight razor.

Yeah, this girl. She gets to me. Bad.

I don't often act without logic, but that's exactly what I've done here.

I've essentially hired Stella—on a trial basis—so that I can see more of her. But in turn, hiring Stella has made her off-limits. Not only would kissing her be a violation of company policy and an unforgivable abuse of power . . . I sense it would be a complication totally separate from our positions at Vivant.

I don't mind complications. I'd do just about anything to get complicated with her.

I'm just not sure she'd want to get complicated with me.

She's made it pretty clear that she thinks I'm the world's biggest cheeseball.

My worst transgression is a parking ticket. While she was in prison, lonely and cold—I'm actually going to break out in hives just thinking about it—I was up here in this cushy office worrying about product displays and purchase orders. Easy. *So* easy compared to what she's faced. And I think that's what she was trying to tell me on Tuesday night when she confided the reason she got convicted. It was a roundabout way of saying we're different.

Too different.

And she's not interested.

Why else would she have run out of here like I offered her moldy toast?

On my way down the hall, I catch sight of my reflection in one of the glass partitions between desks left over from the pandemic. I'm smiling, even though I'm dreading the next couple of hours with every fiber of my being. I'm wearing a bright red bow tie and suspenders and I can already see Stella smirking over them.

Maybe I should skip the meeting and go downstairs to the window box where she's working. Just to be positive she'd smirk. Hell, I'd take a smirk over not seeing her at all. I've held the girl in my arms one damn time and now all I can think about is doing it again. Sitting down with her in my lap, letting my hand roam freely up the softness of her wool tights. Watching awareness dawn on her face that I'm nothing in bed like I am in the street.

Not even close.

Christ, don't think of that now or you'll embarrass yourself.

We reach the entrance to the conference room and Linda, the receptionist who has been here longer than me, comes stomping out with a pinched expression holding a pitcher of water. "They don't want it cold," she says, somewhat hysterically. "They want it room temp. Last time they wanted it freezing."

"Maybe we should have the water blessed by a priest and burn the demons out of them," Leland suggests. "St. Patrick's is only a few blocks away. I could be back in no time."

"Forget the water, Linda. I'll handle them." I lean down and whisper near her ear, "There's a bottle of bourbon in the bottom left-hand drawer of my desk. Go take a swig."

Her shoulders drop down from around her ears. "Bless you, Aiden Cook."

"Leave a drop for me." I chuckle on my way into the conference room. "I'll need it," I murmur under my breath as I come to a stop at the head of the table, taking in my family members and their shared air of impatience.

Closest to the window overlooking midtown is my grandmother, Shirley, and her grandson—my cousin—Randall. Randall will not look up from his phone once during this entire meeting and frankly, I'm good with that. He tends to say things that make me want to pop a blood vessel, Leland-style. Across from my grandmother and cousin sits my father, Bradley Cook. He looks over at me briefly when I walk in, then goes back to studying the skyline.

"Merry Christmas, everyone," I say, taking a seat. Leland flops down into the chair beside me like he's about to get a tooth pulled without Novocain. "I hope you didn't hit too much traffic coming in from Long Island."

"Of course we did," Shirley draws out, fingers wrapped around the straps of the purse in her lap. "This is Manhattan and we're nine days away from Christmas. The bridges and tunnels are full of people wanting to shop."

"For which we are eternally grateful," I say briskly, spreading my paperwork out in front of me. "Where do you folks want to start?"

"Folks?" My father snorts. "Where on *earth* did you come from?"

Shirley cranes her neck to look out the conference room door, probably wondering where Linda is with her room temperature water. With any luck, Linda is feeling no pain right about now. I'm not going to make my receptionist run around for water when I'm sure my grandmother's limousine is waiting downstairs stocked with nine flavors of seltzer. "It's Edna's influence, Bradley," she drawls. "The fault lies with you for sending him to live down south with that loon for so long."

My skin turns hot under my clothes, but I refrain from taking issue with that statement. If Edna were here, she would laugh and say, *Sticks and stones may break my bones, but words are just a representation of the speaker's insides—not me. And not you.*

I clear my throat. "Moving on from family matters—"

"I had to send him. You know my hands were tied there," Bradley slides in smoothly, gesturing to me. "At least he got a decent education while living in Tennessee. I'm not sure how Edna managed to get employed at a prestigious boarding school as an art director, but they obviously knew what they were doing." I'm caught between skepticism and shock that my father just gave me a rare, if roundabout, compliment, but skepticism wins when he tacks on, "So he occasionally sounds like a country bumpkin. You take the good with the bad."

"I suppose," my grandmother murmurs, looking at the door again.

"Yes!" Randall cries out, excited about whatever just happened on his phone.

Shirley smiles at him indulgently.

Leland is blinking so fast and so hard, I already know we're looking at a doctor visit. The tip of his pen has already ripped a hole in the page of his notebook and he's only written the date.

"Down to business," I say quickly when my father tries to continue the conversation with his mother. "Our holiday shopping numbers are not quite back to pre-pandemic levels, but we're getting there and we're making up a lot of the deficit by focusing on online sales and marketing." Shirley snorts at this. She thinks online shopping is tacky. She also thinks shopping in real life is tacky. I have no idea how she does her shopping. "It has been our saving grace through all of this, really, and based on focus groups we've been holding, I believe people will continue to shop this way, so we're increasing the budget for online customer acquisitions."

"Are you sure that's a good idea?" Bradley asks, turning his chair slightly in my direction. "Don't people want a return to normalcy?"

"Yes, sir. And what constitutes normalcy changes. It *has* changed. That's not to say we've completely taken our focus off physical, in-person shopping. As we know, consumers tend to buy more in person or open a line of credit. We're incentivizing in-person shopping through the newsletter and various television spots running through the holidays in the tri-state." My bow tie suddenly feels tighter. "As far as appealing to casual shoppers and tourists, we hired a new window dresser, as you requested, and she's taking things in an interesting direction. I should be able to send you more details once she's finished with her current design. Now, as far as—"

"Oh thank God," my grandmother interjects. "The last girl was an abomination. Who is the new one? Have I heard of her? Please tell me you stole that genius from Saks."

Hang on to your smile. "I did not." I start to tell them about Stella, then hesitate. Not because I don't think she's qualified. Not because I'm afraid they'll disapprove of her past (although they definitely would). But I'm already right on the edge of my patience. If one of them has a negative thing to say about Stella (they definitely would), I'm not going to handle it well. At all. In fact, I'm very protective of her in a way I didn't realize until now. Or possibly when she called me, sounding breathless and terrified, to say she'd gotten locked in the window space and my heart dropped ten stories to the sidewalk below. Yeah, I was protective then and I'm even more so now.

I'm not casting her name out into the viper pit to be torn apart.

But at the very core of me is a need to people please. Especially when it comes to my family. No matter how unlikely it seems that they'll be satisfied with anything I do, I can't seem to stop trying, either. Something will give eventually, won't it?

"She's been hired on a trial basis," I say. "We're going to unveil her initial design tomorrow and go from there."

My grandmother sits up straighter. "But who is she—"

"Begging your pardon, Shirley," I say, slapping a hand to my chest. "I have a conference call shortly. Would you mind if we powered through and I'll update you on the window design situation at the end of the week? Thank you."

Without taking a breath, I address the next few bullet points, but my grandmother doesn't say a word for the rest of the meeting, continuing to watch me through eyes the size of dime slits. Toward the end of my marketing recap, I realize I may have made a mistake. In refusing to give them Stella's name, have I inadvertently drawn their attention to her?

Chapter 5
Stella

With my heart in my mouth, I stare down at the missed call on my phone.

Connecticut number?

There is only one person I know in the state of Connecticut and she's housed in their women's prison. Nicole. She must have found out I've been released, otherwise she wouldn't have called my cell. Is she just calling to catch up? Why didn't she leave a message?

With a familiar pinch in my chest, I leave the window box to find I've once again worked past closing without realizing it. I did the same last night and found myself on the various upper floors, roaming the empty aisles of Vivant to the sound of vacuums humming downstairs. There is something oddly soothing about a dark, empty department store.

For tonight's venue, I choose the luggage section for my stroll. Picking through the holiday displays and boxes of inventory waiting to be shelved tomorrow morning, I can almost hear the buzz of customers lingering behind, even though it's deadly silent in here now. Big, elaborate garlands are hung along the perimeter of the room, Vivant's signature vanilla-and-cardamom scent evident in the air. Walking past a small black quilted carry-on suitcase, I reach down and turn over the price tag, choking over the cost. No holiday bargains in *this* store.

Continuing on my slow journey through Vivant, I lift my hand and massage the back of my neck. I'm sore head to toe from hunching over on hands and knees all day. In the middle of the night last night, inspiration hit and now I've covered the floor in fragmented pieces of a broken mirror, which I smashed up with a hammer—very therapeutic, truth be told—to make the floor reflective. Once I turn on the lighting, where I've suspended a herd of papier-mâché butterflies, the effect should be prismatic and amazing.

Hopefully.

Please be amazing.

Tomorrow is the unveiling of my first ever window display. It could be a massive flop. I could have completely misjudged the direction Vivant should be taking. It's too late to change anything now, though, so I'm trying to keep my head down and focus on the finish line.

And I'm trying really, really hard not to think about Aiden.

Where has he been for the past two days? I mean, it stands to reason that the general manager of a department store would be a tad swamped with nine days left until Christmas. It also stands to reason that he has taken the hint I delivered and no longer plans to bother with me. As a friend, as an acquaintance. As anything. Which was exactly what I wanted.

I just wouldn't mind seeing him around once in a while.

I don't even know what kind of bow tie he wore yesterday.

Or today.

"Oh my God, listen to yourself," I mutter, rounding the corner out of the luggage section into cookware. If Nicole could hear me obsessing over a full-fledged nice guy, she would never stop ridiculing me. I can hear her voice in my head right now. I always can.

Stop trying to be something that you're not, Stella.

We're the same, you and me.

You think you can change, but you can't. People don't change.

Your parents don't understand you.

You said you'd always have my back. Prove it.

I come to an abrupt halt when I hear a clink. Was that in my head?

It sounded like a glass being set down on the ground.

Suddenly, the cookware section is a lot less soothing and a whole lot more haunted, the spookiness exacerbated by the life-sized Victorian-style Santa Claus positioned beside the register. Did he just wink at me?

I should probably just turn tail and sprint for the elevators. Collect my things and come back when it's daylight, like the more sensible employees of Vivant. And that's exactly what I'm about to do—until I see two shiny black wingtip shoes sticking out from behind a display of Le Creuset Dutch ovens. In between the polished shoes and the pant leg, there is a section of red-and-green socks peeking out, and somehow, I know who is attached to those feet.

"Aiden?"

That clink sound is louder than the first time. A beat passes. "Stella?"

Oh dear. It's impossible to pretend that deep voice didn't send a tremor straight through me. I'm still catching my breath from it when Aiden appears behind the display, towering over it—holding a bottle of liquor in his right hand.

"This isn't what it looks like," he says, openly chagrined.

My mouth is already threatening to smile. "Really? Because it looks like you're getting sloshed by yourself, in the dark, in the cookware department."

"Okay, it's exactly what it looks like."

Keeping my laughter contained is near impossible, but I button my lips and keep them sealed. I don't know why. Maybe because laughing at this man and his unique sense of humor is too much of a privilege when I've spent a long time stripped of so many. Laughing with him feels like something a girl with a blowout and peep-toe pumps should be doing. Not me.

Nicole is in my head again telling me I don't share his sense of humor. I'm not like him. I'm unique. Born with a wild streak. I'm like her.

With a swallow, I approach my boss and lean back against the table display, holding my hand out for the bottle. Lips twitching, he hands it over and takes the spot beside me, leaving our hips less than an inch apart. When I tip the bottle to my mouth for a medium-sized sip, I glance over and find him looking at my black-stocking-covered legs, but he quickly glances away, a muscle popping in his cheek.

"Rough day?" I ask, sounding a little breathless. At least I can blame it on the liquor.

"Nah, it was just fine," he says, his tone warm and reassuring.

I raise an eyebrow at him.

"All right." He takes a breath, rolls his shoulders back. "It wasn't what I would call ideal."

"Try again," I say, bumping him lightly with my shoulder.

His laughter makes my pulse skitter. "Okay, you win. It was more messed up than Uncle Hank on New Year's during a full moon. Is that better?"

"Much." I hand him the bottle, trying not to look too closely at the way he wraps his lips around the rim and gulps without reservation. It's not what I would have expected of him. It's better. He's got a five-o'clock shadow all over his jaw, his hair is finger messy. And his bow tie is just a bit off-center. It's crocodiles today. Dressed in Santa hats. "What made it bad?"

He starts to blow it off. I can see that's his impulse and I wonder why. It's like he's allergic to being anything less than positive at all times.

"There was a board meeting today," he says finally. "My father, grandmother and cousin. You could say the family dynamic is on the complicated side." Until he says this to me, I don't realize how starved I am for information about this man. I am literally holding my breath and hoping he continues, only letting it seep out when he does. "I did most of my growing up with Aunt Edna and Uncle Hank. The rodeo clown, too, but like I said, he didn't last long." Aiden crosses himself. "Edna never planned on having kids. She's a free spirit. Shocked the hell out of me when I first arrived. There I was, coming from this . . . tense and sterile environment and suddenly I'm in the care of this woman who collects wind chimes, embraces nudity and laughs at inappropriate moments, like when we're passing a fender bender on the highway. But she never gave me anything but her best."

I'm so caught up in his story, I forget to think before I speak. "If she's the reason you're so Aiden-y," I murmur, "she did a great job."

A slight crease appears in between his brows, as if he doesn't know whether I'm complimenting him or not. "Aiden-y?"

A flush creeps up the back of my neck. "Yes, you know. Nice. Honest. The kind of guy who gives an ex-convict a second chance and wears crocodile bow ties." Seconds pass and he just goes right on looking at me, probably reading between the lines of every breathless word out of my mouth and figuring out that I've developed a teeny-tiny crush on him. Itty bitty. Microscopic. Definitely not big enough to make every nerve ending in my body gravitate so quickly in his direction that I feel off balance leaning against this table right now.

Definitely not.

Being around Aiden is like . . . I've been wandering around in the dark and suddenly I've spotted a big, crackling campfire. *Please don't let any of this be showing on my face.* "Is Edna responsible for the bow ties?"

He seems to be having trouble gathering his train of thought, taking a few seconds to drag his attention from me to the store laid out in front of him. "She is, yes. I was down in the dumps when I arrived in Tennessee. My father and his new wife needed some space to get acquainted back in New York—and I guess they just kept on needing it." He clears his throat. "Anyway, none of the kids in my new school wanted to hang out with the 'lanky Yankee.' That's what they called me, and I have to admit, it has a nice ring. Much more creative than Fiber Gummies Greg, who sat behind me on the school bus. He had some digestive problems."

A corner of his lip tugs and I watch it with such rapt attention, it's embarrassing.

"Anyhow, Edna started putting me in a bow tie for school. She told me no one can be anything but happy while wearing a bow tie. I thought she was crazy, but I had nothing to lose. So I tried it and . . . the bow tie made me feel like someone else. It was a shield of sorts in the beginning. They weren't making fun of me, they were making fun of some kid in a bow tie. And when that kid laughed along with them instead of skulking off, the outcome was a lot better. In a way, I guess the bow tie conditioned me to be a good sport." He reaches up and tugs on his crocodiles absently. "All the time."

What am I going to do with this heavy, uncomfortable object that seems to be sitting on my chest and pressing down harder by the moment? "Do you ever feel like ripping it off and going skulking again?"

"Sure I do," he says, squinting over at me. "Today in the board meeting, for one."

"Why?"

Aiden shrugs a big shoulder. "When I'm around my family, sometimes I forget to be grateful Edna raised me. Sometimes I can only focus on the fact that I was sent away for so long."

I study the hard planes of his profile, the way his fingers seem jumpy where they hold the bottle. "It makes you feel guilty, doesn't it? Being anything less than happy."

He frowns over at me. It's not a mean frown. It's a thoughtful one and it gives him a different kind of appeal. Sexy and intense. A small section of hair loses its battle with gravity and flops onto the center of his forehead where lines have appeared. His total absorption in our conversation makes my skin heat, my tummy muscles performing a weird flex. Why? I think because . . . this is a man who pays attention. This is a man who doesn't miss anything. Apparently after a life of constant variables, I'm attracted to that. To someone who doesn't need to be told the sky is falling. He's the one who has already built a shelter. "Yeah. I do, uh . . ." He clears his throat. "That's what it is. I'm impatient and irritated around my family. And that makes me feel guilty."

"You're supposed to be better than that."

"Right." He nods. "Yes."

"You are. But you can't be better *all* the time. No one can, right?"

I take the bottle he offers, but I don't drink from it. Instead, I twist the heavy glass base of the bottle on my thigh, just grateful to have something to do with my hands. I have this uncharacteristic urge to talk, to share with this man. Maybe because I sense he needs a distraction. Or a friend. I don't know. But it's so easy to open my mouth and speak. I fear nothing from him, especially judgment.

"I've been in New York just over a month. I needed to get used to the process of things again. Using money, getting change back— even that was weird. I did a lot of sitting on benches and watching people walk their dogs. And it's such a chaotic place, New York. There are sirens and labor strikes and traffic congestion and delayed trains. But the chaos of it really highlights the good things, you know? Like two people meeting in the park. Two people out of a *million*. Just connecting paths in the center of buildings and avenues and so many other humans. On purpose, they connect. It seems like it should be impossible in a place so massive. If there wasn't all this wild commotion around them, meeting in the park might not be so beautiful." God, I'm rambling. My hand tries to wave everything I said off, but the bottle sloshes, so I stop and search for a way to make myself sound less fanciful and ridiculous. "All I'm saying is . . . maybe the positive power of the bow tie only has to extend so far. Maybe it's okay to loosen it up once in a while and let yourself feel or express some bad stuff. It'll only make the good that much more valuable." I sigh. "Everyone's got some yuck."

I'd have to be dead not to feel the way his gaze has settled on me. It's magnetic. Even more so when he continues to consider me in thoughtful silence for stretched-out moments. "Thank you. I'm going to think about that for a while. Probably a long while." A beat passes. "What's your bad stuff, Stella? I know we didn't even scratch the surface the other night."

"Mmmm." I hum into a small sip of bourbon, the liquor burning a path down to my stomach. "We're talking about you now, not me."

He's undeterred and I need to stop drinking this bourbon because his body warmth is beginning to suck me in. A few more sips and I won't see anything wrong with laying my head on his sturdy shoulder or pressing the sides of our thighs together. "Your application said you went to high school in Pennsylvania," he says, drawing me out of my dangerous thoughts. "Are your parents still there?"

Discomfort packs in tight below my neck. "Yes."

"Are you going home to them for Christmas?"

"No," I say on a forced laugh. "No, I'm not."

He doesn't say anything.

Seconds tick by as he waits for me to fill the silence.

And suddenly, there I am doing it. Knowing he is going to be kind and nonjudgmental about this particularly messy subject makes me feel like I'm rock climbing, but at least I've got a sturdy harness. "My parents didn't want me living at home after release. I stayed one night before my father drove me here." I avoid looking at him. "I don't blame them. They were pretty good parents, even if we never really related to each other and I took them for granted. Now . . . they've had just enough time to get back on solid ground with their friends and community after . . . everything. I can't show up and disrupt their lives again. My presence alone would do that. It doesn't matter if I've . . ."

"Changed?" He's doing that intense concentration thing again. "Have you? Are you different than you were before?"

I take a moment to think. "In some ways, maybe. But it's harder than people think. To just *change*. To stop being the kind of girl who steals her parents' car in the middle of the night to joyride. Or spray-paints her name in neon orange on the side of the town water tower. Worse things when I got older. And it's like . . . the insecurities that drive someone to do those things? They don't just erase themselves." I roll a shoulder. "Change is hard."

He tilts his head, prompting me to look over. "This trouble you got into . . ." he starts, cautiously. "You couldn't have gotten into it alone."

Nicole's face materializes in my mind. She could be right there in front of me, reaching for the bottle of bourbon. Even imagining my ex–best friend here makes me feel like a fraud. Like I'm pretending to be something I'm not.

Oh, you're having a heart-to-heart with this guy? Baring your soul? Poor little Stella.

Gut churning, I push off the table, banishing her voice with determination.

I don't want Nicole here. There's no room for her around the campfire.

Boundaries.

This man—my boss—he gave me a chance to fulfill a dream I never thought I'd ever have a shot at. He's inherently good. I can't say that about many people I've met in my life. Maybe I can't even say it about anyone. And I just want to make his night slightly better after he's given me this chance to . . . do something. Make a mark.

Okay, I don't even need Nicole here to call me out on that being corny. But screw it.

"I have an idea."

He sits up straighter. "Yeah?"

What am I doing? I don't know. Flying by the seat of my tights, I guess. Just trying to distract him, take his mind off the unwarranted guilt of being slightly less than happy for a while. "We have fifteen minutes to find the perfect Christmas gift for each other. We're not *really* buying them, of course. We'll put them back afterward. It's just an exercise. You can choose it from anywhere in the store." I pull my phone out and check the time, laughing inwardly at the way Aiden has come to his feet and started to rub his hands together, completely game for this spontaneous idea. "It's ten forty. We have until ten fifty-five. Meet in the first-floor break room. Go."

The man takes off running.

He runs like an athlete, no dorkiness detected.

It's in that moment that I discover something I'd missed. Something monumental.

Aiden Cook has a firm, thick bubble butt.

My jaw unhinges and I have no choice but to let it hang there, the time ticking away on my own challenge just so I can watch those gorgeous buns move until he disappears around the corner. Not before they engrave themselves on my brain, though. Holy. Cakes.

When I realize I'm standing there, hypnotized by the booty, I shake myself.

Move.

I turn on a heel, mentally running through the departments in my head. What would I buy Aiden for Christmas? Menswear has bow ties, but that's too obvious. I don't know his shoe size. He probably has amazing luggage already. I'm not choosing him a new cologne to mess with perfection. I already like the way he smells too much.

This task is way more intimate than I realized.

I chew my lip over that fact on the way down in the elevator—but my worries are interrupted when it hits me. Oh yeah. I know exactly what to get him.

Twelve minutes later, I jog through the empty aisles of glass cases toward the break room door, gift in hand, positive I'm going to beat him there. I've never been in a long-term relationship with a man, but it's common knowledge they are terrible shoppers, right? He's probably still upstairs rifling through blouses and sweating bullets.

My notion pops like a bubble when I skid to a shocked stop inside the break room door.

Not only is Aiden there waiting, his wing tips are kicked up, ankles crossed on the rectangular table, hands stacked behind his head. Two steaming mugs of hot chocolate sit on the table beside him, marshmallows bobbing on the surface.

In between the mugs is a long black velvet case.

"No way," I breathe, waving a hand in his general direction. "You found my gift *and* had enough time to make cocoa?"

The slight darkening of his cheekbones has to be a figment of my imagination. He can't have a bubble butt *and* be a blusher. That's got to be illegal. "You might say I've got a mental inventory of everything in the store."

"That tracks," I mutter.

I move closer to the table, my heart picking up speed with every step I take closer to him. Keeping my features schooled as much as possible, even though I'm ridiculously excited to exchange gifts—when was the last time I did this?—I turn a chair to face him and sit down, trying to cover as much of his present as possible with my hands. As I'm taking my seat, he drops his feet from the table and inches closer, watching each of my movements thoughtfully, as if he'll be writing a detailed report about my mannerisms later tonight.

"Who starts?" I manage to say, parched.

Aiden slides the black velvet box across the table. "Ladies first." He leans back in the chair, crosses his arms, his right knee starting to jostle.

"Oh my *God*, look at how excited you are. I bet you have a Christmas song playlist, don't you? December first, that thing is on random twenty-four seven."

"Wrong." He winks at me. "I start it the day after Thanksgiving."

An unrestrained laugh tumbles from my mouth before I can stop it or even think about swallowing the sound—and his knee stops bouncing abruptly.

In the ensuing silence, the only sound is Aiden exhaling unevenly. "Now, that's a laugh worth waiting around for, Stella." Then, more to himself, "I was wondering if you were ever going to let me hear it."

My insides are flailing, but I manage a scowl. "Just don't get used to it."

"Getting used to it would be impossible. But trying to hear it again?" His voice matches his eyes now. Smoky. "I don't know if I'll be able to help myself."

He's not near enough to kiss. Not even close. Based on the havoc his words wreak in my belly, however, he might as well be speaking from above me, his strong body pressing me down, down, down. "M-maybe I'll just open this," I manage, wrangling open the box with the desperation of a ten-year-old being gifted an Xbox.

Please be something that distracts me from my boss and his effect on my libido. My . . . chest. Specifically, inside my rib cage and slightly to the left.

Until I open the box, I don't stop to consider what might be inside. But when a necklace glitters up at me from the red velvet lining, I realize I was stupid not to have anticipated jewelry. It's a *jewelry box*. It's just not what I expected. Not from Aiden. Somehow it seems too forward. Or . . . like there's an expectation attached. From this man, though? I don't know how to react. Was I totally off the mark about his personality?

"Stella." I glance up to find him looking worried. "You hate it."

"No. It's . . . beautiful." I search for the right words. "A necklace."

Aiden takes the box back and removes the thin gold rope, holding it up. Now that it's out of the box, I can see a hook at the bottom that wasn't visible before. "Not a necklace. It's kind of a fancy key chain, I suppose. For around your neck. I thought you could wear the key to the window box, so you don't get locked in again."

"Oh." The word blows out of me, along with my sense of disappointment. In flows the opposite. A sense of comfort. Relief. Appreciation. Not only did he pick out my gift quickly, he picked out the perfect one. "That's really thoughtful," I say, stumbling over my words. "I'd love to get this as a gift, Aiden. Really."

He lets out a breath, chuckles. "It was touch and go there for a second."

"My mistake. I should have known . . ." I trail off, shaking my head. "Okay, your turn." I start to hand over the gift, then hesitate. "It seemed like a great choice until right this second."

"Aha. You've got the gift giver heebie-jeebies. Totally natural." He doesn't try to take the small box from me, but sits and waits with his big hands resting on his outstretched thighs. "Whatever it is, it won't be as bad as Aunt Edna's gift on Christmas of ninety-four. She took me out in the backyard in my pajamas and taught me how to field dress a rabbit."

"*What?* Jesus!"

"She nailed the surprise element. I'll give her that."

Blinking, I hand him the gift. "Consider me cured of the heebie-jeebies, I guess."

He weighs the box in his hand, his dark brows drawing together. "Huh. I can't figure out what this is. Which department is it from?"

"No hints. I might not pull off a Thumper-slaying level of surprise, but mild shock would be nice." I realize *my* knee is bouncing now and reach down to stop it.

Aiden follows the action and smiles.

"Open it," I clip out, crossing my arms.

"Yes, ma'am," he drawls, drawing off the deep brown leather of the top. "Binoculars."

I wait for a reaction. And I don't get one.

Of course he would choose this moment to be stoic. His expression is giving away nothing. "Uh-huh. Binoculars," I say, as he continues to look down at them in a considering way. "You know . . ." I uncross my arms and wave a hand between us. "You know, because you're always looking up."

Wow, says Nicole's voice in my head. *What a try hard.*

"I love them," Aiden says, turning them over in his hands. "Thank you."

The genuine appreciation in his tone makes me feel good. Too good. Better than I've felt in a long, long time. The combination of pride and pleasure is almost a shock to the system.

"It was just a game. Anyway . . ." I come to my feet so quickly, I nearly upset the chair. "Tomorrow is the window unveiling, so I should probably catch the train soon—"

"I'd already given some thought to what I'd get you for Christmas. That's how I found the neck chain for your key so fast," he says in a low voice, shaking his head. "Hell, I shouldn't be telling you that."

He . . . he'd already thought of what he'd buy me for Christmas? That weight on my chest from earlier continues to press down, but now it's lower, too. Over my belly button. Everywhere. My lungs aren't working as efficiently as usual. I'm standing now in front of his chair, so close that our knees would touch if I shuffled forward ever so slightly. "Why shouldn't you tell me that?"

The way his eyes lift and rake over me quickly, filling with smoke, is my only answer.

"Oh." I wet my suddenly dry lips. "Because of the rule. I . . . read it in the handbook."

"Did you?" Without breaking eye contact, he sets the binoculars on the table. "What did it say, Stella?"

His use of my name in this instance seems . . . heavier. An anchor dragging along the ocean floor. Or is that my neglected hormones playing tricks on me? I'm going to feel like a moron if I'm totally misreading the situation and this annoying attraction is completely one-sided. If he's just being nice and my social skills are too out of practice to see it. "Well." *Just say it. Get it out.* "It said there is a strict non-fraternization policy between any member of management and an employee of the Cook Corporation."

He nods, searches my face. Seems to be deciding whether or not to say something. "Unless . . . those two people were to sign some paperwork with human resources. Acknowledging their intention to date and releasing the company from any liability. It's called a love contract—and I know, it's a little on the nose." The chair creaks under him as he shifts, visibly restless. When his gaze ticks back to mine, his eyes tick deep with meaning. "But with the love contract signed, two people would be free to do whatever they want."

"What *do* they want?" I whisper, before I can think better of it. Before I can remind myself of all the reasons getting any closer to Aiden Cook would be a mistake.

He's my boss. I'm trying not to break rules anymore. Trying to figure out what and who I'm going to be in this giant world. A world I've been absent from for a long time and still seems like an alien planet to me most of the time. Breaking the non-fraternization rule wouldn't put me in prison again, but it would jeopardize my dream job.

A job I barely qualify for to begin with.

All of this is at the forefront of my mind, yet when Aiden stands, his height forcing my head back, I can't move away. His gaze slides down the slope of my cheekbone, landing on my mouth. It dawdles there, heats, traces down to the hollow of my throat, leaving electrified skin in its wake. Then it falls away with a curse. "What would these two people want? I can't answer that for you." He releases an expulsion of breath. "I only know I think about you to the point of distraction. The board meeting wasn't the only reason I was drinking tonight. I had to stop myself from going downstairs. I knew I'd end up here again, feeling like I'd melt unless I kiss you."

Oh boy. How am I supposed to keep from collapsing into a puddle of goo let alone continue to keep the barrier between us up when he goes around saying things so baldly honest and romantic? "But the rule," I whisper lamely.

"Yeah. The rule." A line snaps in his cheek, thought churning behind his eyes. "I need to be extra vigilant about that rule with you, Stella. There's already an imbalance of power. Boss. Employee. Then you throw in the fact that I hired you with what some people might call a black spot on your résumé. Whether you're qualified or not—and I believe you are—I have to worry that maybe on some level, you feel indebted to me. You shouldn't. But if I took advantage of that, of you in any way . . . I feel sick just thinking about it."

My knee-jerk reaction is to reassure him that I don't feel indebted. It would be a lie, though. There isn't a single other department store in Manhattan that would have hired me straight out of prison. None but this man with his optimism and willingness to look at the person, not the paperwork. But my attraction—which, I'm very worried could extend beyond a chemical reaction—has nothing to do with gratitude. I'm *earning* the chance he gave me. I'm working myself to the bone for it, and hopefully that will become obvious tomorrow. Hopefully I won't let him down.

But the tug and ripple in my belly is separate.

It's chemical. Organic. Not bred of any thankfulness or sense of obligation.

No, it might be the purest thing I've ever experienced.

What worries me more is the squeeze in my chest when we're close.

I need to back away now. Make some excuse to go home, cut off the magic that is brewing around us relentlessly, making the red garland sparkle where it hangs above the coffeemaker. Giving the Christmas lights a more romantic twinkling glow. My feet don't even feel like they're touching the floor. *I knew I'd end up here again, feeling like I'd melt unless I kiss you.*

"You have to say something, Stella." He laughs softly, his eyes concerned. "Feels a lot like that first-day-of-school, no-clothes dream."

He's so vulnerable, standing there, having taken a leap and bared himself to me. I want nothing more than to reward him for that courage. I want to reward myself with *him*. But for what? I'm not right for this happy-go-lucky man. God, I'm all kinds of *wrong*. When I walk through the main floor of Vivant to use the bathroom or break room, the jewelry saleswomen guard the cabinets. They eye me up and down. They either know about my prison stint or they've decided there is something undeserving about me.

I'm barely out of Bedford Hills a month and I'm trying—I'm trying so hard to be a good person. The kind of person I always scoffed at growing up. I've gone straight. But I haven't even proved to myself that I can do it yet. What if I'm fooling myself? What if I backslide? How many women did I meet while serving my time who were released, then ended up back inside? I'm not better than them. I'm *one* of them. I was there for a reason.

And now I'm *out* for a reason. One I haven't had time to grasp yet.

Why does none of this seem to matter when he's looking at me with his heart in his eyes? It takes me a moment to speak. To get enough air into my lungs to respond. "Paperwork . . ." I push through stiff lips. "I mean, that feels like a big step. Feels . . . official."

He's already nodding. "I know. If there was another way to try this, try us—"

"I know."

"It's more than making sure you're not seeing me out of some misplaced sense of gratitude, Stella, even if that's my main concern." He gestures to himself in kind of an exasperated way. "I'm a rule follower, you know?"

"I do. And that's okay. That's *good*."

"Rule follower," he repeats, thoughtfully, his forehead knitting. As if something just occurred to him. "Stella. Can you do me a favor?"

I eye him dubiously. "What is it?"

"Name one other rule in the employee handbook. Besides the non-fraternization policy, I mean."

Heat seeps out of my pores like molten metal, engulfing me.

I don't know the other rules. I only skipped to that one. *Oh God.*

"Sorry, what?" My airways shrink to the size of licorice. "Can you repeat that?"

I don't like the knowing smile that transforms his features. I don't like it one bit, even though I experience my own relief that he's no longer looking out to sea. Lost.

Mainly, I'm panicked, my head tipped all the way back to meet his eyes, the rich male scent of him fuzzing up my brain waves. "Name one rule in the handbook. Besides the one saying I can't take you out. Can't . . ." He drags his full bottom lip through his teeth, a low sound kindling in his throat. ". . . bring you home to bed. Without signing paperwork."

Bed.

Aiden's bed.

It would be amazing.

Big and sumptuous and heavenly. Especially with him in it.

"I, um . . . well, there's the one rule that says . . ."

"The one that says employees must enter and leave through the rear entrance on weekends?"

"Right," I say brightly, snapping my fingers between us. "That's it. That's the one."

His eyes twinkle. "There's no such rule in the handbook, sweetheart."

Even as I glare up at him, I can't be anything but impressed. He caught me. He caught me considering what could be between us, and now there's significantly less restraint radiating from his body. A change that makes me nervous, while also making my toes curl in anticipation. *Of what?*

"Well played, Cook." I place my hands on his chest with every intention of pushing us apart, but his pecs flex as if starved for my touch and his eyelids droop, his nostrils flaring, and I can't remove my touch for the life of me. Now I'm just standing in the break room feeling up my boss, scrubbing my hands lightly up and over his hard slabs of muscle, then back down, watching him enjoy the treatment so openly, so eagerly. "Fine, you caught me, okay?" I try to swallow the choppiness in my voice. The arousal. "I was curious."

"About us," he clarifies, studying me. "If it could happen."

Despite warning signals from the back of my mind, I hum in affirmation and he grins the grin of a lifetime. It's so gorgeous and bright, transforming every one of his features, I almost liquefy in the face of it. "Maybe," I whisper. "But I—I'm not paperwork curious."

His expression doesn't dim a single watt. "If you don't mind, Stella, I'll be sticking around until you are."

He leans down and kisses my forehead, tucking a loose wisp of hair behind my ear. Then his eyes take one last lap around my face and he takes my hand, guiding me out of the break room. He leaves me outside the entrance to the storage room where I've been working most of the week, emerging a few seconds later with my purse and jacket. He holds the puffer open so I can slide my arms into the holes and I can't help but savor it. The first time anyone has ever held my coat for me.

"How are you feeling about tomorrow?" he asks, his vibratory thrum just beside my temple.

"I don't know. I don't know what you meant by 'sticking around.' That could mean anything, really. Are you threatening to woo me or something? I don't get—"

"Stella," he interrupts with a smile in his voice. "I meant how are you feeling about unveiling the window in the morning."

My face has to be magenta. "Oh. Sure." I duck my head under the guise of lining up the zipper of my jacket. "A combination of nervous and . . . more nervous. Mostly." When I straighten, his curiosity and patient attention on my face make me want to say more. "But no matter what happens, I'll know I didn't take short-cuts or pass on any ideas because they were too hard. I'll know it was my best effort. I have the sore lower back to prove it."

He makes a sympathetic noise, circling around the back of me. Before I can guess his intention, he slips his hand beneath my jacket and runs a firm thumb up the center of my lower spine. My shameless moan is echoing off the walls of the main floor of Vivant. "If only we had the proper paperwork filed. I'd be taking you home for more of this." His thumb digs in, circling on top of my sore muscles. It feels so good, my vision doubles, my head falling back on my shoulders. "I'd do my part. A hot bath would do the rest." From behind, he rests his mouth on my ear, his hand settling on my waist very briefly, squeezing. "Tell me you want to hear what would happen next, Stella. Give me permission to say it."

"Permission granted," I say with embarrassing quickness, because who wouldn't? Who wouldn't want this beautiful man rasping secrets into their ear?

Aiden prowls around me slowly, stopping when we face one another. The hand on my waist has been dragged low, along the small of my back, and that's where it remains now, burning me through my clothes. "Once we worked out the strain in your back . . ." He leans in and settles his mouth on top of my ear. "We'd work on making the right parts of you nice and sore, wouldn't we?"

"Aiden," I breathe, half admonishing, half stunned. I really thought I had a read on this man. He's a wholesome rule follower who believes the best in people. A man who has a few demons lurking but is innately good at his core. Now we're throwing a dirty streak into the mix?

Good grief.

"I tried to warn you," he says, taking my hand and leading me out of Vivant onto the street where bitter Manhattan cold does its best to cool my flaming cheeks. "I'm not always nice."

"Oh, don't worry, I remember" slips out.

His lips twitch while he's flagging me down a cab. "I was hoping you would."

At this time of night on the avenue, taxis are in abundance and one slows to a stop at the curb immediately. Aiden hands the man a twenty through the passenger side window, tells him to keep the eventual change and opens the rear door for me. I'm tempted to make an issue out of him paying for my ride home—I'm fine with walking or taking the train—but it's late, I'm ready to drop and getting to my bed faster sounds like an ideal plan. "Thank you."

"Hey. You took my mind off the board meeting and saved me from a bourbon hangover tomorrow. It's the least I can do." I take a seat in the back and look up at him. "Good night, Stella," he says, a little hoarse, looking me over top to bottom as if memorizing me. "See you bright and early for the unveiling."

"Yes." I swallow hard. "I'm definitely not thinking of skipping town or anything."

"Hey," he says seriously, making me look up in time to catch his wink. "When in doubt, remember Penguin Chernobyl."

For the second time tonight, I laugh and he pauses in the act of closing the taxi door, as if waiting for the full sound to play out before finally pushing it shut, leaving us separated by glass. He shoves his hands into his pockets and stands back on the curb, looking so perfectly old-fashioned and debonair in the streetlamp glow, I can barely catch my breath.

And I lose it completely a half mile into the ride when I find the long, slim, black velvet jewelry box in my jacket pocket containing the gold key chain necklace.

Chapter 6

Aiden

I don't sleep a damn second all night. Around 3:00 A.M., I give up trying and order two dozen donuts through Postmates. Most of them, I plan on bringing with me this morning to the unveiling of Stella's window, but I eat three before I've even set the box down on the counter.

And I wonder why my tailor always has to make space accommodations in the seats of my pants. This butt is courtesy of baked goods and there's no getting around it—that fact *or* my ass. Hell, though, it's good and sturdy and I carry my own padding with me.

Can't beat it with a stick.

I pick out a fourth donut—a green-and-white-striped masterpiece with chocolate reindeer bits and pieces—and pace past my eight-foot Douglas fir to my living room window. The reflection of white lights blinking on my tree blurs together with the lights of the city as I look out over the skyline toward Chelsea. Where Stella lives. I didn't anticipate being this nervous. I should have taken a peek at the window in advance and given her time to make changes, if any were necessary. I'm confident in her. She's smart. Insightful. She's punched in early every day since Tuesday and left Vivant late. If the window isn't a success, it won't be for lack of trying.

Maybe this trial period was a bad idea. If I'd just hired her without the moratorium, there wouldn't be so much riding on this reveal. And it was only going to be low-key, a few of my managers, some key staff and our social media rep would be there to witness the moment. But on the way home last night, I got a text from my father saying he and Shirley would be outside Vivant at 6:00 A.M. for the unveiling.

Stella doesn't need that pressure. And the last thing I want is them digging into her background and making an issue out of her record. I'm prepared to stand by my decision. I'm prepared to protect her in any way I can, but if the window isn't a home run, the board will make both of those things as difficult as possible.

Stella already has her own family problems, she doesn't need the judgment from mine. I've been in that seat many times, faced the disapproval, felt it burn layers off my skin. The thought of that happening to her when she's already so raw from the last four years, has me pacing back and forth in front of the wide window, the half-eaten carcass of my fourth donut lying forgotten on the ottoman tray.

There's a huge part of me, a protective part, that toys with the idea of rescheduling the unveiling, but I don't know that it would stop my family from descending on the proceeding like vultures. Nor do I want Stella thinking I lack confidence in the final product.

With no clear solution in sight, I duck into my second bedroom-turned-gym and start lifting weights. I throw myself into some pull-ups in the doorway and rush through crunches—because I hate them—in the hopes of blowing off this stress that's plaguing me. But when no amount of exercise seems to loosen the tension in my midsection, I finally relent, admitting to myself that there's only one thing that will help.

The very second I give myself permission to beat off, I tent my sweatpants. My dick gets hard so instantaneously, I get dizzy on my march to the bathroom. Undressing quickly, I turn on the shower to hot and step in underneath the spray, reaching for the soap before I'm fully wet. Lathering my palm with suds. As soon as I close my eyes and press my forehead up against the misty tile of the shower wall, there's Stella. Topless in those tights.

Pouting at me.

She thinks that glare makes her look so ferocious, but it's the hottest damn thing east of the Mississippi. Makes me want to work to get her five percent crooked and one hundred percent perfect smile back. Makes me want to find out which buttons have to be pushed to erase the wariness in her eyes—and glaze them right over.

Damn, though. I hate that this feels like a violation of the rules. I'm doing something seedy when I'd rather be dating her out in the open. I want to pursue her the right way. Instead, here I am, gripping my cock and feeling my balls tighten with the ungodly mixture of lust and shame. "I'm sorry," I whisper against the mouth of Imaginary Stella. "For what I'm about to do to you." She's sitting on my desk in the office—an ethics violation if I ever heard one—and she's playing with her tits. Peeking up at me through her bangs, fingers teasing her nipples into little points.

One soapy stroke of my erection and I'm already panting.

Am I a kind man? Yeah. To a fault, some might say. But the niceness slides right off of me now, circling the drain. The only time I've ever been able to completely cut loose is during sex. My mind turns off and my body engages. There is still an expectation for me to meet, but it's a different one. Giving pleasure doesn't require me to be kind. Or smile when I don't feel like it. And the permission to drop my guard and *go* is exhilarating.

In the past, women have been unable to connect with one of my two sides. They either want an all-around gentleman, thus re-coiling from my aggressiveness in bed. Or they don't even make it past coffee with me, assuming I'll be too nice in all other aspects, as well. Including the bedroom. Without the benefit of proxim-ity, Stella might have fallen into that latter category. Thank Christ that didn't happen. There isn't a chance in hell I could have forgot-ten about her like I did the other women.

"Don't apologize," she murmurs, teasing the seam of my mouth with a light sideways drag of her tongue. "Just make it extra good for me, okay?"

"Fuck that, I'll make it great," I growl against the tile, the grip of my hand cinching tighter, speed picking up already. "Just let me in."

Looking me in the eye, she opens her thighs wide, so perfectly wide, showing me her damp pussy and the strip of trimmed dark hair. Goddamn. She scoots to the edge of my desk and walks her fingertips up the center of my chest, wrapping her hand around my tie. "Show me what it feels like to be yours, Aiden."

"Yes," I grunt, not even sure I'm going to make it to the end of this fantasy before I blow. It's too much, hearing her say she wants to be mine. Because I can't deny that when it comes to Stella, I've been experiencing an unfamiliar sense of . . . greediness. I want to gather her up and *learn* her. Better than anyone. As far back as I can remember, I've envisioned myself in a committed relation-ship. Someday. The idea of coming home every day to the same person and knowing how they want to be pleasured, what they like to eat, how to coax them out of a bad mood . . . God, I've dreamed of that. To be depended on like that.

To depend on someone else to know what I need even when I don't.

The way Stella did tonight. Distracting me with that game.

I've been in relationships that *should* have been ideal. On paper, they were partnerships that fit the bill. Good careers, ambitions, similar hopes for the future. But I've never had this extra-sharp carve of lust for someone and also wanted to sit next to them on the couch in matching robes and slippers before. With Stella, it's both. Hunger *and* affection. Which is insane—I've known her less than a week. Crazy talk. Yet here I am, fucking her in a frenzy on my imaginary office desk and already thinking about how good it'll feel to cuddle her up afterward, once I've drained her of anything resembling energy.

I'll be the big spoon.

She'll tuck her tush into my lap and we'll argue about china patterns.

A rough sound claws its way out of my throat and fuck. *Fuck.* Pleasure stops teasing and digs in deep, firing me to the edge of agony before releasing me to drop, drop, drop. *Jesus.* Thinking about picking out side plates with Stella has sent me into the throes of my best orgasm in recent memory, my knees nearly buckling from the monumental rush, the lightening of the tight weight between my legs, that hot, milky substance sliding down the tile below me.

Just before that final spurt, I grind my forehead into the tile and think of Stella knotting my tie in front of the bathroom mirror, both of us dressed for work and trying to drink coffee on the fly—and I groan loudly through clenched teeth, stroking myself furiously over the finish line, slumping forward with both of my palms flat on the tile, my rib cage expanding and contracting in quick pants.

Good lord, I've got it bad.

* * *

I ASSUME I'M going to be the first to arrive, but when my town car rolls to a stop outside Vivant, Stella is there in the near darkness, sitting on the lip of the Vivant front window in her signature boots, tights, sweater dress and puffy jacket, listening to her headphones.

Right away, I'm hit with a prickle of guilt over this morning's activities. Not only did I fantasize about her body, I had the nerve to pick out dinnerware without her input. Double shame on me. If I wasn't worried about her freezing to death, it might have taken me a few more minutes to tamp down the guilt, but when I see her blow warm air into her hands, I smack my hand down on the button to lower the window.

"Stella." She doesn't look up, probably because her music is too loud. I call out to her again. This time she shoots to her feet and pops out an earbud. "Come wait in here with me. It's warm and I've got donuts."

"Say less." She crosses her arms and kind of stomps toward the car with her head down against the wind. Plates and saucers with a basket weave pattern are dancing through my mind as she climbs into the car beside me, her wary blue gaze traveling between me and my driver.

"Stella, this is Keith. Keith, Stella," I say. "We're unveiling her window this morning."

"Ahhh, very nice," Keith says over the talk radio station, catching Stella's eye in the rearview. "Those penguins are going to be a tough act to follow. I do *not* envy you that. No, I don't. Who does not love a little waddling penguin, eh? No one. Everyone loves them. Now they're making Santa's toys? With little tools in their flippers? Forget about it." He does a half turn. "But I'm sure yours will be amazing, Stella."

Stella extends a hand. "Donuts, please."

"Thank you, Keith," I say, dryly, giving him a polite nod as I roll up the partition window, leaving me and Stella in the quiet. When I settle the box of donuts in her lap and lift the lid, she sucks in a breath and smiles, making my chest tug. "I don't want to influence you one way or the other, but the peanut butter and jelly donut was made by God himself."

She soundlessly repeats the words *peanut butter and jelly donut*. Makes a considering face. "Too risky. It might give me flashbacks to second grade and the last thing I want to think about this morning is Todd Peterson dipping his PBJs in lemon-lime Gatorade." She winces. "Too late. I'm thinking about it."

"And here I thought I was weird for putting cool ranch Doritos in mine."

"No, that makes you a visionary." She points to one of the flakier, powdered ones. "What is this one?"

"S'mores."

"Sold." She plucks the donut from the box with two fingers and rotates it a few times, looking for the best spot to bite. When she finally sinks her teeth into the crust and moans, my Adam's apple gets stuck behind my bow tie. Is it hot in here? I reach up and adjust the air-conditioning vents, only to remember it's the middle of December and the car is being heated, not cooled. "Aren't you going to have one?" Stella asks me.

I cough into my fist because I suspect my voice is scratchier than a porcupine with psoriasis. "I already had my usual three and a half this morning."

Stella blinks. "Impressive." She hesitates to take a second bite. "I'm going to save the rest for when I have coffee—" I'm already holding out my metal travel mug. After a beat, she takes it from me, steadying it in her lap. "Thank you."

"Don't thank me yet." I sigh. "I have some news."

The donut stops midair on its way to her mouth. "Uh-oh."

"Yeah." I push a set of fingers through my hair. "The board decided to be here for the unveiling. Found out late last night." The sound of her gulp fills the backseat. "It doesn't change anything, all right? I'm going to run interference as much as possible."

Her gaze cuts over to me. "I don't need you to do that, Aiden."

"They can be unnecessarily cruel sometimes. It's one thing to have it directed at me, but you?" Baked goods churn in my stomach. "No. I can't have that."

"And I don't want special treatment," she says softly. "Would you be acting as a buffer between any other window dresser and the harsher parts of their job?"

I close my eyes. "No."

It's impossible to describe what happens inside of me when I'm around Stella. It's like someone is stripping wallpaper in my chest, replacing the Sheetrock, nailing up new artwork.

"This is a trial run, right?" Across the console, she nudges me in the side with her elbow. "Let me go through the trial. I can handle it."

"Are you sure? Keith could have us in Mexico by Monday."

"Aiden," she scoff-laughs. I like how easily my name comes to her. Even more than that, I love the way her eyes meander over me. Down my chest and stomach. The fly of my dress pants, briefly. She must think the black fringe of her lashes is hiding her checkout mission, but they're definitely not. Does she think of me when *she's* in the shower? Has she touched herself in bed remembering what it felt like to have her legs around my waist? "I like your bow tie this morning. Are those walruses with wreaths around their necks?"

"They sure are." I reach up and pull the sides to tighten it. "Found this one at the Union Square Christmas market two Decembers ago. Only one of its kind. Unless the salesgirl was just pulling my leg."

Stella rolls her lips inward, suppressing a smile I would have paid admission to see bloom to its full potential. "Something tells me she was being honest. I can't imagine anyone but you walking around with a walrus bow tie." A few seconds tick by. A few seconds when I can only think about leaning across the seat and licking the taste of marshmallow and chocolate from her mouth. "Do you have ties for every season? Or is it just Christmas?"

"Christmas only. The rest of the year is just a basic rotation of colors. Red, black, blue."

"Christmas is special to you."

"Yeah. It is." Stella is always trying to focus our conversations on me. I'm torn between letting her—maybe she's not comfortable enough to reveal things about herself yet—and changing the subject to her, instead of me. Maybe it's my apprehension over Shirley and Bradley having access to this girl who I want to wrap in blankets and ferry to Mexico, but I'm feeling anxious to know more about Stella. Now. Before the window unveiling. Before anyone else has a chance to chip away at this moment with her. "Is Christmas special to you?"

She looks up quickly. Then forward. "I have good memories of it. That calm feeling of everyone being sealed into the house for a full day, nowhere to go because nothing is open. My parents were always working—constantly—I was a latchkey kid. But

Christmas . . . it was the only day of the year when they didn't take work calls. Or rush out to meetings. My mother usually burned a pie and Dad would sit on the floor of the living room and read whatever World War II book my mother bought him." She stops to think. "Those memories are special."

"Did you always have a tree?"

"Yes," she says slowly, as if trying to recall. "Up until middle school, maybe. We stopped decorating so much as I got older. We were barely having meals at the same table anymore. I guess it didn't make much sense to create an atmosphere for us to be together. We were all just doing our own thing." Her expression turns wry. "I was doing my own thing. I need to take responsibility for that. The thought of being parted from my friends for even a day turned me into teenage Godzilla."

"Fear of missing out."

She nods, scratches at a spot on the knee of her right stocking. "I really could have done with some missing out. My parents tried to warn me that I was . . . slipping. Down this treacherous slope. But I didn't listen." A beat passes. "It's weird. When you're younger, you think you know everything. Then you get older and live in constant awareness of how little you actually know and understand."

"An age-old curse," I agree, soaking up her insight like a sponge. We seem to keep ending up in these moments, confiding in each other—and I don't want them to stop. We've only known each other a short time, but I've never been more comfortable talking to anyone. It's like a new portal of the universe has opened up and suddenly . . . the bond I've never had with anyone is being offered to me in a forbidden package. But I can't stop untying the strings. "Your parents. How is the relationship now?"

"Awkward." Her brow knits. "I want to have a relationship with them as an adult. But my adulthood was sort of . . . put on hold. Now I'm trying to find a reason for them to like me, be proud of me, before I reach out for something meaningful. I don't want to mess up a second time."

That confession tightens my chest. I want to dig in, want to question her about everything involving those rebellious years, but I can't throw a dart directly at the bull's-eye or I sense she'll clam up. Christmas seems to be our jumping-off point into more serious topics, so I stick with that, hoping she'll jump with me. "What was your tree decorating style growing up? Did you start at the top or bottom? Strategic placement or haphazard?"

A quiet smile twitches her lips. "Oh, strategic. All the way. I would sketch it out with crayons beforehand."

I tip my head toward the covered window. "Sounds about right. You stopped getting the urge to plan it out once you'd grown up?"

"Yeah, that would have meant I cared about something. The horror." Staring past me out the window onto the avenue, she seems to forget herself for a moment. "My friends would have laughed at me. Nothing worse, right? Nicole—"

When she cuts herself off and doesn't continue, I duck my head to catch her line of sight. "What about Nicole?"

Stella becomes fidgety. "My best friend came from a difficult family situation. They moved from apartments to motel rooms and back. Her father had some substance abuse issues and couldn't keep his jobs longer than a few weeks. She was over at my house a lot. Eating, spending the night. My parents were really generous. They were there for her as much as they could be, with their jobs being so busy. But of course she was defensive. Of course she was resentful. She was a kid in this unstable situation that was scary and uncertain." She stops for a moment. "When she started party-ing and shoplifting . . . I went with her. I was her best friend. That's what best friends do. They have each other's backs. They don't let them go out alone. And somewhere along the way, I just got so absorbed. She was my new family and if I did anything without her, she'd get hurt. I'd feel guilty. I never even told her I was tak-ing online college courses after high school." She wets her lips. "That's when I knew something was wrong with our friendship. The fact that she wouldn't like me pursuing a dream. But I still couldn't break it off. And then it was too late. I agreed to hold up the restaurant, telling myself it would be the last time I caved. That I was going to let the numbness wear off. I *missed* myself."

I have to bite down on the inside of my cheek so I don't reach across the seat and pull her into my lap. Stella is this incredible blend of strength and pain and self-awareness. And I can't even imagine the courage it took to apply for this job. To type out her mistakes on a page, show up and move forward and pursue some-thing she loves after having her life veer in such a drastic direction from where it started. "And now? Do you still miss yourself?"

A line appears on her forehead. "I don't know. I've been paused for four years. I'm still trying to hit Play again." Her gaze drifts over to Vivant. "No, I *am* . . . hitting it. I'm hitting Play and trying to pretend I know what happens next. But really, I'm just walking into it blind."

"You're not alone in that, Stella. Most people have no idea what to expect from the next calendar day, let alone year. Look at 2020." I wave a hand. "Actually, don't."

Laughing quietly, she shifts a little to face me, crossing one long leg over the other. A physical subject change—and I'm going to let her have it since I already got a lot more than I was hoping for.

"You don't walk into anything blind, do you?" Her eyes narrow playfully. "Except maybe . . . decorating your office."

Surprise leaps in my rib cage and pops right out of my mouth. "What?"

"You decorate your own office, don't you?"

Wow. I can hear my own heartbeat. "How did you know that?"

"I . . . don't know." Her expression proves she's puzzled. "When you carried me to your office the other night, I just knew. You're so tidy and tucked in, but I think . . ."

"What?"

God help me, there's a pink flush creeping up her neck. Pinker than the frosting on the strawberry shortcake donut. "I think you like to get messy sometimes." She jolts a little, as though caught off guard by the sensuality in her tone, sitting up straighter in the seat. "I mean, I bet you don't plan out *your* Christmas tree decorating strategy."

There's no way she realizes how rare it is for someone to see into me like this. Does she get right to the heart of everyone or is it just me? I really don't like the idea of her looking this deep with anyone else. I want that insightfulness all to myself. Jesus, I'm jealous of the possibility of her giving that gift to someone else who may or may not even exist. What is this girl doing to me? Is it possible she could appreciate my lighter *and* coarser sides?

"That's exactly right," I say, trying to keep my tone even when I'd like to drag her beneath me on this seat and feel the rasp of those tights on my hips. "Christmas should be a little messy."

Her still-pink cheek twitches. "You manage the wrong department store for messy."

I point at the establishment in question. "That's for other people. Not me."

"You don't want your family store to reflect you in any way?"

"Maybe it already does. Tidy and tucked in on the surface. Messy behind the scenes." The window is fogging up behind her and it takes me a few beats to realize why. We're both starting to breathe harder. I know damn well I can't just pluck her off that seat and sit her in my lap. Can't slide my hand up the inside of her sweater or let her feel my hard-on against her ass. I meant what I said last night. About being a rule follower. About making sure Stella wants me—authentically—and not because of gratitude. Or obligation. Or pressure because I'm her boss. The man who overlooked her prison record. I'm trying so hard not to lay a finger on her until I'm positive, but God, it's getting more difficult by the second.

We're in the back of this car, alone, it's half-dark outside and she's in those dang soft-looking tights, looking at me with heavy eyelids, her tits rising and falling, ripe fruit asking to be stroked and sucked. One would think I didn't churn one out in the shower this morning for all the blood rushing to my cock. Making it thicken and rise.

On top of it all, her mouth would taste like marshmallows and chocolate.

Who knew God would forsake me a week before Christmas?

"Stella . . ."

"Love contract. Paperwork. I know." She leans forward. Toward me. Scoots a little closer on the seat. As if in a trance, she reaches out and traces the line of buttons down my white dress shirt, stopping an inch from my belt buckle. She draws that hand away quickly, but I catch it. Without thinking. I lay it flat over my heart and she makes this half whimper, half gasp sound, probably because that damn organ is going a million miles an hour and there's no pretending it isn't. "Aiden . . ." she murmurs, dragging her gaze up to my mouth and leaning in. And of course I'm leaning, too, ready to meet her halfway on everything from kissing to china patterns.

When we're an inch apart, the sides of our noses touch, her expulsion of breath bathing my lips, my hand moving of its own accord, reaching out and fisting the section of her jacket that curves into her side, pulling her toward me, my dick turning to steel when she shudders.

"Tell me you're wearing the key chain necklace."

"I'm wearing it," she says, her breath hitching. "Under my clothes."

The gold resting on her skin. Heating. Staying with her all day. God, I love knowing that. It appeases the foreign possessiveness she stirs in me. Possessiveness I should be fending off or refusing to entertain, but I can't seem to help it. I've only ever had this semi-twisted feeling for her and I don't know how to turn it off. "Tell me you go home and think of me," I demand against her mouth.

"I go home. And I think of you." One second ticks by. Two. "I think about that time in the elevator you told me you can be downright rough. I think about it a lot."

A fire lights in my head, my lower body. She's squirming on the seat and it's painful to know what that means. What her body is communicating. If I laid her down on this leather seat and dropped my hips down, punched them a little and rocked some more, she'd moan. We'd wet up the seam of her tights in a matter of seconds. I know it better than I know how to fashion this bow tie around my neck. Even though we've never been physical. "Is that what . . ." I stop myself from asking what I want to know. This is not the time, place or circumstance.

"What?" She moves closer, her hip pressing against the outside of my thigh, and now she's got ahold of my jacket lapel, gripping it tight. How long have we been on the verge of kissing? It's like some unique brand of torture foreplay crafted by the two of us. If our tongues touched right now, I swear to Christ I'd come. "Ask me."

"Is roughness what gets you off?"

She moans at the question, and I'm panting now, turning, dragging her closer, ready to yank down her tights and lick her until she forgets her own name. My question is out there. Hanging. I can't take it back, no matter how inappropriate. No matter how much I wish the timing were different. "Yes. And thinking of you being . . ." She squeezes her eyes closed. "Turned on. In the office. For me. Trying to hold it together. You're hard and sweaty and you need relief, but there's nothing you can do about it."

"I didn't realize you had a camera pointed at my desk."

Her breathy laugh seals the deal. Completely robs me of scruples and ethics and restraint. I'm going to settle her onto my lap and unzip my pants. There is no way in hell I can live another second without the wet squeeze of her pussy sliding lower and lower, cradling me. Feeling her move, listening to her whimper. If we move slowly enough, the car won't rock. Maybe. *Jesus.* I'm not even sure I can make myself care about being caught when I'm this hungry for her. "I need you, Stella," I growl, turning us, positioning myself to be straddled—

A horn honks loudly.

Two, three honks.

I'm lost in a stupor, my thoughts sticky and lost in an unrecognizable pattern. Who is honking? What year is this? I don't know, but I'm halfway through dragging an employee onto my lap in public. Having sex with her—all formalities tossed away like a batch of burned cookies. The sun has begun to rise while we've been . . . not kissing. Just grabbing clothing and breathing hard and confessing fantasies. I could live my life doing this. I could keep going through the next seventy Christmases, tasting her chocolate breath in my mouth and listening to her tell me she thinks of me erect and sweaty at my desk. That it gets her revved up.

But someone is honking and I'm outside Vivant. My place of *work*.

Possibly taking advantage of an employee.

The lining of my stomach burns. "Stella," I manage, swallowing, settling her gently back on the opposite side of the backseat. "I'm sorry. Jesus. I got carried away."

"We both did, Aiden," she responds, dazed, repeatedly curling messed-up strands of hair behind her ears. "It's o-okay."

I want to argue, but I get distracted by the swollen rosiness of her mouth. Her red-stained cheeks. The fact that her hips keep shifting around, as if I've left her unsatisfied. Of course I did. I started something I can't finish. Yet. Something I might not ever be able to finish if she doesn't like me enough to make this . . . situation between us official.

With that troubling thought in my head, I turn and look out the back window of the town car, inwardly wincing when I see my father and Shirley stepping out of their limousine, Randall skulking two feet behind them. They nod at someone up ahead and that's when I see the store managers have started to gather, Jordyn, the first-floor supervisor, among them. Either none of them have seen us or I'm exceptionally lucky to have so many discreet employees.

I turn back to the girl beside me, still trying to compose herself on the seat—I can relate. I'm not sure I'll ever be composed again after what we just did. But this moment isn't about me. Or even us. This is Stella's time.

"Remember," she says, addressing me before climbing out of the car. "You don't have to protect me from criticism. Let me hear their opinion. I have to be able to handle it, okay?"

It costs me an effort to nod, but I manage a stiff one.

Watching my relatives out of the corner of my eye, I feel my earlier nerves bubble back to the surface, accompanied on the growing tide of protectiveness I have for Stella. But mostly, I'm proud of her. For coming out of her pause. Moving forward. And I hope like hell that whatever is on the other side of the paper is enough to keep her pressing Play.

Chapter 7
Stella

When I was in fifth grade, my school PTA held a mock art gallery opening. Sculptures and paintings created by students were put on display in the gymnasium. Parents could walk through and buy the items. Of course, it was kind of customary to purchase your child's creation, and looking back, it was mainly a way for the PTA to make a lot of easy cash. And I remember it feeling just like this. Skin vibrating, muscles taut, so hot that I'm cold.

There is something about revealing art that is so personal, so vulnerable. The concept for this window came straight out of my head. No one approved it. No one said, yes this will work. It's a flying leap. It's believing in an idea—and since *everyone* has ideas, this is when the impostor syndrome kicks in. What makes me think *my* idea was going to stop foot traffic on Fifth Avenue? What makes me think I'm artistically gifted at all?

Just like at that PTA art show, it's my parents whose reactions mean the most.

But this time, they're not here. They're not going to show up with big, enthusiastic smiles on their faces, armed with praise and a suggestion that we stop for celebratory ice cream on the way home. They don't even know I have this job.

Maybe they've completely moved on with their lives and aren't thinking of me at all.

That possibility threatens to take the wind out of me, so I push it away. I remind myself that if I can do well at window dressing, if I can prove to myself what I'm capable of, I'll eventually attempt to prove it to them, too. I'll try again with my parents. In time.

Up ahead, some of the upper management employees are gathered at the window. Jordyn is there, along with Mrs. Bunting, the head of human resources, who I met on my first day. I notice she seems to be on familiar terms with Aiden's grandmother, who is skeptical of me right off the bat. She watches me approach the way a house cat behaves when their owner brings home a puppy. Can't say I blame her. I'm probably younger than she was expecting, went a little heavy on the eyeliner this morning—an attempt to keep Aiden at arm's length that clearly didn't work—and now I'm exiting a foggy-windowed vehicle with her grandson. Not to mention, my eyes are still crossed from . . . whatever just happened.

What *did* just happen?

I think Aiden and I almost skipped kissing and went right to the main event. In a parked car on one of the busiest avenues in the world. I've never lost myself like that with a member of the opposite sex. Granted, I haven't even breathed on a member of the male species in four years, probably longer, but I would remember the feeling of having my stomach levitate, my intimate flesh squeezing, heart going bananas inside my eardrums. I definitely would recall feeling safe and cherished and *required*.

Unable to stop myself, I turn and glance at Aiden over my shoulder. I'm not the only one who is shaken up. Little sweat speckles soak through the front of his white dress shirt, his bow tie is a touch off-center and that curl graces the center of his forehead. His gaze travels from me to his family ahead and darkens with . . . I don't know. It's hard to tell. Worry, yes. But there's a sort of fierce protectiveness in those depths, too, that gives my knees the consistency of wet paste.

When he returns his attention to me, I lift one corner of my mouth to let him know I'm good to handle whatever his family throws at me. Even though I'm not exactly *sure* of that fact. All I know is I've already gotten too much special treatment recently. From the judge, the prison system itself and now Aiden.

If my window isn't a success, I need to take that result on the chin. And if I don't get another chance to prove myself, well, most people don't even get a first one, right?

I just really, really hope they like it, because this has been the best week of my life. I spent the last three days decorating a Vivant window—for Christmas, no less. And it was a constant rush. Hours sped past in colorful blurs of enjoyment and creative impulses. Not only that, I had the means to follow those urges and watch them come to life. There is nothing, no job in this world, I want to do more. But as I come to a stop about ten feet from the glass, forcing a smile for Jordyn, that nervous PTA art show feeling has me convinced the paper will be torn down and there will be a pile of dirt sitting on a plate.

What if the last three days was a hallucination?

Something warm and solid brushes against the back of my fingers and I realize Aiden is standing next to me, his hand grazing mine in secret. His jaw is bunched up tight, but his eyes are reassuring. Confident in me. But they turn wary when his father and grandmother darken the sidewalk in front of us.

"Aren't you going to introduce us, Aiden?" says the grandmother, her sharp attention zipping upward from my secondhand combat boots to my cat-eye makeup.

"Shirley, Brad, I'd like you to meet Stella Schmidt. Stella, this is my grandmother and father, Shirley and Brad Cook."

I hold out my hand and they stare at it for a moment, before Bradley does a shoulder roll and we shake, followed by the same from Shirley, though she more or less just drapes her limp hand into mine and suffers through the handshake like it's an indignity. I start to marvel over the fact that these two people are related to Aiden, but then I remember Aunt Edna.

God bless Aunt Edna, wherever she is.

"I'm definitely unfamiliar with your name, as I suspected I would be," Shirley says, her warm breath clouding in the December air. She pulls her ankle-length coat tighter. "Where exactly have you worked prior to this?"

I can practically feel Aiden coiling like a spring beside me.

My own palms are growing damp in the laser sights of this woman. She'd make a good prison guard. None of us would cross her. *Here comes Hawk Eyes, hide the nail polish.* It has been a long time since I needed to impress someone. Most of my teenage years into my early twenties was about *not* caring if I impressed people. "I have a background in fashion merchandising, but this is my first time dressing a window." I force a smile onto my face that comes suspiciously easily, probably thanks to the amount of smiling I've been doing with Aiden. "I'm very grateful for the opportunity."

"Yes." Her gaze ticks from me, back to Aiden's town car. "*How* grateful is the question," she mutters dryly, the words meant for my ears alone.

At least I think I'm the only one who hears Shirley's comment until I turn around to find Aiden looking pale. Jaw bunched. His gaze tracks over my features and I can tell he's not going to let that comment go unaddressed. Quickly, I shake my head at him, reminding him to let me handle whatever is leveled at me this morning. I meant it when I said I don't want any more special treatment. Even if everyone hates this window, at least I'll have earned the outcome by myself, whether it's good or bad.

Aiden remains poised on the edge of irritation for another moment, then swallows hard and quickly lifts his phone to his ear. "Seamus, you can start taking the paper down." He listens. "Thank you."

"I want to stand next to the guest of honor," Jordyn announces, coming up beside me and hooking an arm through mine, dragging me closer to the window and away from Aiden's relatives. "Excuse us." I'm still reeling a little from Shirley's comment but fight through the nausea in my middle and focus on the moment ahead. "Don't mind that woman," Jordyn says out of the corner of her mouth. "You could present her with a swimming pool full of chocolate and she'd still look like she just ate a turd."

I disguise my laughter with a cough. "Thanks for the save."

"Welcome." She squeezes our linked arms and addresses the assembled crowd. "We finally get to see what's had this girl scurrying in and out of the store from morning until night."

"It's going to be great," one of the other managers assures me, knocking back the final gulps of her coffee and sighing wistfully at the paper cup. "That was terrible. And yet, I need more."

"We love the red dress display you created on the first floor. People have been coming in just to pose with it for Instagram," says another, pronouncing Instagram in three distinct syllables. "Maybe you could do something like that in lingerie? We could use a boost!"

My ribs stretch to accommodate the warmth building in my chest. "I'd love to. I would. But I'm technically only working on a trial basis." Even as I say this, my mind is filling out with a list of ideas. "But . . . I guess you'd have to appeal to men. Make it accessible to them. They are the ones who'll be buying expensive lingerie this time of year—"

The rapt attention of my co-workers snaps in two when the first strip of paper drops from the window. My lips clamp shut. The only thing being revealed in the window is Seamus and he's grinning down at Jordyn like it's Christmas morning and she's the pile of presents beneath the tree. "This motherfucker," she mutters, waving her hand at the admiring custodian to hurry up and finish stripping down the paper. "Uh-uh. Nobody wants to look at you. Keep moving."

Seamus chuckles, the sound muffled by glass, and he tugs down another strip. Now some of the design begins to come into view behind him. The swarms of butterflies dangling from invisible fishing line from the ceiling. The refracted light being projected on every wall, courtesy of the mirror pieces adhered to the floor. Another piece of paper comes down and there's half of the red dress, then eventually the whole thing. I went with a vintage black metal wire form with an antique stand, unearthed from the bowels of Vivant's storage space in the basement, and I mentally rejoice in that choice now, because in the early morning light, the throwback to the past makes the display look as though it has been transported here from another time and place.

"Oh," Jordyn whispers. "Wow. I was bracing myself just in case it sucked, but you went the hell off. It's beautiful, Stella. If you don't get hired full-time, I'll wear elf ears until January."

The manager of the lingerie department turns with a thumbs-up, swiveling back around quickly so she doesn't miss the next length of paper coming down. And then it's completely revealed, for everyone to see. Somehow I know without looking that Aiden is standing beside me, and I flex my fingers, brushing them up against his bigger ones. Briefly, his middle finger snags around mine and holds, before we drop our hands away.

I gather my courage and look up and over at his face, finding him transfixed by the window, but saying nothing. Holding my breath, I follow his line of vision to the bold, copper-colored stenciled lettering on the glass. GIVE THEM A NEW BEGINNING.

An odd sound reaches my ears and I realize everyone is clapping for me.

Oh God.

There's a rise of pressure under my breastbone that I don't know how to handle. Hot moisture pushing on the backs of my eyes, threatening to come out. Blinking rapidly, I swallow hard and say thank you, my face flushing when I clearly sound like I'm trying not to cry.

Why? Because you designed one good window?

Nicole's voice filters in through everyone's hushed chatter and makes a roost in my head. Maybe this time I even invited her voice, needing it to bring me back down to earth before I get carried away. That's what my best friend always used to do. She'd remind me how fleeting the high from an achievement could be, while our friendship was forever. It's hard to allow myself the moment. It's hard not to temper this rush of satisfaction with a reminder like, *yes, but your next window could be terrible.* But when I look back at Aiden and find him smiling down at me with untempered pride, I shut out the negative voices, including the loudest one. For now. And I let myself coast on this wave of happiness. Relief.

"I don't get speechless very often, Stella," he says, shaking his head. "But damn. I don't have the words to do it justice."

"This calls for vodka," Jordyn stage-whispers to the group, garnering their attention. "Happy hour drinks after work."

"Done."

"I'm in."

"*Coffeeeee.*"

Jordyn gives my arm a final pat, then joins the rest of the managers. I'm left standing beside Aiden, and I savor the next few seconds. The dash of cabs racing down the avenue behind us. The icy wind on my cheeks. The smell of bagels and garlic and perfume and gasoline that seems to forever linger in the atmosphere of the city. I savor the momentary lack of impostor syndrome and marvel at the giant opening it leaves behind. The endless possibilities of what I could fit inside that unoccupied gap.

Until Shirley and Bradley block my view of the store window, I honestly forget that they are still here. Shirley's features are no less pinched than they were before, but Bradley's expression is utterly blank. At least until he looks at Aiden and his eyes widen a little. Probably because Aiden is giving off serious *don't fuck with her* vibes that are trying really hard to turn me on, despite the fact that I asked him to remain neutral. The vagina wants what it wants.

Still, I raise my eyebrow at him and he lets out a very long breath.

"It's . . . flashy. I'll say that. But is it really in line with the class and sophistication of Vivant, Aiden?" Shirley asks, turning slightly to regard the window. "I worry this feels like a desperate grab for attention."

Aiden smiles with teeth. "I think we can all agree that store windows are *supposed* to be an attention grab. They exist for that very purpose."

Bradley clears his throat. "We've always done well with the subtle message that we don't need anyone's business. That we're allowing it."

Somewhere close by, Jordyn makes a gagging sound.

Aiden still manages to hold on to his affable expression. "Now, I'm not sure anyone is buying that message anymore. Not when they walk into an empty store." On the surface, Aiden seems like his usual positive self, but upon closer inspection, his bow tie is literally quivering. He's having a harder time with the criticism of my window than he's letting on, but he's respecting my wishes to let it be voiced out in the open where I can hear it. He's not shutting it down, though I suspect he wants to. And this isn't unusual for him, is it? To be suppressing his feelings for the greater good. I still remember what he said as we shared that bottle of bourbon in the cookware department. When he confided in me.

"I'm impatient and irritated around my family. And that makes me feel guilty."

"You're supposed to be better than that."

"Right." He nods. "Yes."

I'm hit with a smidgen of guilt for asking him not to protect me. He's obviously already quelling more than enough of his opinions and urges. My fingers twitch, wanting to reach over and smooth the sides of his bow tie. Calm it down. Then maybe slide those exact same fingers up into his hair. Pull his face down to mine and tell him he's better than anyone. All of them.

Okay, I'm definitely falling for this man. Falling pretty fast.

Nose-diving—without a parachute.

Shirley speaks again, interrupting my thoughts. "Are we going to bring in the kind of clientele"—she gives me a once-over—"that we want, though? We don't want to alienate our current base."

My stomach wads up like a wet paper towel, my wool tights suddenly itchier than usual, but I take a cue from Aiden and put my chin up. I can handle this.

Meanwhile, Aiden's bow tie is going to start spinning around like an airplane propeller at any second. "I firmly believe this window will boost our foot traffic to sale numbers and we're going to take a couple of days to prove that. In the meantime, I've seen enough to make Stella a permanent hire."

"Why not wait for the data?" Bradley asks, brushing lint off his lapel.

"Yes," Shirley says, narrow-eyed. "What is the big hurry?"

"She has time to design another window before the Christmas Eve rush. It's not fair to ask her to do that without a contract."

Not a single muscle moves on the grandmother's face. "I suppose. And I assume she's been through orientation with Mrs. Bunting in human resources?" Her eyes lock in on me. "Read through the handbook and its various clauses?"

My face heats, pulse kicking into high gear at the base of my neck.

This woman may or may not know what happened between me and Aiden this morning (still not totally clear on that myself), but she suspects *something* is between us. The fact that we got out of the same car looking stoned is likely evidence enough—and she doesn't like it. Neither does his father, who has the disapproving expression of a Puritan villager. While the impostor syndrome is still blessedly missing for my professional feat, I'm now experiencing it for a very different reason.

How must I look standing beside Aiden?

Probably a lot different from the women he's dated before. They were likely graceful and tasteful and tall. Never had their mug shot taken. Of course his family would be concerned about the possibility that he's spending time with A) an employee and B) a sad, knock-off goth girl who had to use clear nail polish to treat a tear in her tights this morning. I'm about as approachable and welcoming as a vampire bat. Aiden is like a walking Baby Ruth bar. Sweet and savory and sort of old-fashioned. Makes a person happy just looking at it.

"Yes, I've gone through orientation with HR," I say, before Aiden can answer. "I'm aware of employee . . . protocol. It was so nice to meet you. If you'll excuse me . . ."

I manage a smile as I walk away, approaching Jordyn where she scowls at Seamus through the glass and the other managers are taking selfies with the window. Two women jog by our group but come to a stop and walk backward when they see the red dress glowing beneath hundreds of butterflies just off the street. "Oh shit, I just found my dress for Brian's Christmas party," says one of the joggers. "I won't mind that his ex is there if I'm wearing that."

"*She's* going to mind."

"Good."

Laughing, they high-five. "What store even is this?" They back up to read the decades-old carving on the top of the building. "Vivant. I'll swing by on my lunch break."

I'm breathless by the time the women start running again. I never got past hoping for approval from Aiden, from the board. The fact that I just witnessed the effect of my window in action is such an unexpected miracle, my hand flies up to cover my mouth while the managers crowd around me, poking me in the shoulders and giving me hip bumps.

"Remember," Shirley calls out while climbing into her limousine, interrupting our celebration. "When you're in public, you're representing Vivant. Please act accordingly."

Everyone quiets down again.

Aiden is standing in the empty sidewalk space between us and his departing family, watching me. Torn between pride and disquiet. As if he already knows in advance what I decide two seconds later. No more touching. No more after-hours alone time with this man. I'm officially an employee of his store, his family would obviously be horrified if our relationship developed into something serious—and who am I kidding even *pondering* such a thing? I've got a four-year delay in figuring out where I fit into this world, but I know definitively that he doesn't fit with me. Not with his identity so authentically curated.

Aiden Cook is out of my league, might as well admit it. He's a class act. He's real and incredible and I blew my chance with someone so altruistic and wholesome the night I held up a restaurant at gunpoint. He'd give us a try—he's said as much. But I'm even more positive now that he would stick with me, even if we weren't the right fit. He's a fixer. A loyalist. He's already bandaged one of my broken wings. I can't let him run around underneath me while I try to fly.

Right now, I need to focus on this miraculous opportunity I've been given and stop wishing for even more. Stop wishing for . . . him.

* * *

I'M SITTING ACROSS from Jordyn on the rooftop of a hotel. In a bar called Monarch.

Plexiglas runs along most of the perimeter of the space, attached to an overhead tent, keeping out the December cold while still allowing for a view. The fact that it's after ten on a Friday night means the place is standing room only, and it's a wonder we managed to find a little corner of the lounge seating area to order drinks. Technically, I cannot afford this place—yet—and that is weighing pretty heavily on my mind, but Jordyn bought the first round and I can't help but get absorbed in her story about the man who came into Vivant this afternoon and bought seven pairs of diamond studs to give to his employees for Christmas.

Jordyn leans into our circle, her martini glass half-full, a lemon twist floating on the clear surface. I would marvel over the fact that she can be so animated while telling a story and not spill a single drop, but her every movement is graceful and I'm no longer surprised. "First of all, that's some spooky sister wives shit. If I get those earrings as a gift from my boss, I'm pawning those things before end of business day. Who wants the same jewelry as six co-workers? This man wouldn't listen, of course. He knew best." She takes a small sip, shivering as the vodka goes down. "Would you keep them, Stella?"

The bar might be way more upscale than I'm used to—and my night out hat hasn't been worn in a while—but this isn't a totally foreign setting to me. Sitting with people I half know, drinking, letting myself slip into a slightly numb state where I don't overthink every word out of my mouth. The vibe is completely different, however. We're not trying to decide how we're going to top the previous night or what wild stunt we can get away with. That lack of peer pressure is more intoxicating than the alcohol.

Is this what adulthood feels like? I could get used to it.

"No, I'd sell the earrings, too. But I would invest some of the profit and buy fakes. Maybe wear them to the office a few times to earn points."

Everyone laughs, including Jordyn. "Did you hear that? This one is wise beyond her years. And that is why . . ." She raises her glass. "Our store was packed full of new customers today. They didn't have black American Express cards, but dammit, we take Visa, too."

We clink glasses, cheering. Someone starts a chant about having an ambition for commission, but the sound dies down abruptly when Seamus swaggers onto the scene. The saleswomen and managers gape at the custodian and his slightly sideways Yankees hat, but he only has eyes for Jordyn. I watch carefully for my friend's reaction and notice the leap of pleasure on her face before she hides it behind a wall of irritation.

"What are you . . . following me now?"

"Nah, I was invited." He scoots in between Jordyn and one of the perfume girls, grinning like a jack-o'-lantern. "Get you another one of those fancy drinks, Miss Jordyn?"

"I pay for my own drinks," she snaps.

"I know." He shakes his head slowly. "It's a damn crime."

Jordyn rolls her eyes, but she's battling a smile. As someone who made fighting smiles into a lifestyle, I'm sure of it. "If I let you buy me a drink, you're going to read something into it and there is nothing—let me say that again—*nothing* to read. This book is out of print, as far as you're concerned."

He doffs his hat, pressing it to his chest. "I just want to quench your thirst, my queen."

"Oh my—" Jordyn covers her face with her free hand. "Fine. Go. Just go. It's a lemon drop martini." She pins me with an incredulous look when he walks away, moving triumphantly through the crowded rooftop on the balls of his feet. "I can't even deal with that kid."

I make sure no one else is paying attention before I speak. "You like him."

Jordyn does a double take.

"You. Like." I pause for effect. "Him."

"I take back what I said about you being wise."

"What is holding you back exactly? From giving him a shot, I mean."

"I'm sorry . . ." she draws out. "Did you miss the fact that he's a baby compared to me? And hello, he is the weird friend from every sitcom you've ever watched." She makes a show of crossing her legs. "He doesn't get to date the main character."

The act of grinning reminds me of Aiden and I get a little twinge in my throat. He won't be here tonight. I mean, I highly doubt it. The general manager doesn't come out with his employees. There's probably something in the handbook about it. I should probably get to perusing more than the non-fraternization policy. Anyway, he's not going to be here and that's a good thing. We are boss and employee moving forward. That's all.

I glance at the door before I can stop myself. Looking for his big shoulders. That bow tie.

Dammit.

"Stella." Jordyn waves her hand in front of my face. "We were talking about me."

"Right." I breathe a laugh, realizing I'm being somewhat of a hypocrite. "Forget I said anything. I'm not telling you who to date. If you're not interested, there's a good reason."

Jordyn nods. "That's right. I'm just, you know . . . he'll lose interest. Men always do." Some of her usual self-assuredness slips. "My ex-boyfriend sure did. A day before our wedding."

A weight drops in my belly. "Oh. Jordyn, I'm sorry."

"Don't be. I'm better off," she says quickly, shrugging. "But if a man with a 401k who wants children can't even commit for the long term, Seamus sure as hell can't, either. He's still wet behind the ears. A caretaker is what he needs. And I'm not here to check some older woman box for him, you know?" When I start to respond to that, she slashes a hand through the air to signal a close to the discussion. "I don't say this very often, but enough about me. Have you got your eye on anyone?"

That grin.

The Tennessee drawl.

How he holds me.

How easy it is to talk to him.

"No," I say gruffly, surprised when it hurts to deny a bond with Aiden. Stomach-plunging hurt. "Nobody yet. Maybe in the New Year."

She hums, scrutinizing me a little too closely. With an exaggerated movement, she turns toward the entrance of Monarch. "Totally unrelated, I wonder if Mr. Cook will actually show up this time."

I choke on a sip of my drink. "Totally unrelated. Sure."

Jordyn pats my knee. "Don't worry, I'm the only one who saw you two in the backseat of his car this morning. I distracted the other managers by telling them I saw Michael B. Jordan on the street corner."

"Thank you." I have no idea where to start explaining this, but oddly, I find myself mostly concerned with how this will reflect on Aiden. He's right. As the one who holds professional power, he'd be ten football fields further into the wrong than me if word got out.

"Look, it's complicated. It can't go anywhere obviously. And . . . I just don't want you to think I got hired because there's something going on between us. He wouldn't do that. *I* wouldn't—"

"You don't have to tell me that, Stella. Your work speaks for itself. And I'm not judging, okay? Whatever your secret is, it's safe with me."

She holds eye contact until I nod and finally let out the breath I'm holding. "What did you mean about him actually showing up this time?"

"There's nothing going on between you and Mr. Cook, but you want to know more, right?" She tosses back her head and laughs. "Classic."

Wincing, I hide behind my martini glass.

"I just meant I always invite him to happy hour, but he never shows. He's . . ." Absently, Jordyn glances over at where Seamus is standing near the bar, her spine snapping straight when she sees a woman approach Seamus with a flirtatious smile, trailing a finger down his shoulder. "Excuse me? Hold that thought."

I have to press my fist to my mouth to keep the laugh from bursting out. Because Jordyn is on her feet and on a mission, maybe even an unconscious one. A moment later, she's tapping Seamus on the shoulder. He looks relieved by the interruption, then full-on shocked when Jordyn pulls him away from the other woman and out onto the dance floor.

With a kick of hope in my chest for the lovesick custodian, I take my half-finished apple pie martini and stand, crossing to the other side of the enclosed rooftop. There is a break in the heated tent leading out into the open air and I step through it now, resting my elbows on the wrought-iron barrier that runs the perimeter of the roof. I forgot to put on my jacket, but the cold air is welcome on my skin, overheated from the crowd and, let's face it, being called out by Jordyn. I sip my drink and watch 35th Street bottlenecking below with Friday night traffic, the top of the Empire State Building peeking out over the buildings, lit up in red and green.

What is Aiden doing tonight?

A successful man in his early thirties should be on a date.

How often *does* he go out—and more importantly, with who? Who gets to sit across from that man and have absolutely no reason *not* to pursue him? What must that be like?

In the hopes of loosening the knot in my throat, I start to toss back the rest of my drink, but my glass pauses when someone else steps out onto the outdoor section. A guy I don't recognize. Older than me by a few years. Two eyebrow piercings, a tattoo climbing up the side of his neck, skinny jeans and a bomber jacket. Attractive in a sharp way. He smiles at me in kind of a conspiratorial manner, like it's a relief that we've found each other. Two misfits in the sea of well-dressed and upwardly mobile young professionals. It says *we don't belong here, do we?* It's a sentiment that reminds me of Nicole, and my scalp prickles uncomfortably in response.

He leans an elbow on the wrought iron and nods at my glass. "What's that fancy shit you're drinking? Get you another one?"

Once upon a time, this guy would have dazzled me. I would have mentally simpered about his boldness and his air of rebellion. But right now? Tonight? I can only hear that deep voice textured with Tennessee in my ear. I can only sniff the air for the cheerful scent of zesty peppermint and wonder what he's doing. The necklace he gave me last night is between my breasts, pleasantly heavy, the window box key attached to the end. I've enjoyed having it beneath my clothes all day, a constant, secret touch. What did he do with the binoculars?

"Uh . . . hello?" prompts the real-life man in front of me.

"Sorry, I'm going to—" *Pass.* That's what I'm going to say. But I never get the chance, because Aiden steps out onto the roof looking like a bear who has just stepped in a steel trap.

Chapter 8
Aiden

Oh. Oh shoot.

What in God's green earth is this scorched feeling tearing through my esophagus? Feels like I just drank a pint of gasoline and swallowed a match. Maybe I did. Me breathing fire right now doesn't seem all that far-fetched. Who is this tragic-looking fellow in the tight jeans standing so close to Stella? His wolfish expression reminds me of Uncle Hank at the church bake sale—and I don't like it. He can't have her.

That's obviously not my decision, but logic doesn't seem to matter when there is a hole burning straight through my chest. I just want him gone. Now. Is this her type? They could easily be a couple. Young, cool. Outsiders. I've never felt like more of a bumbling dumbass in my life, coming out here and interrupting their conversation. I'm the boss walking into the break room during lunch, gossip screeching to a halt around me, everyone going from comfortable to formal.

With Stella, it isn't like that. The fact that I sign her paycheck doesn't color the way she acts around me. Maybe because of the way we met. Or maybe just because she's Stella. But Jesus, maybe I read too much into that? That feeling of being . . . different. To her. The way she's different to me. Not like anyone else. I don't have a lot of friends, since I didn't grow up here. Stayed down south right up through college and the first five years of running the honey business, before moving back to New York to step in as general manager. Most men my age in this city are settled down or workaholics, and I fall into the latter category.

But I haven't felt alone since meeting Stella.

It's possible I'm just a regular acquaintance to her and I have *zero* right to step out onto this roof and send this pierced gentleman packing, but my heart seems to be in control of my mouth. And my heart is not handling the sight of her standing with another man well *at all*. It's lodged up underneath my bow tie, beating two hundred miles an hour.

"Hey, buddy," I say, giving the kid a broad smile and jerking my thumb over my shoulder. "There's some woman out here looking for you. Says she's your mama."

"My . . ." He straightens, his features going from man on the prowl to confused boy. "Are you sure? She lives in Milwaukee."

I'm already nodding. "I could pinpoint a Wisconsin accent in the middle of a hailstorm." I move my flattened hand up and down until his eyes widen. "She's about yay high?"

"Whoa. That is her." He shakes his head like he's trying to wake up, looking at Stella and then the opening leading back into the bar indecisively. "I guess I should . . ."

Well, I *was* starting to feel bad about lying, but he's really weighing his options, isn't he? Continue flirting with my Stella or going to find his mother who has flown all the way from goddamn Wisconsin in the blistering cold a week before Christmas. My conscience is clear.

"Oh . . ." I cup a hand around my ear. "I hear her calling you. Tommy . . . Tommy . . ."

"Braxton."

"*Braxton*, right. Hard to hear over all the noise." I give him the smile I normally reserve for Leland when he's in a bad mood—which is often. "Better catch her before she gives up and leaves."

His shoulders slump. Still visibly confused and skeptical, he gives Stella one last, longing look before skulking back into the bar and disappearing into the crowd where he belongs.

I return my attention to Stella and find her mouth hanging open. "Aiden Cook," she scolds me slowly. "You better hope Santa isn't watching."

With that hot gasoline burn easing a little in my chest, I look up at the sky. "Santa, if you're listening, please bring Braxton some new jeans for Christmas."

"Aiden!"

"I'm concerned about his breathing. Think of his mother."

"You are out of line," she whispers, a corner of her mouth jumping. And standing out here in the cold, the night air blowing the bangs off her forehead, I complete my plummeting free fall for Stella Schmidt. She's had me twisted up like an angsty pretzel since I saw her standing outside Vivant the first time. There's something about her that makes me feel like a more authentic version of myself and I don't have an explanation for it. I just have the facts.

"Is that your type?" I ask, before I know what I'm doing. The gasoline feeling hasn't subsided. I can still see them together, bonded by their nonconformity, and this churning inside of me isn't satisfied even though he's gone. "Is that the kind of man you like, Stella?"

Her smile is gone and two little twin lines pop up between her brows. "I haven't . . ." Am I reading her wrong or is she mentally pep-talking herself? "Look, I haven't been around men in a long time. I have no idea what my type is anymore."

That's far from a satisfying answer, but at least she didn't give an outright yes. That's probably what I deserved for asking such a personal question. Christ, I'm her boss, asking what type of man interests her. That's not right. Unfortunately, the darkness of the rooftop combined with the buzz of Friday night makes me feel a million miles from her employer. We're two people who most definitely fraternized in the backseat of my car this morning and now we're alone, tension gripping the air along with my lowest stomach muscles. I'm trapped in this jealous purgatory and . . . I sense she could have easily broken me out of it but didn't.

Why?

I freaked her out with talk of the love contract. I came on too strong, too soon.

Now she's laying down boundaries and I have to respect them, despite wanting to carry her out of this lounge in a fireman hold. Away from Braxton and whoever else has bright ideas about approaching Stella when she's all I think about anymore.

With every ounce of my garnered willpower, I back toward the entrance, confused by the way her face falls. Further baffled by the quick step she takes forward. "I'm sorry," I say. "I shouldn't have come."

"Aiden, wait."

Whatever she says will be out of guilt and I'm not putting that pressure on her. I've done enough. "I'll see you at work, Stella."

"*You're* my type," she blurts.

The music behind me stops.

Or maybe I just can't hear it anymore over the wind in my ears. "What?"

"Oh my God," she groans, slapping her hands over her face. "I can't believe I just said that out loud. I can't believe it's *true*. You've given me a weird bow tie kink and nothing else is appealing now. It's *terrible*. All I was thinking when that guy offered to buy me a drink was, why? He doesn't have any stories about Aunt Edna. What can I possibly get out of this?"

Ah hell, I have to yank on my collar. It's choking me.

Pulses are rioting all over my body, the center of my sternum gathering up tight.

She means what she's saying.

I'm her type.

She likes my Aunt Edna stories.

"Stella—"

"No, hold on."

It's probably a good thing she interrupted me, because I am on the verge of proposing marriage. Or at the very least a weekend in Vermont in one of those cozy cabins with a fireplace and whirlpool bathtub. "Okay, I'm holding on."

She paces away a few steps, then approaches me slowly, wetting and re-wetting her lips. "Here's the thing. If it was up to me . . ." She blows out a breath, shakes her hands like they've been asleep. "I'd suggest we work out this attraction just between us, you know? Without any of the paperwork."

Ah, Jesus. My cock very much likes the idea of working out our attraction. Likes the flushed cheeks she gets from talking about it. She's turned on. By me. I'm almost grateful enough to forget the rest of what she said. Almost. "Without the paperwork, Stella . . ."

"I know. I know you're opening the company up for a big mess—"

"No. Well, yeah. But no, that's not my reason for wanting the paperwork, Stella. I don't want this thing between us to be . . .

dishonest. Or something we sneak around and do behind the scenes. I want to be better than that for you. You deserve better than that."

A skeptical laugh whooshes out of her. "Aiden . . ." She rubs at her throat. "I wasn't finished explaining. I'm . . . I'm not in any position to make a personal commitment that huge. Filing paperwork with HR is *huge*. And you're so far ahead of me in life while I just had one good step in the right direction today, you know? It's all so new. *You're* so new."

"I get that," I say honestly. Quietly. "I get that, Stella."

"Thank you." Her hand lifts and slides up the center of my pecs, rubbing there, her unfocused gaze landing on my mouth. "So we're at an impasse. I like you. I want to go to bed with you. Badly. But I won't ask you to compromise yourself by forgoing the paperwork. Or asking you to be dishonest."

I want to go to bed with you. Badly.

Jesus. Jesus, I'm hard as a rock.

There has never, ever been a time in my life when lust or anything this remotely selfish got the better of me. Tonight is different. It's Stella. I need to be inside of her. I need to lick her skin and feel her orgasm grip me. Watch her shatter and shake and sweat. I need to *fuck* her. Rough. Like she wants it. Like I *need* it. But once I know what it's like to taste her, to pin her down to the mattress and *take*, I'm going to want more. More than I've even come close to wanting with anyone. More than sex. I already do. And I'll have sold this relationship short. I'll have turned her into a dirty little secret and I'll be too addicted to stop coming back for more. There won't be a chance in hell of her doing this right once we do it wrong.

"It's okay, Aiden," she murmurs, studying my face. Dropping her hands away from my stomach. "I mean that, it's okay. You're . . ." She steps away. "You're a good guy. A nice guy. I respect that—"

I catch her wrist, those words ringing in my head. *You're a good guy. A nice guy.* She's said things to this effect before. The urge to prove her wrong has always been there, but it's a physical demand now. Heavy and consuming. It's unacceptable to me—Stella thinking I don't have the right disposition for her. That maybe I can't satisfy every need she has because I'm not selfish enough. Not mean and demanding and gritty enough.

That guard I've never dropped outside of the bedroom hits the deck. Fast. And I let it. I let the demand for physical pleasure— hers and mine—bleed in and blur the line of what's allowed. What's appropriate between me and Stella.

Blood pounding in my head, I pull her toward the dark corner of the roof that is the farthest out of view from the bar. She gasps when I press her up against the brick wall with my body, letting her feel every hard inch of her effect on me.

"Aiden," she breathes, going pliant, eyelids fluttering.

I drop my mouth to her ear, inhaling the singular scent of her. "Do you want some proof I can be more than a nice guy, sweetheart?"

Stella nods, letting her head tip back and hit the wall. "Yes. Anything. Yes."

Anything.

Permission granted, I reach down and yank up her skirt.

As soon as I get the garment bunched up around her waist, my hand is delving down the front of her tights and panties. My middle finger parts the flesh of her pussy, finding her hot and slippery. Perfect. She's already whimpering when I slide that digit high and tight inside of her, so firmly and without warning, she shoots up onto her toes, her thighs dancing around my hand. "Oh my God. Oh my God."

"Nice guy?" I slip my middle finger out, almost the whole way, then push it back in accompanied by my ring finger. "I'll fill this tight, little thing up so full, you won't know whether to open wider for it or slap me across the face."

The awareness that transforms her features is satisfying. I'll admit that. I lust for this girl more than I've ever lusted in my life and now she realizes I have what it takes to gratify her. That's not to say she was totally skeptical before, but she can't know how close I've been paying attention to try and determine her preferences, painting a picture of what it would take to get her off good and hard. She gave me a hint the night I carried her up to my office, her eyelids turning leaden when I settled her butt on the edge of my desk and let myself linger between her thighs for a few seconds. She arched her back and panted once, twice, like she'd die for that quick, dirty release. A boss going to town on his employee after hours, right there on top of the profit-and-loss statements.

And again this morning in my car, her pulse ticked faster, more insistently when I grazed her lips or jawline with my teeth, the tighter I fisted her clothing, the more anxious she became. No soft and slow for Stella. Yeah, I've got her number. It's the same as mine.

I curl my fingers inside of her and rotate them, watching her pupils dilate in the moonlight. Her mouth opens in a soundless O and then her tits start to labor up and down. "Please, Aiden." She fists the front of my shirt, half tugging me closer, half pushing me away. And she's turning slicker by the second. "Please, please, please."

"Tell me I'm your type again."

"Y-you're my type," she gasps.

"Not that tattooed child." I enunciate every word and feel her pulse around my digits in response. "Not anyone else, either. Just me."

"Oh. *Ohhh* my God. J-just you. Yes."

Gratified as hell by that instantaneous agreement, I pull my fingers halfway out and sink them back in fast, hard, and watch her mouth form my name without a sound, feel the clench of her little muscles around my digits. "That's it. Good girl, Stella." God, I need to experience that tightening on a much lower part of my anatomy. Need to feel her milk me.

Need her now.

I'm taking her home. There's nothing else to it. There's a warning in the back of my head telling me I'll regret letting my hunger for Stella trample my willpower, but right now all I can think about is getting her alone and planting myself so deep inside of her, her thighs will still be shaking on Christmas morning. I can only think about getting rid of the density gathering in the deepest regions of my loins. Calming *her* inner frenzy, as well. Letting my guard down the rest of the way. A way I've never done with anyone. Physically. Mentally. All of it.

When voices from inside the bar seem to grow louder, traveling closer to the open-air rooftop, I lumber through the fog of hunger and remind myself where we are. As hard as it's going to be to stop touching her now that I've got that perfect slickness wrapped around my fingers, there's no choice. *Goddamn.* Reluctance grits my teeth as I slide my hand out of her panties, fixing them back into place and tugging down her skirt, resting our foreheads together while we get our breathing under control. Some people walk out onto the roof behind us, lighting up cigarettes, but I don't recognize any of the voices and we remain just like this until finally, my brain is able to form semi-coherent thoughts.

"I'll go downstairs first. Wait five minutes and follow me. I'll meet you outside."

Stella's eyes lift to mine, searching. "I'm pushing you to do this and it isn't you. I can't . . ."

I panic when she shakes her head, beginning to slip out from between me and the wall. But I press her back firmly to the brick, letting her feel my hard cock. I look her in the eye as I do it, cupping her chin in my hand and lifting. There's a part of me that knows she's right. This isn't me. Sneaking around. Hiding what I feel and want and know is right.

And because I never want to be anything less than one hundred percent honest with Stella, I tell her exactly what I'm thinking. Exactly what's in my head and heart. "Being dishonest is not me. You're right. But it's not *you*, either. I don't think it ever was. We're going to meet somewhere in the middle tonight and find out who we could be. What that could feel like." I drop my mouth to hers and kiss her for the first time, pressing my tongue deep into her shocked mouth, moaning in my throat when she responds, her body melting against mine, our tongues stroking like they've been starved for contact. She's about to scale me like a rock-climbing wall, and while I want that more than my next breath, I pull away, panting, before we can make a scene. "Meet me downstairs in five minutes."

Chapter 9
Stella

After Aiden leaves, I lean against the cold brick wall on the rooftop for a few minutes trying to catch my breath. Then I pull the quickest goodbye in history, which consists of me passing by the lounge section where everyone is sitting with my phone pressed to my ear, grabbing my jacket and mouthing *I have a family thing okay bye*. I definitely take note that Jordyn and Seamus are sitting beside each other. Jordyn looks nothing short of dazed and Seamus might have just won the lottery for the triumphant set of his chin. I'll definitely be getting the inside scoop tomorrow. For now, though . . . I'm apparently going home with my boss.

No. He's more than that.

He's Aiden.

And . . . I've never felt like this. Never had these fluttering fingers of sensation in my belly over anyone. Or this hot-cold tremor in my knees. As I step into the elevator and hit the down button, I'm worried I'll burst into hysterical laughter at any moment and freak out the other passengers. But oh my God, *my body*. What did he do to my body? Inside and out, I'm a mess of shivers and hormones and need. I actually *need* him.

His hands. His voice. His mouth. His weight against me. Above me.

I let the bow tie fool me, didn't I?

When he told me he could be downright rough, I didn't fully comprehend his meaning. Or maybe I thought he was exaggerating. He wasn't. This man just yanked up my skirt in public, touched my body like he'd been studying it his whole life and *growled* at me. Possessive things, jealous things that should turn me off, but oh lord, they don't. The fact that a skilled lover is lurking beneath the surface of this buttoned-up gentleman has skyrocketed his appeal to the moon and I've been carried along with it. I'm without gravity. Floating.

I loved his fingers inside of me. Every brutally wild second. Loved his jealous words in my ear, especially because he's so conflicted over them. It's bad but he can't help it.

He's going to rock my world tonight, isn't he?

Dammit.

When I step out of the building downstairs, Aiden is waiting at the curb, leaning against the side of his black town car. A muscle leaps in his cheek when he sees me. Without coming up from his lean or taking his eyes off me, he opens the back door and nods for me to get inside. It's such a smooth move, the panties are almost incinerated straight off my backside.

Oh man, I like this. I like that Aiden came here for me. That he told Braxton to get lost and now he's bringing me home. This man thinks about me in his spare time and changes his plans to include me. The boys in my memory made any time spent together seem like an accident. Almost like they didn't want me to get the wrong impression that they cared. While Aiden . . . he's the epitome of care. And for some reason, he's decided to offer the warm security of his presence to me. He's offering me a relationship. A constant.

More than once, he's stated plainly what he wants from this, from us. My impulse is to give it to him. To march into human resources and check the right boxes, cross the *T*'s and dot the *I*'s. But that would put me all in. I'd be invested. More importantly, I'd be telling *Aiden* I'm invested—and I have barely started investing in myself. I'm just starting to find my sea legs. The world is this massive place without the prison walls keeping me penned in. Every day, I'm trying to walk the same path, hoping it will wear into a permanent walkway. A constant.

But it hasn't yet. Not completely.

Everything is still foreign. This *version* of me is foreign.

Last time I was free to make my own decisions, most of them were bad ones. Now I'm supposed to believe I can just magically be this person who makes the right choices? That I can just step into this role of a professional? A girlfriend?

And Aiden . . . I know he senses the uncertainties in me. That he wants to be my knight in shining armor. I can't let him. I can't take advantage. But maybe if we can just . . . explore being together quietly for a while, someday soon I'll be healthy enough to be my own knight. Healthy enough to sign my name on a dotted line beside someone like this.

Like Aiden.

The man who is currently sliding into the rear leather seat beside me, twining our fingers together. Asking for my address, then giving it to Keith. I catch a glimpse of the driver's face in the rearview mirror—and he's definitely battling a smile. But he reaches up and presses a button to raise the partition and once again, it's just me and Aiden, my cheap puffer jacket pressed to his expensive knee-length winter coat, his height and size making me feel almost dainty in comparison. And when he presses a firm thumb to the pulse at my wrist, it's like he's touching me everywhere at once.

We both watch as I cross my legs tight, tamping down the free fall below my belly button. Both of us let out a shaky breath.

"Traffic isn't bad going downtown," he says, tracing a slow circle onto my knee with his middle finger. "We should be there in less than ten minutes."

My nod is jerky.

Ten minutes.

Then I can turn my mind off. I'm not going to think about paperwork or how I couldn't possibly be the right person for this man. I'm not going to speculate on what Nicole would say about my shaky new life. I'm just going to let myself feel, let myself get lost and ask questions tomorrow. Or the day after that. I'll know when I get there.

Hopefully.

"Did you say hello to Jordyn or anyone?" I half whisper, the restraint between us thin enough to be slashed to ribbons by a decent gust of wind. "Upstairs, I mean?"

He exhales, shifts in his seat. "No. I started to head over when I arrived, but I didn't want to stop everyone midconversation. Or make everyone tense. They have to be on their best behavior all day. No sense in forcing them into it after hours, too."

"What?" I scan his face to make sure he's serious. "You're not that kind of boss, Aiden. If anything, you'd put them at ease."

He nods, but he clearly doesn't believe me. "Thank you, Stella."

"I really mean it, though." This is crazy. In my need for this man to understand he's wonderful, my heart is *pounding*. What is happening to me? "You really don't think your employees would enjoy getting to know you more?"

"Not everyone likes my Aunt Edna stories, Stella."

"Well, they're wrong."

"I mean that as kind of a metaphor. For . . ." Absently, he gestures to himself. "This. Me. Sometimes people just want to complain. They don't feel like they can do that around me. Take Leland—my assistant. Sometimes I haven't even said good morning yet and he tells me to stop judging him." I'm deep in a fantasy about giving this faceless Leland a swift kick in the ass when Aiden continues. "Thing is, sometimes I want to complain, too. Want to just give in and call it a bad day. It's just that . . . back when I had a lot of those, the positivity is how I learned to cope." His brow furrows. "Now I don't know how to do anything but lean on it."

"Even when you're unhappy," I say softly.

"Yeah." I move our joined hands into my lap and he watches it happen. Swallows hard behind his collar. "I don't enjoy being unhappy, so I ignore it." His gaze lifts, tracing my features in the near darkness, streetlights hiding and revealing his face at intervals. "For the record, I'm the furthest a man can get from unhappiness right now."

Goose bumps tickle to life along my arms, warmth pooling in the lowest region of my belly. "Good. I'll try and keep you that way tonight."

"Me first," he says thickly.

Our uneven exhales mingle in the warm backseat. The sexually deprived part of me wants to climb onto his lap in this moment, but there's an even more compelling desire to dig deeper into what he's telling me. To know Aiden better. It's like a gasoline tank has sprung into existence inside of me and until it's full of Aiden facts, I'll be running on empty. "When *are* you unhappy?"

He starts to talk, stops. Lets out a husky chuckle. "It's even hard to admit it out loud." I squeeze his hand and he transfers our joined grip to the hard slab of his thigh, the pad of his thumb rubbing circles on my knuckles. "Vivant was in trouble around five years back. My grandfather had passed and they were getting ready to close the doors. I'd made some money on a side business down in Tennessee, while I was still in school. Did I ever tell you Uncle Hank was a beekeeper? Well, I went door to door selling that honey in mason jars until we had enough capital to package it properly and buy into trade shows. We sold out and it went from there—"

"Hold on." I press a hand to my chest. "I'm still picturing you ringing doorbells in your bow tie. You must have made a killing."

Aiden winks at me. "You're not wrong."

"I bet the local Girl Scouts were beside themselves."

"There were some toilet-papering incidents. A few surly eyes. But eventually we carved out territories to make it fair."

I'm back to wanting to crawl into his lap. Maybe tuck my head under his chin and press an ear to his throat, so I can hear the timbre of his voice right at the source. *Settle down, Stella.* "Okay, so you're taking the honey industry by storm . . ."

"And a few years after I graduated from State, Hank and Edna are able to pay off their mortgage and buy a second vacation home down near the Gulf."

In the midst of this story, Aiden unhooks my seat belt and pulls me into his lap sideways, dropping his chin onto the crown of my head. I let it happen in a daze. Is he . . . a mind reader? I don't have time to pursue that line of thought, because he's speaking again and the burr of his voice is vibrating down the side of my neck, making each and every one of my nerve endings sing an aria. Oh this. This is way too perfect. I'm melting like butter on a hot plate.

"Around that time, Vivant was getting ready to declare bankruptcy. I'd never had a close relationship with my father or grandparents, apart from yearly visits and phone calls. But they needed my help. I came to New York thinking I would buy into the family business . . ." He shakes his head, messing up my bangs in the process. "I don't know, maybe I was a young idiot who wanted to be a hero. To be the kind of son they wouldn't ever consider sending away. In hindsight, I made our relationships worse. Now they resent me for coming in and turning the ship around. And I don't know any other way but to try and make them happy."

Unwittingly, he's hit the bull's-eye on why I hesitate to sign the paperwork. To take the leap across the chasm. Because this facet of Aiden's personality, this responsibility he feels to inspire happiness in everyone, reminds me of something I think about and regret every day. My parents tried to make me happy and I rebelled anyway. I'm a different version of the same bad guy in the story he's telling and he doesn't even realize it. Will he? What then?

I swallow down that worry and refocus. "Sometimes people just aren't in a place to receive happiness, you know? And it's nothing you're doing wrong. It's just that they don't *want* to feel it. Or they don't recognize happiness when it's handed to them, so they take a foreign feeling and turn it into something that makes them comfortable. They wouldn't know themselves if they stopped obsessing over their own shortcomings or their past mistakes . . . and just let you in. They don't know how. But it can't be your job to teach them, okay? You get to take advantage of your own happiness. You're allowed to keep it if they don't want it."

Something is butting up against my shoulder and it takes me a second to realize it's his heart. Shifting a little, I press my palm there to experience the thrum up close, my gaze drifting up to meet his. And I'm so screwed. I'm so *incredibly* screwed because he's looking at me like I've just unlocked the secrets of the universe, instead of issuing a roundabout warning about myself—and then he's kissing me like we have thirty seconds until civilization falls. This is how he chooses to spend it. With his fingers plowing into my hair, his lips coming down hard on mine. Pressing my mouth wide so he can ride the ridges of our tongues together, his groan cracking in the middle and turning into a growl.

It's like someone tossed a match into a puddle of kerosene.

One second, I'm almost lulled by his story and the next, my libido is dancing furiously in a top hat and clogs. I twist my butt in his lap and feel the bulge rise, gasping when his hands rake down out of my hair to unzip my jacket in one long zing, his hand delving inside to play with my breasts. Yes, *play* with them. He doesn't honk them like an old-fashioned bicycle horn or turn them like a doorknob. He brushes his fingertips over my nipples, teasing them into little peaks, then he squeezes the full mounds gently, in turn, grazing his teeth down my jawline as he does it, before returning to my stiff nipples and stroking them, firmer this time, through my sweater dress. "Oh no," I whisper, my breath catching, one hand curled in his collar, apparently. No idea when that happened. "Oh no. What are you going to do to me?"

This is a question I'm asking on more than one level.

Thankfully he only picks up on the most obvious one.

"Tell me what you want done, sweetheart. I'll bring you inside and do it," he rasps, raking his open mouth up the most sensitive portion of my neck. "As many times as you want."

"That's too many options. That's a diner menu. I need like . . . a—a prix fixe."

What an utterly ridiculous thing to say. And yet he nods like

I'm a normal person speaking in perfect English. "Let's start at the beginning." Searching my eyes, he bathes my mouth in an unsteady exhale. "Are we getting each other off?"

I nod. And I keep on nodding.

Nod nod nod.

His eyes close briefly and I think he might whisper a quick prayer. "I can use my fingers," he says hoarsely, toying with the hem of my skirt. "My tongue. We can keep our clothes on and I'll just rock us into it, make you come in those little tights." That big chest of his starts to rise and fall faster. "Or I can fuck you good and rough. You decide, Stella."

Wow. Okay.

I'm squirming now in his lap, my body so restless for fulfillment, the tiny muscles between my legs are almost painfully taut. Pulsing. I've never been given power like this. I'm being given control and, ironically, it makes me feel safe enough to let it go. "I want you. Any of those ways. Yes to everything." His hand is already sliding up my leg, beneath my skirt, where he rubs two knuckles against the juncture of my thighs. "Ohhhh, right there. Please. But I don't want to plan, Aiden. I want to just do whatever feels right. Okay?"

Looking me in the eyes, he cups me between the legs. Through the soft wool of my tights. His big palm conforms to the protrusion of my sex and he kneads me there, a muscle popping continuously in his jaw. "If you want to stop, Stella, you tell me. You feel like we're doing something wrong or the fact that I'm your boss makes you feel pressure—"

I stop his words with my mouth, drawing him into a long, reassuring kiss that leaves us both panting, his fingers rubbing in the *exact right spot*, turning me sodden, his erection thick and hard against my buttocks. "I'm not thinking about the fact that you're my boss right now. Or that we work together at all. You're just Aiden." I circle my hips, making his breath stutter, his pupils expanding to block out the green. "And I need you."

The town car pulls to a stop outside my building.

We can't stop kissing for long, dizzying moments, my thighs beginning to feel funny, like jelly. Am I going to have an orgasm now? In the backseat? No. No . . . I want to make it inside. I want this out-of-control feeling to continue. "We're here," I whisper, dazed and laboring for air.

"I know," he growls, jiggling his middle finger against my clit, right through the damp wool. "Come on, sweetheart, give me one."

Oh God. *Oh God.*

I'm the one who said she didn't want a plan, right?

I'm getting my wish.

My teeth clamp down on my bottom lip and I stare up at the spinning ceiling of the town car, reaching through the opening of my jacket to play with my nipples, imitating Aiden's movements from before, my lower body moving more and more restlessly, dragging my bottom side to side on his arousal. Sensation gathers, familiar but different for all the intensity. For the fact that Aiden is the one bringing this down on me. And then he presses two fingers tight, tight, tight to that bundle of nerves and I let out a strangled sound, pleasure coursing down my middle with the power of a white water rapid, pulling up roots and annihilating me.

"Christ, that's beautiful. You're so fucking *beautiful*." His voice doesn't sound natural, doesn't sound like classic Aiden, but the Tennessee in his voice makes him familiar, welcome, regardless. Maybe even mine? At least for tonight? I don't know, but I find myself wrapping my arms around his neck and clinging my way through the climax, hiccupping into the minty sinew of his throat.

Letting him kick open the door of the car, exit onto the sidewalk and carry me into the vestibule of my building. "Your bag is in my hand, Stella. Take out the key."

What is a key?

What is a hand?

I don't know these words right away, but thankfully my vocabulary comes rushing back and I fumble to do what he asks, letting us into the building with shaky hands. I'm still floating on a river of bliss, but when we pass a sign that says HEY APARTMENT TEN. PLEASE STOP PISSING IN THE HALLWAYS, it hits me that I'm bringing this man, this wealthy honey entrepreneur turned department store owner, into my tiny, messy rent-controlled apartment full of secondhand furniture and unreliable Wi-Fi. "Um . . . oh." I tap his shoulder when we reach the door of my apartment and he slowly sets me down, keeping a big hand settled on my hip. His mouth lands on the side of my neck, raking upward toward my ear and I whimper, crushing my keys in my fist. "I—I don't know about this."

His hands leave my body immediately, settling on either side of me on the doorframe. "Okay. Damn. That's okay."

"This apartment . . . it belongs to my uncle. Most of the furniture belongs to him. It's not what you're used to, I'm sure. I can't even remember if I made the bed and our neighbor never stops smoking weed, so my bathroom smells like a dispensary—"

"Stella." He exhales in a rush, head tipping forward. "I thought you were going to tell me it doesn't feel right because I'm your boss."

"No. No, I'm just . . ." I jerk a thumb over my shoulder toward the apartment. "I guess I'm a little self-conscious."

Aiden nods, a corner of his mouth ticking up on the way to kiss my forehead. "Well, don't be," he says, right up against my temple. "Aunt Edna didn't even have indoor plumbing until I was in seventh grade. Had to walk across the yard in the middle of the night to use the john. If your weed bathroom is indoors, this might as well be the Four Seasons."

My self-consciousness drains out through my fingertips and toes, leaving me boneless between him and the door.

Three things hit me at once.

One. He's not just saying those words. He means them. Aiden Cook will find a way to see the apartment behind this door as a wonderful place, because that's what he does. He sees the good. The bright side. And somehow I sense our economic differences will only be an issue if I allow them to be. If I dwell on them.

There's no way he'll let me.

Two. I am now turned on by Aunt Edna stories. God save my wretched soul.

Three. I might be falling in love with this man. Real, authentic, no-escaping-it love.

Saying those words out loud seems like a far-off dream, way in the future. Maybe one that will never come to fruition. But for tonight, I can show him exactly what I'm feeling.

That's safe. That's what I have for now.

Wrapping a hand around Aiden's tie, I slowly back into the apartment, pulling him with me.

Chapter 10

Aiden

Touching Stella, kissing her, feels good in an indescribable way. Feels like where I belong. Grounded and needed and accepted.

I've got her pressed up against the wall of her entryway. She's unknotting my tie and I'm pushing the jacket off her shoulders, learning the shape of her tits through the material of her sweater dress. The way she arches her back for the downward stroke of my palms, the mewling sound she makes when I pinch her nipples, tells me she has sensitive breasts. Licking and sucking the peaks will help make her wet for me. Based on the frenzied way we're kissing, she's going to need that crucial slickness sooner rather than later.

God.

Goddamn. She wraps a leg around my hip and I dip, surge up between her thighs, pinning her to the wall and grinding into the heat of her pussy, making both of us groan. And I don't think we're going to make it any farther than this wall, right beside the door. We've barely managed to twist the dead bolt on the door to her apartment—no, her uncle's apartment—and I could come already from the feeling of her pliant curves molding to my muscle, the way her eyes implore me. Now, now, now. They don't have to say it out loud for me to know what she wants. I want it, too. I *need* her.

"Aiden," she whimpers, her fingers beautifully clumsy on the buttons of my shirt. She pops them open all the way to my waist and pushes the sides of the garment wide, her breath releasing like the steam of a teakettle. "No. No, you're . . . there's muscles under here. I'm getting Clark Kent transforming into Superman vibes and I'm not mad about it." We smile against each other's mouth and that shared moment makes me think of china patterns and Vermont and the nine million other things I want to do with this girl.

Including fuck her so well her pussy clenches every time I walk into the room.

But you're not only doing this because you want her. Need her.

You're here to prove a point. Prove you're not too nice.

I have an ulterior motive—and that's not right, is it?

That unwelcome thought has me avoiding eye contact with Stella, dipping my head down to taste her incredible neck. Drag my tongue up the side of that smooth column and become drugged by her scent. Rich, girl musk and crisp night air and a hint of peach. If she tastes even remotely this good between her thighs, I'll never come up for air, I swear to God.

But even as I'm reaching up beneath her dress to peel the tights and panties down to her knees, I'm looking at the apartment out of the corner of my eye. And it's definitely not hers. It's temporary. There is nothing artistic or feminine about it. Stella has only just landed.

In fact, it seems as though her belongings are gathered neatly in one corner of the tiny living room, as if she's afraid to take up space. A hairbrush, phone charger, a bottle of lotion. My pounding heart wrenches sideways at the sight of them crowded together in one spot. I want to address it. Want to talk about everything under the sun with her. But that's not why I came here, is it? More importantly, that's not why she brought me here. I came to scratch our itch for each other and hopefully create a permanent one. The kind that needs to be appeased over and over again.

The kind that might inspire her to sign the papers to make this right.

Because I am definitely in an employee's apartment right now. I'm not judging where she lives. God, no. It's just that I can't ignore the power imbalance between us when it's staring me right in the face.

Yet I've got her tights and panties down around her knees now. She uses her feet to drag them the rest of the way off, kicking them aside—and Christ, now her pussy is bare. I haven't even seen it yet and I'm already moaning, my hands fisting in the sides of her dress to yank it up, get her naked from the waist down.

"Let me see how sweet it is," I rasp, molding her hips in my hands, trailing my fingers inward toward her exposed flesh. "Let me feel how wet."

"Please." Her nod is disjointed, her eyes glazed over, locked on my face. "Touch me."

I lean back enough to watch my fingers meet her bare pussy for the first time. We both watch as my middle digit trails through her dark, tidy strip of hair and disappears between the soaked lips. They close around my touch with a wet sound that tightens my balls painfully, her smooth heat dampening my finger more, more, especially when I find that bud and tease it, reveling in her choked intake of breath against my mouth. "You bring me here to fill this up with cock, Stella?" I add a second finger, rubbing them both up and back over her clit gently—until her thighs start to flex, then with more pressure. Faster. "You going to need me to push it in slowly or all at once, huh? What's going to make you come the hardest?"

"I don't know," she says, gasping when I push my middle finger inside her tight channel, flexing it, feeling her stretch around me. "I don't . . . r-remember anything before this. Four years, no sex. No, longer. Longer."

"Don't do that," I heave into her neck, fingering her roughly now, in, out, deep, like I sense she needs. "Don't remind me I'm breaking your dry spell. Jesus, I won't last five seconds."

Her laugh is breathy, almost euphoric. "That's such a man thing."

"Oh yeah? You're not turned on knowing you're my first since before lockdown? Maybe longer, because I can't remember a damn thing before you, either, sweetheart?"

"Fine. Maybe a little, yes." She sinks her teeth into her bottom lip, her cunt flexing around my knuckle. "Maybe a lot."

This girl. I want to run away with her. Elope. Go on safaris. Sink down to the bottom of the ocean holding her hand. Just everything. And now her fingers are unfastening my belt buckle, stopping every few seconds or so to stroke her palm down over my straining cock, massaging and teasing it, scraping her fingernails down my abs. "You're about to come on my fingers again, aren't you?"

"Yes," bursts out of her, just as she gets my zipper down.

"Go on," I pant against her mouth. "You're allowed to love getting fingered when I'm the one doing it. Get that wet stuff all over the man who brings you the fuck home."

With my zipper down, my cock pushes out into the scant space between us, still housed in my white briefs. I'm hard as iron, so help me God. So stiff I'm leaking. I've never needed anyone so bad in my life and I never will again. That's an intuition written in stone. And I just need to get Stella on her back. Now. I need her nails scoring my back and her knees hugging my rib cage. That's what I need—but when she slides her smooth palms down my chest and stomach, gripping my erection and giving me a *perfectly tight* hand job through my briefs . . .

I look down at the part in her hair. My tie on the floor.

At some point, she dropped her purse. Her employee badge has spilled out onto the floor of the entryway. Stella has a lopsided smile in the photo. A nervous one. It's her first day of work. First major chance, major leap she's taken since being released back into the real world. And she's taking it in my store.

My conscience rears its head.

No. Please.

It's too late, though. I'm her boss. I'm her boss and there's the proof, staring up at me.

I've stopped kissing her. My fingers are pressed deep inside of her, but I'm no longer moving them. She looks up at me questioningly, the pace of her breath frantic, her sex pulsing around my touch. There's no way I can leave her unsatisfied. There's no way. I just need to get out of my head about our imbalance of power. I need to trust what's happening here. What's between me and Stella. It's the real deal. I feel that in my fucking bones. And the reason I am forgoing formalities, the reason I've bucked the rules and brought her home tonight, is so she'll see me as more than a nice guy. So I'll have a chance to make this last.

Plus, Jesus, I need her. I need her so bad, I can't unclench my molars. The weight between my legs is pounding and unbearable. I want to be the closest to her anyone has ever gotten. Want to pump deep and watch her forget about anyone and anything but me.

"Aiden?"

"Yeah, sweetheart. I know," I say hoarsely. Rallying. Focusing. I stoop down and throw her over my shoulder, striding to the back of the apartment. Entering the only room besides the bathroom. A small bedroom the size of a closet—and again, her things are neatly organized in one single corner. But I'm not going to dwell on that and make her self-conscious. Nope. Not going to think about packing her suitcase and moving her into my place and putting her things *everywhere*, on all the surfaces and in multiple drawers. Because we haven't gotten there yet. This is my audition to be her boyfriend, right? As of now, I'm just her too-nice boss whom she doesn't even want to be attracted to.

That last thought has me pinning Stella down on the twin-sized bed a little too roughly, my body coming down on top of hers. Giving her my full weight, watching those eyelids flutter, listening to her excited moan.

"Does that make you hot?" I push her knees open. Fast enough to make her suck in a breath. I savor the sight of her parting flesh. The telling sheen that runs from her slit to the pucker of her asshole. *Gorgeous.* "You like to be reminded that I'm not so nice once I get your panties off?" My hips drop into the cradle of her thighs, shifting slowly, the friction worth dying for. "You want this mean fuck?"

"*Yes.*"

I'm hard as nails. She wants this. All I have to do is peel down my briefs and give us the forbidden fuck we're both dying for. I've worked her up so thoroughly with my fingers that she'll probably come after one thrust—and if she doesn't, there's more where that came from.

"Aiden." Her breath saws in and out, her fingers twisting in the sides of my open shirt. And I realize I've started to dry hump her, my teeth clamped and tugging on the lobe of her ear. "Please, please, please."

I reach down, intending to lower the waistband of my briefs, take myself out and drive home inside of her. But it's like an invisible force is stopping my hand from performing the action. I know if I peel away that last layer of material, that will be it. I'll be inside Stella. I'll have defied my conscience. Betrayed her trust, even if she doesn't realize it now. Yet.

There's a good chance I'm just overthinking this, right?

Yeah. Yeah, I just need a minute.

But she doesn't have a minute. Her beautiful body is writhing beneath mine, she's naked from the waist down—wet, so tight and wet—and before I register my own movements, I'm stripping her completely. I'm throwing her dress onto the floor and indulging myself in the sight of her bare skin, her dusky-tipped tits, the swells of her hips and dips of her sides. *Incredible, perfect girl. Stella.* And she's shaking with the need for relief.

"I've got you, sweetheart. Open your thighs wider for me." I'm slurring, drunk with lust. My voice unrecognizable. But she hears me and does as I ask, as I beg, dropping her knees wider by another inch as I skate my tongue down the center of her torso, over her belly, parting the flesh of her pussy in a hungry lick. And *my God*. Her taste is nothing short of incredible. Peachy and female. For *me*. "Goddamn, Stella. If tight had a taste, this would be it."

If possible, when she moans at my honest praise, her thighs flex violently and fall open even wider, her fingers tunneling into my hair. And this? I can do. I can fuck her with my mouth, because it's about her pleasure, not mine. Fine, I'm letting myself get away with a technicality, but there isn't a way in hell I can keep my tongue off of her wet, willing pussy when she needs an orgasm so bad. Regret wouldn't even begin to cover how that would leave me, because she'd be unsatisfied and *all I want to do* is satisfy her.

To that end, I watch the planes of her nude body shift and undulate while I tap the tip of my tongue against her clit, push two fingers inside of her and start to lick that bundle of nerves in earnest. Eager, fast, thorough. I pump my fingers deep, quickening the pace along with her breaths, reading her, watching. Waiting. When her grip tightens on the strands of my hair, I purse my lips over her clit and apply gentle suction. In contrast, my fingers are twisting, searching for that spot and finding it. The proof is in the way she begins to speak in gibberish, her heels finding purchase on my shoulders.

"Aiden. Oh . . . oh God, Aiden. Please don't stop. Don't, don't, don't . . ."

I growl into the suction to let her know there's no way in hell I'll stop when she's shaking like this. When her stomach is hollowing out and her nipples are in hot little points and her sex is beginning to ripple around my fingers. *Go on, sweetheart. Give it to me.*

I've never heard a purer sound in my life than Stella's scream of my name.

Never felt anything better than the twist of her fists in my hair. Her thighs draw up around my head, hips jerking, her relief wet and warm against my tongue and lips. Desperate to give her more, give myself more, I continue to stroke that place inside of her, teasing the pad of my finger over the coarseness, and Stella gives and gives, body straining until she grows limp on the bed in front of me, the taste of her pleasure making me dizzy.

So hard I almost can't stand it.

I lever myself up onto an elbow and memorize the sight of her flushed body, the vulnerability she's allowing herself with me. To be naked and needy, so honest with her reactions. Like she trusts me.

Trusts me.

Those words are ringing in my head when Stella sits up, gorgeous and seductive with her lids at half mast, so beautiful she makes it hard for me to breathe, and takes hold of my open shirt, tugging me closer. Promises in her eyes. "I want to give now, Aiden. Give you what *you* need." She looks down at my lap and releases a rocky exhale. "Please."

One move. One move and I'd be on top of her. I wouldn't think of anything but her tight heat around my cock, wouldn't feel an ounce of this conflict or guilt over being her boss. Over our relationship beginning with me giving her a chance to shine as a window dresser. But I'd hate myself afterward for leaving those unknowns between us. And God, the trust in her eyes—that seals the deal. I can't do this.

"I'm sorry," I say thickly, grasping her wrists until they let go of my shirt. "I can't, Stella. God, I want to so bad, but I can't."

My dick hates me. When I climb off the bed and zip up my erection with a wince, I'm pretty sure he adds "new owner" to his Christmas list. But that disgust is nothing compared to how much I loathe myself as I stumble toward the door of her bedroom. Have to go *now*. I don't trust myself to maintain this resolve for much longer, especially if I see the disappointment transform her face.

"I don't know, Stella." I swallow past the lump in my throat. "I guess I am too nice for you, huh?"

Turning away from her stunned expression, I walk out of the apartment, then the building, the cold air practically hissing as it meets my fevered skin. But later . . . later I've never been colder in my life, because I'm pretty sure I've just blown it with the girl I've fallen for.

Chapter 11
Stella

I t's Saturday morning. My first official day as an employee of Vivant.

Until now, I'm not really sure it has sunk in. I was given this crazy, once-in-a-lifetime chance—and somehow I delivered. I met expectations. Possibly even exceeded them. Enough to be hired full-time. Is this the point where I call my parents? Would they be proud of what I've accomplished in a short span of time? Or should I wait until I've managed to hold down the job a little longer before I attempt communication?

Wait. I'll wait. Just to make sure this is really happening.

Decision made, I continue completing the new hire paperwork spread out on the table in front of me in the human resources office. When the holiday season is over, I won't always work on weekends, but with a second window to design before Christmas Eve, there are no days off.

HR emailed me this morning with a request to come by their office and upgrade my badge, fill out a W9. As I go through the process of becoming the full-time window dresser, I keep expecting Aiden to show up in the doorway of the office, to make some kind of sense out of what happened between us last night, but he never arrives.

Can I blame him for avoiding me? God, I *really* messed up.

I guess I am too nice for you, huh?

The form I'm filling out blurs in front of me. What was I thinking letting Aiden break his rules? I couldn't have been more encouraging, tempting him to ignore his conscience and do the wrong thing. One kiss and I stopped thinking of his conflict, my physical need hopping into the driver's seat. How selfish can I get?

As if in response to my inward question, my phone starts to vibrate in my pocket. My pulse spikes at the possibility that it could be Aiden. Not that I can answer it right now. Not under the hawk eye of Mrs. Bunting. Does she watch everyone this closely or is it just me? *Stop pretending you don't know the answer to that.*

With a half smile in the woman's direction, I tug the phone out of my pocket—

And my heart sinks down to the carpet when I see "York Correctional Facility" on the screen. Nicole is calling me again.

My palms perspire so quickly, the phone almost slides out of my hand onto the floor. I want to ignore the call. Dr. Skinner would tell me that's okay. Boundaries are healthy. If I don't want to interrupt the rebuilding of my life with a reminder of the past, I'm allowed to make that choice for myself. But after last night, after Aiden walking out of my bedroom looking so torn and upset with himself—thanks to me—I find myself in need of reinforcement. In need of something familiar. A rock to grab onto as I'm floating quickly downstream, a little overwhelmed by the pace at which my life is happening after four years of stagnancy.

That's the thing about our friendship. Messing up isn't merely acceptable, it's encouraged. It's hard not to seek out validation when I'm feeling terrible about last night.

My friendship with Nicole wasn't, isn't, healthy. I know that now. But it was my constant growing up. And I was *her* constant. I let Aiden down last night. Am I really going to let Nicole down, too? If she's calling me again, for the second time in a week, there has to be a reason. Even though there is a sense of foreboding in my stomach, I can't decline the call when she has nowhere else to turn.

I don't want to walk out of human resources before I'm finished, but I also don't want to miss the call, so I answer and keep the phone down on my thigh. "Excuse me?" I ask the human resources director, who arches an eyebrow at me. "Am I all set or do you need me to fill out anything else . . . ?"

Her smile is pinched. "All set, Ms. Schmidt. You can go. Please remember to keep your badge visible at all times."

"Yes. Will do."

I rise and leave the office, entering the warehouse-like space that holds merchandise and veer toward the rear exit door—mostly used for employee smoke breaks—waiting until I'm outside to press the phone to my ear.

"Nicole. Hey."

"Nice of you to answer. And with such enthusiasm, too!" There's a long pause. "Excuse the hell out of me for being excited to hear my best friend's voice for the first time in years."

A kernel of guilt wiggles its way into my throat, despite hour upon hour of counseling from Dr. Skinner that suggested I should feel the opposite. It's a lot easier to recognize a toxic relationship when there's some distance. But having their voice, their character up close and personal is different. There's nostalgia and reminders of the good times attached to that voice. I . . . *should* be excited to speak with her, as well. Shouldn't I? I once referred to Nicole as my sister. We went through puberty together and we vowed to grow old in a condo by the ocean. Countless nights of our youth were spent sneaking out, huddled up behind the local liquor store talking about the adventures we were going to take as soon as we had the money. A few words from Nicole and I can smell cigarette smoke, burnt hot dogs from 7-Eleven and peach schnapps or whatever terrible liquor I pilfered from my parents that wouldn't be missed.

"Yeah, hey, I'm sorry." I pinch the bridge of my nose, wincing at how little time it took me to start apologizing. "I just didn't expect the call."

Being that we were in prison for the same crime, we were not on each other's approved caller list, so no phone calls were allowed. We've written letters over the years, but they definitely grew strained and thinned out toward the end of my sentence. There was always a tone of resentment from Nicole's letters because of my actions the night of the robbery and the fact that my sentence was shorter because of it.

Nicole sniffs. There's some shouting in the background. A security door slamming. Familiar sounds that make my stomach turn over like a rusted car engine. "That's fine," she says. "So where are you?"

I stare down at my feet, fighting to swallow. God, I don't want to tell her. I don't want anything to touch the fragile construction of this new beginning. It's barely in its infancy. I'm proud of the steps I've taken, but she'll find a reason to put it down. "Home," I croak, then clear my throat. "I went home. I'm at my parents' house." Several seconds tick by. I can feel my pulse hammering at the side of my neck.

"Really?" Her laugh is like a recording from the past. "Because I spoke to them a few days ago. When you wouldn't answer my call, I tried them instead. Can't say they were happy to hear from me, but they did say you were in New York at your uncle's place."

My whole body feels hot.

Like my beating heart has expanded and taken up every corner of my insides.

"We always talked about going there together. Getting jobs, taking advantage of the cheap rent and saving up our money. Using it as our jumping-off point."

"I remember," I say through stiff lips.

"Why would you lie?"

"I don't know." The winter sun is blinding. It's cold, but I'm sweating. "I'm just . . . look. I'm trying something new. I'm starting over."

"Without me, sounds like," she adds flatly.

Yes. Say yes. This is my chance to set the boundary. I practiced this for years with Dr. Skinner. Why are the words sticking in my throat? Words that are written in a notebook at the apartment, so I wouldn't forget.

I take ownership of my bad decisions. Every single one of them. Those bad decisions were made alongside Nicole, though. They were made with a lot of pressure on my back. Saying no to anything made her defensive. Any time I questioned her, she broke me down. Accused me of thinking I was better than her because I was raised with middle-class advantages. And she kept up until I just gave in, scared to drive a wedge between us. Because at that point, she was the only one I had. I'd alienated everyone else. Or she'd done it for me.

"Whatever, it's fine." She laughs. "Don't include me in your plans. I'm used to being left behind, right? My parents didn't even come to my parole hearing."

"Parole hearing," I echo, cymbals crashing in my ears.

Nicole hums. "I thought I was calling to give you good news, but maybe you want me to stay in here and rot while you're 'starting over' in New York."

I lean back against the building, my legs no longer able to support me. "You got parole?"

The robotic recording starts to play, telling us we only have thirty seconds left.

"That's right. Guess they decided to be lenient with me, too. It's about time something went my fucking way, right?" She pauses. "Do you have a car?"

"No."

Her sigh fills my ear. "Guess you won't be able to pick me up."

She leaves it hanging there. Automatically, my mind scrambles for a solution. A way to get me to Connecticut so I can be there when she walks out. So I can help her. I had someone there, didn't I? My father might have been tight-lipped and distant, but he showed up. Brought me home to Pennsylvania, gave me enough money to start me off in New York. It's an advantage that Nicole doesn't have. I'm selfish if I don't do something to help. I can't just pull up the rope ladder and leave her trapped in the basement. "I mean, I can send some money. I don't have a lot left and I won't get my first paycheck for another week or so—"

"You got a job? What is it?"

I shake my head, even though she can't see me.

No. No, I won't tell her about this. I can't. She'll hate everything about it. If I think I'm dealing with impostor syndrome now, her reaction to me having such a high-end job will take the cake. *Score another one, Stella. Some people are born with it all.*

Our time is running out.

"*Ten seconds remaining,*" chirps the voice.

"I'll send the money," I mutter, right before the line goes dead.

Nausea pitches in my stomach as I stare down at my phone. It's not that I wanted Nicole to stay locked up forever. I wouldn't wish that on anyone. But I had my chance to establish my intentions to move on without the stickier obligations of our friendship and I blew it. The opportunity passed and now . . . now I don't know what's coming. I suspect Nicole wants to pick up right where we left off, though. She has no choice. Nowhere else to go. What am I going to do if she comes here? I can't turn her away.

The rear door opens with a loud creak, making me jump. One of the salesgirls steps out and lights a cigarette, waving the smoke away so it doesn't cling to her black uniform. I catch the door behind her and she smiles wearily at me when I pass. I don't realize how much the call has thrown me off balance until I step into the rear merchandise room of Vivant and everything looks fuzzy around me. A conversation between two stock delivery guys sounds unnatural. I need to make a list of art supplies and props for the next window I'll be designing. It's my first day as a real employee and the morning is already getting away from me. My legs are like gelatin, though. Am I shaking? *Pull it together.*

I'm almost to the door of the merchandise room when Aiden appears in front of me.

And wow. Wow. He's beautiful and strapping and familiar and bright. Like orange slices and coffee after weeks of being served cold oatmeal and lukewarm water. Just like the night he saved me from the locked window box, I want to throw myself into his arms again and cling for dear life. A hug from him would fix everything for a little while.

"Stella?" He's holding something in his hand—a small stack of envelopes—but when he sees me, his face transforms with concern and he drops them into his jacket pocket, coming forward. His hand reaches out to cup my face and I'm poised to moan at the welcome contact, but he hesitates. Looks around at the employees coming and going from the room, some of them openly watching us, and lets his hand drop away.

If the phone call with Nicole drove a dagger into my middle, it has just been yanked out, sending blood spurting from the wound.

"Are you okay?" he asks quietly, brows knitting together. "You look upset."

Of course I'm not okay. I had this man in my apartment last night. I had his beautiful mouth on mine, his presence warming me, making me feel secure and happy and hopeful and treasured. But he couldn't be corrupted. I should be ashamed of myself for trying. I *am*. I almost made him do something he would have regretted. Something that would have compromised his rare, genuine integrity. He was right to leave. He'll be right to move on. And I'm definitely not going to take advantage of any more kindness from him. Or lean on him about my best friend and the ominous tone of our phone call.

"I'm not upset." I force a smile, marveling at the fact that it's painful to stand so close to him without touching. How did that happen so fast? "I'm fine."

He scrutinizes me in silence. "I know I probably ruined this thing between us last night," he says for my ears alone. And for the first time, I notice the black U-shaped shadows beneath his eyes. "Believe me, I've been thinking about it nonstop, Stella. Going back and forth between kicking myself and being sure I did the right thing, wanting better for you than secrecy and lies." He rakes a hand through his hair. "Maybe you just think I'm a self-righteous jackass now. I don't know. But you can talk to me."

I want to. Badly. I want to bury my face in his peppermint-scented neck and let it all pour out. He'd probably have really good advice, too, even if he's definitely never had a friend get released from prison or experienced the conflicting emotions that come along with it. Aiden has done enough for me, though. I need to start doing for myself. Speaking of boundaries, I'm his employee. I'm *only* his employee. He established that the hard way last night and I respect him for it. So I need to swallow my feelings for him and start acting like a professional. Someone he hired to do a job.

"Thank you. Really. But I'm fine." I start to move past him, holding my breath so I don't get a catastrophic whiff of his aftershave. "I have a lot of work to do."

"Stella, wait." God, he looks miserable. All he wants to do is the right thing, but I am definitely the wrong thing. He just needs a little time and breathing room to realize it. I assume he's going to assure me again that he can still be my confidant, but instead he offers me one of the envelopes from his jacket pocket. "Christmas party invitation," he says in a gravelly tone. "Sorry for the short notice. It took us a while to find a venue. Our usual place never reopened after last year. It's this Thursday night—Christmas Eve. Kind of a tradition to close the store early and celebrate a successful season." His chest rises and falls. "If you don't have plans."

Finding it hard to keep eye contact with Aiden when he's radiating so much intensity, I open the envelope, scanning the scripted invite for a location.

The High Line Hotel.

I've never been there, but something tells me it's ritzy.

What would I wear? Nothing I own, that's for sure. I don't have a single thing that would be suitable for a place that warrants a scripted invitation. There's almost no chance I can go. But I also can't bring myself to lie about already having plans. Not to this man. I'm already lying to him about being fine. "I will try my best to be there," I say, still looking down at the invite. "Oh. It says to bring a plus-one."

"I'd rather you didn't," he says in a rocky voice, drawing the rapt attention of the smoking salesgirl who is passing by, on her way back to the main floor. "I don't have any right to ask you that. I'm not ready to let go of the belief that you're mine yet. Whether it was ever true or not." He exhales, as if impatient with himself. "Just come alone. For my sanity, please."

Somehow I want to laugh and cry at the same time. "Aiden . . ."

"I should pass these out and get back to work before I embarrass myself." He swallows, his eyes running a lap around my face. "Have a good day, Stella."

He's gone before I can respond and I know it's for the best to walk away. Just walk. And with a squaring of my shoulders, I do. But I can't help but glance backward as I leave the merchandise room and I find Aiden watching me go with his heart in his eyes. As for my heart, it stays locked inside my throat for the rest of the day.

Chapter 12
Stella

I t's the Monday before Christmas—the last week to shop before the big day.

I'm sitting cross-legged in the window box eating a ham sandwich from the deli, the glass no longer able to muffle the increasing din of humanity crowding the sidewalks outside. The exclamations as they pass my red dress window make me smile into a bite, but it fades pretty fast when I remember the morning of the unveiling. Aiden's face when he saw it. The way we touched in the backseat of his car, pulling and pushing at each other like we didn't know what to do with all of the gravity between us.

Avoiding each other turned out to be the only solution. I haven't seen him since Saturday morning when he gave me the Christmas party invitation. Although, when I unlock the window box every morning and step inside, I swear the scent of peppermint is lingering in the air. Then again, that might just be wishful thinking on my part. I mean, come on. It's not like he's coming in here and pining for me before the store opens.

Right?

I'm not ready to let go of the belief that you're mine yet.

"Hey!"

I squeak a little when Jordyn clicks into the window box on a pair of electric-blue heels, wiping away the visions in my mind of a yearning man in a bow tie. Almost.

"I came to check your progress."

There's something a little jumpy about my new friend's demeanor today. Even after knowing Jordyn for only a short period, though, I know better than to ask what's on her mind right away. We'll get there eventually. Or more likely, she'll reveal something under her breath and pretend I wasn't supposed to hear it.

I swipe some sandwich crumbs off the lap of my black skirt and stand, re-tucking the edges of my dark green, long-sleeved shirt into my waistband—and I did not wear this to be festive. Definitely not. The green is just a coincidence. "It's coming along well," I say, looking down at the mannequin that is the focal point of the window. "It's nice not to be in a huge rush with this window. I can take my time with Norma."

"Excuse me," Jordyn says. "You named the mannequin?"

"Oh, she has a whole persona. She's thirty-nine. A single, career-driven lady who is about to make partner at her firm. But with one month to go until she turns forty, she realizes how little self-care there is in her life. When was the last time she pampered herself? Never, that's when. And she isn't planning on it now. There is work to be done." I reach down to brush the fine edge of Norma's bangs. "She has some good friends, though. College roommates. And they know her better than she knows herself. They see she's only doing for others. All she gives herself is pressure. So they give her the gift of rediscovering her physical beauty with a smoky eye kit from Chanel and the 24k Gold Mask from Peter Thomas Roth."

"Ah, that's why you asked me to order more stock." Jordyn steps back, seeming to look at Norma in a new light. "I see what you're doing here. You're treating the window as her mirror. It's like a two-way glass into a woman's bathroom and she's getting ready for the night."

"Everyone has an inner voyeur. It'll be impossible to pass by the window when a woman is looking right at them applying mascara."

The corners of Jordyn's mouth lift into a smile. "You kept your word. This is definitely going to send customers running to the other departments." She runs a finger along the collar of Norma's cherry blossom silk robe. "They're going to want this little number, too. You spoke to women's apparel about having extra on hand?"

"Yes, ma'am."

"Good, I might have to snag one for myself," Jordyn mutters, tugging on an ear.

There's my opening. "Oh? Have you got someone to impress?"

"Haven't decided yet," she says breezily, clicking to the other side of the window to examine the candle sconces affixed to the rear wall. "Would you believe Seamus asked me to the Christmas party on Thursday? He wants me to walk in with him. Like a couple. I'm going to look like a chaperone taking her step-nephew to the prom or something."

"Uh . . ." This has me genuinely puzzled. "You're not *that* much older than him, Jordyn. And if he's not bothered by it— understatement—maybe you don't have to be?"

She chews on the inside of her cheek. Crosses and uncrosses her arms. "Listen, I swear I don't have a type. Nothing like that. But my ex happened to be younger by three years and he liked to remind me of that. He'd point it out all the time, sort of implying that he could be out partying, instead of home with me. Like I was forcing him to be there. Like he was doing me a favor."

"And now you hear his voice in your head, no matter how badly you want to block it."

"Yeah." She looks at me, expression shrewd. "You have some experience with that?"

I nod, but keep my lips clamped together. This thing with Nicole is too current to speak about. It's not in the past yet. "Is Seamus similar in any other way to your ex?"

"No. God no. For one, Seamus can dance." She curses, shakes her head. "We shared a little kiss at a staff party once. It was smooth, I'll give him that. But Friday night? I did *not* see the hip movements coming. He was giving me a dick preview. That's what it was. A dick. Preview. He's actually got me wondering about the feature presentation now. Dammit."

My sides hurt from the sudden need to laugh. "Answer without thinking. Do you want to go to the party with him?"

"Yes." She tilts her head back and groans. "Fuck my life."

"Sorry."

Jordyn sighs, fluttering a hand as if to shoo away the topic of Seamus. "Speaking of the Christmas party, you're coming, right?"

Not a chance.

I avoid looking at her, stooping down to gather up the empty soda can from my lunch and some balled-up napkins. "I'm not sure yet. Maybe?"

"How do we make that a definitive yes?" She seems to be choosing her words carefully. "I know you haven't gotten that first check yet—and I was in your shoes once. If you need to borrow something? Or we can talk to womenswear about discounting a dress for you—"

Jordyn is cut off when a security guard walks into the window box. He's followed by two more security guards.

Mrs. Bunting from human resources brings up the rear, clutching a folder to her chest with my name on it. "The one in the green shirt. That's her—Stella Schmidt. She's our only employee with a criminal record and I'd like her searched, please."

The ground tilts beneath me.

In the matter of a second, I'm ice-cold. My teeth are chattering, the sandwich in my stomach threatening to come up.

"Searched for what?" Jordyn demands to know.

"I was alerted about a flagged inventory report. We are missing two very expensive pairs of earrings. *Diamonds.* Miss Schmidt has been here after hours every night for a week. She must have found a way into the locked cases and taken them. There's no other explanation."

"I didn't take anything," I wheeze, pressing a hand to my pitching stomach. "I swear. I didn't. I—I don't have access to the display cases—"

She snorts. "I'm sure someone like you has ways."

Am I terrified right now? Oh yeah. I'm shaking so hard my muscles are beginning to ache. But there is also a part of me that's oddly relieved. I'm not getting special treatment. I'm getting what so many of my fellow inmates spoke about. The unfair, unfounded suspicions, the assumptions placed on them by society. I'm finally getting a glimpse of that—albeit on a much smaller scale—and I'm almost grateful it's finally happening. The other shoe is dropping. My luck has run out. Ironic that I didn't do the crime this time, but so be it.

"I'm going to get Mr. Cook," Jordyn says, jogging from the window box.

My throat is closed up too tight to call after her. What would I say anyway?

No? *Don't* get Aiden?

There's no one else to intervene on my behalf.

Unless . . . he believes I took those earrings.

As I'm led out of the window box and through the riveted main floor, the security guard holding my purse at his side, my left wrist locked in his other hand, I can barely feel my own embarrassment. I'm too busy envisioning Aiden's disappointment, hot pressure blooming behind my eyes at the possibility of it.

* * *

Aiden

A re you sure I can't send a driver to pick you up on Thursday?" I ask Edna through the receiver of my office phone. I'm picturing all kinds of sweat-inducing scenarios that end in my tiny aunt getting abducted or lost in the wilds of JFK airport. "I'll come get you myself."

"I'll hear of no such thing," she says, cackling down the line. "You don't have time to traipse out to the airport in the middle of your busiest shopping day of the year. I'm an independent woman—" She muffles the receiver. "Hank, if you roll your eyes at me one more time today, I'm going to carve them out with my painter's knife."

I know better than to utter a single syllable when Aunt Edna and Uncle Hank are having one of their classic stare-downs. It's a scene I can picture in my head clear as day and it's probably taking place in their screened-in porch. Paints and canvases and half-drunk glasses of sweet tea are taking up every surface. Hank is probably patting at the sweat on the back of his neck, watching

Edna on the phone like it's a spectator sport, never actually getting on the horn himself.

"As I was saying, I'm more than capable of getting a taxi to the party. Just send me the address and don't worry about a thing. Save your fretting for coaxing me off the dance floor."

She curses when something scatters in the background. A mason jar full of beads or some such art supply. "I'll clean that up later. Now, are you going to tell me about the girl or are we going to drag this out another twenty minutes?"

I sit up a little straighter in my chair, shooting a glance toward Leland. Keeping my voice low, I say, "How did you . . . ?"

"You're doing a hell of a lot of sighing, Aiden Cook. Tell me what's up."

"You are," Leland stage-whispers from across the office. "Sighing a lot."

"You can hear this?" I shoot back, pointing at the receiver.

He becomes engrossed in something on his computer screen.

I sigh again. Loudly. Lord, how many times have I done that? No wonder Edna is onto me. I sound like a deflating bouncy castle. Feel like one, too. It's not getting any easier keeping my distance from Stella. Granted it's only been two days since the last time we were face-to-face, but a year might as well have passed. I woke up in the cookware section at 3:00 A.M. this morning with a whiskey hangover and had to do the walk of shame past a dozen judgmental mannequins to the outside world where I took an Uber home to shower. Now I've got a headache and a big chunk carved out of my chest. Sighing doesn't relieve me of the hollowness, so I have no idea why I'm doing it or what it's for.

Maybe when a man is flat-out miserable, his body insists on letting the world know about it. Like an unconscious cry for help. I have the heartache version of a man cold.

Reaching toward the front of my desk, I brush a finger over the binoculars she picked out for me the night we traded gifts. "I wish I had something good to tell you," I say, trying for a chuckle but it sounds like someone stepping on a bullfrog. "You'd . . . love her."

There's a pause. "Well, if I'd love her, she can't be stupid. I'd consider it pretty stupid if she let you get away."

"It's complicated."

"Complicated is a love triangle with a rodeo clown. *Hank*." The zing of metal on the other end of the line tells me she's made good on her painting knife threat. Or at the very least, she's brandishing it like a weapon. "I swear. Roll your eyes one more time. I never loved that clown like I love your crabby ass. But we lived in the same house and you hadn't spoken to me in *nine months*. Nine. Not a 'bless you' or a 'how's it hanging.'"

There's a grunt in the background.

"I'm crazy about you. But I'll still carve out your eyeballs."

Grunt. This one more affectionate.

Edna returns to the conversation with a sniff. "I can't convince Hank to come with me to New York. He thinks there are too many people in our local Dairy Queen, let alone Fifth Avenue."

I picture Hank standing in the middle of Times Square in his coveralls and it almost makes me want to smile for the first time in days. "You'll bring him back something nice."

"I'll consider it. Now, back to this girl. Why is it complicated?"

There isn't a whole lot I can say in front of Leland and that's the issue, isn't it? I want to talk about Stella freely, but even the fact that I am harboring a reservoir of feelings for her is against policy.

The company's *and* my own personal one. Damn, I've wanted to break the rules every other minute since I walked out of her apartment. I've gone down to her window box just to catch the scent of her, to stand in the space she occupies every day and feel close to her. Countless times, I've thought to myself, *Go downtown. Make love to her. She will come around. She will see that we're right.*

There's a roadblock inside of me, though, that I can't seem to bypass.

I won't sell us short or start a relationship with a lie. I won't inadvertently put her in a position to feel . . . required to stay with me—or worse, sleep with me—because I employ her and she doesn't want to lose her job. By now I hope she has some confidence that would never, ever happen, but assumptions are reckless and I won't make them, especially in this case. Especially with someone who is crossing a vulnerable bridge in her life, like Stella.

All of this reasoning doesn't keep me from missing her, though.

From needing her like hell.

I didn't even turn my Christmas tree lights on this morning. Just sat there in the dark like a sad sack wondering if her apartment in Chelsea gets sufficient heat.

"You're sighing again, Aiden."

I drag a hand down my face, bristle scoring my palm. Did I forget to shave?

"I'll tell you about it when you get here, Edna—"

My office door flies open. Linda, the receptionist, is standing there shoulder to shoulder with Jordyn. Wait. What is Jordyn doing all the way up here? She manages the main floor. And now she's approaching my desk in a hurry, gesturing for me to hang up the phone. I don't know how I'm positive in this moment that something isn't right with Stella. I just know.

"Sorry, I have to go, Edna. Call you back." I drop the phone into the cradle and it takes me a few seconds to place it correctly, my hand is suddenly so useless. "What's wrong?"

Jordyn twists and twists the bracelet around her wrist. "Stella . . ."

That single word and I'm winded, my vocal cords tightening. "What happened?"

"Look, Mr. Cook. There is no *way* she did it."

My phone is ringing. Two lines. What the hell is going on? I'm not answering. I'm not going anywhere or speaking to anyone else until I have the story. My muscles are seized up in anticipation of moving. Figuring out what's going on and *moving*. "No way she did what?"

"They're claiming she stole some earrings," Jordyn explains, her outraged expression making it crystal clear what she thinks of the accusation. "I didn't wait to hear the rest. I just came to get you. But I think security will have taken her to human resources."

Jesus Christ. I'm already standing up, moving toward the door, Leland running to catch up with me. Wind is roaring in my ears. The concept of pressing the call button for the elevator makes no sense, so I don't even bother. I go for the stairs.

She has to be terrified.

This is my fault. This is *my* fault. I hired Stella and assumed no one would question that decision. That they would accept the fact that she has a troubled past and treat her with the same respect as everyone else. Like any other employee. I'd just lead by example and everyone would follow suit. That was naïve of me—I can see that now. Now she's been brought *by security* to the back office. Like a criminal.

Anger filters in through the shock and denial.

It crowds into my throat and burns down my esophagus.

Cold perspiration has already soaked the back of my dress shirt by the time I reach the lobby floor and burst through the steel door. I hook a right and rush through the entrance of the first office on the left. Two security guards and Roxanne Bunting, head of human resources, turn to look at me. The guards are stoic but Roxanne looks nothing short of smug, setting off a wild hammering in my temples.

"Where is Miss Schmidt?" I ask through my teeth. One of the guards takes a step back, wisely recognizing that I'm on the verge of imploding.

"Mrs. Bunting asked us to bring her to the back room."

I stride past them, intending to find and reassure Stella that this mess is going to get straightened out. But I'm brought up short when I see my grandmother sitting behind one of the desks, a cup of tea steaming at her elbow. Behind her, my father leans against a file cabinet, twisting the gold watch around his wrist. My gut plummets.

Here it is. This is the T I didn't cross, isn't it? This is the disaster I didn't see looming.

"Hello, Aiden," my grandmother says blithely, leaning down to blow on her tea.

"Aiden," sighs my father with a lazy nod.

My gaze travels to the closed back door, everything inside of me protesting the fact that Stella is on the other side. Scared. Probably worse than the time she locked herself in the window box. Heartburn detonates in my chest with a vengeance just thinking about it. "What are you doing here?" I ask Shirley and Brad.

My grandmother blinks, as if the question is absurd. "Apparently we can't trust you to keep our affairs in order. Dear Roxanne was kind enough to give me a call and let me know some issues were being overlooked. Such as the fact that a felon has been hired behind the board's back."

"I am responsible for hiring. I don't need permission or approval."

"Well, clearly we need to change the hiring procedure." She shoots a look at the closed door. "I knew something was off about her at the unveiling. And I always trust my instincts."

"I thought something was off, too," my father interjects, frowning.

"Yes, you get credit, too, Brad," Shirley assures him, without turning. "Shrewd as ever."

This is where I would normally make nice. Say something to smooth ruffled feathers and keep the peace. It's how I was taught. I was given kindness and even-temperedness to combat the feeling of being lonely. Cast aside. And the resentment that came with it. I'm an outsider in this family and I've been giving my relatives what they want, hoping they'll accept me. But I realize in this moment with absolute clarity that I don't want to be accepted by them. God, no.

I no longer accept *them*.

I'm not going to quell this anger inside me. Not this time. That would be doing myself *and* Stella a disservice. She deserves to have someone pissed off on her behalf. And I'm not responsible for making everyone comfortable, especially when they're in the wrong.

I can't wait another second to get my eyes on Stella, so I take two final steps to the door and push it open. She jolts at my entrance, her back going ramrod straight. She's not crying, thank Christ, but she's shaking. She's shaking like a leaf and the sight of it goes through me like a javelin. "Aiden . . ." Clenching her eyes shut, she shakes her head. "Mr. Cook—"

"Don't say another word," I interrupt, as evenly as possible when the girl I've fallen for has essentially been arrested on my watch—and now she's calling me mister.

Her face loses even more color. I'm working on softening my tone enough to tell her everything is going to be all right, when I hear Shirley whispering with Roxanne and red trickles into my vision. I turn away slowly from the back room, noting absently that Leland and Jordyn are shoulder to shoulder in the doorway, visibly invested in the proceedings. Furious for Stella's sake. And that's when I start thinking semi-clearly. Enough to know what has to be done.

"Jordyn, lock the registers on the main floor and bring the sales staff in here."

My floor manager's eyes widen. "All of them?"

"Yes. All of them."

Jordyn takes off her heels and runs. She's getting a raise.

"They're working, Aiden," sputters my grandmother. "The store is packed. We can't just shut down the main floor on a whim."

My jawbone is going to crack, my teeth are grinding so hard. "You think it's a whim to accuse someone of stealing?"

"Oh please," snorts Brad. "I'm sure the girl is used to it."

Roxanne laughs quietly at my father's remarks, drawing my attention. "Mrs. Bunting. When were you informed of the inventory report that showed the earrings were missing?"

She shifts uneasily over being the new center of attention. "Last night around five thirty. Before I left for the day."

"And even though I was working upstairs until at least eleven o'clock and my personal phone is always open for calls, you decided the best thing to do was alert my grandmother about the issue. Is that right?"

"Roxanne has been working here since me and your father ran the store, Aiden," says Shirley, as if that is an adequate explanation.

"Ran it into the ground, you mean," I say.

The wind sails straight out of Brad, sending him into a coughing fit.

My grandmother's teacup freezes on the way to her mouth. "Aiden, what has gotten into you?"

"It's finally happening," Leland whispers. "He's losing his temper. Get the popcorn."

Now that I've apparently brought the room to a standstill, I focus on the human resources director. "Mrs. Bunting, I might have excused the breach in protocol if you didn't seem gleeful over an employee being falsely accused of stealing merchandise. You may keep your position through New Year's and then I suggest you find another place of employment. You don't represent this company in the manner it deserves. Or rather, that the employees deserve."

Roxanne's mouth drops open.

Shirley lurches in her seat, visibly indignant. I assume she's going to complain about Mrs. Bunting being fired, but instead she says, "*Falsely accused?* The girl was in prison!"

"First of all, she's done her time. And she came out with enough courage to try again," I rasp, trying as hard as I can to keep my composure. "She didn't take the damn earrings. I'll bet my position at this company on that." I hear a soft intake of breath and turn long enough to catch Stella's bemused expression. Did she assume . . . I'd found her guilty? No. No way. "Second, Grandmother, I'm glad you noticed the store is packed, because it has a lot to do with Stella's window and the attention it's bringing to Vivant."

"Through the internet," she mutters, rolling her eyes.

"Yes, through the *internet*. Where attention comes from, Shirley." For the love of everything holy. "Look, either you're in the business of judging employees based on their contribution to the store or you're doing it wrong. It appears to be the latter, so I suggest you stay home from now on. Board meetings are canceled until further notice. Merry Christmas."

"You can't just cancel—"

"Oh yes I can. I have a controlling interest in this company. Sixty percent, if you'll recall. Those meetings are just to humor you." Leland has produced a lighter from out of nowhere and is waving it side to side in the air like he's at a Foo Fighters concert.

My father snorts, his expression finally losing some of its perpetual boredom. Resentment twists his mouth, instead. "You hold those meetings so you can remind us we would have declared bankruptcy without you playing the hero."

I always suspected how my father felt, but to have it said plainly is a sock to the stomach. Anger and resignation help me recover. "You're wrong. Today is the first time I've brought it up since I took over as general manager. I held those meetings thinking it might bring us closer together as a family. That's all I ever wanted in coming back here. I wasn't rescuing the store to hold it over your heads. Maybe in a way, I wanted to prove I was worth keeping around this time, but mostly, I was trying to *be* someone to you." Something unknots inside of me like a ribbon, the ends fluttering free and fading into nothing. "But I'm no longer interested. Not even a little bit. Being something to you means being less to myself." I shake my head. "Thank God you sent me to Edna."

My father looks down at the ground sharply. If I happen to glimpse a hint of regret in his eyes, I don't get any pleasure out of it. Sensing a presence behind me, I turn to find Stella standing in the doorway of the back room. If I didn't know any better I would say she's in shock. *God*, she's so beautiful. But she's staring at me like she's seeing me for the first time. Is that a good thing or a bad thing?

I don't have a chance to ask because Jordyn is back, ushering members of the sales team into the small human resources office with the brisk efficiency of a flight attendant. Once the half dozen of them are packed like sardines into the room, I speak. "Listen up, everyone. I want to start off by saying no one is going to be penalized for coming forward. Understand? We're smack dab in the middle of the busy season, after a long lull. It's easy for merchandise to get misplaced. But I need you all to think carefully now, sort back through the last couple of days. Did anyone show two pairs of earrings and forget to lock them up? Or maybe had a customer accidentally walk off without paying? It wouldn't be the first time—"

"Were they diamonds?" comes a voice from the group, but I can't tell from where.

"Yes," Jordyn responds quickly, scanning the faces of each employee.

A young woman with a red side braid steps forward and slaps a hand across her eyes and starts talking in a high-pitched rush. "I'm so sorry, Mr. Cook. A man put them on sort of an unofficial hold yesterday afternoon. I know we're not supposed to put jewelry on hold during the Christmas season, but he was so sweet and he just needed until Thursday to get paid, so I . . . They're in the back of register number three. In the spare change compartment. He couldn't choose which pair, so I tucked them both away. He was going to decide by Thursday. I just didn't want someone else to buy them. Oh God, please don't fire me. I'll never do it again."

As the girl has been giving her explanation, the tension has slowly ebbed from my chest. Not because I was worried Stella took the earrings. No, sir. The relief at having an explanation, having it *over* for her, is just so steep, I feel like I'm flying down a hill in a wheelbarrow. Again. Pulled that stunt when I was eleven and knocked out a tooth for my trouble. "Thank you for telling the truth. No one is getting fired. Especially for helping a fella impress his sweetheart." I trade a smile with Jordyn. "You can all return to the floor now."

There's a chorus of thank-yous and shuffling feet as everyone files out.

My father, Shirley and Roxanne look chastised, but none of them look prepared to issue an apology to Stella, reinforcing everything I've said and done since walking into human resources.

Jordyn sends Stella a warm wink, preparing to follow her charges back to the main floor, when Seamus sticks his head into the office, a broom in one hand. "Sorry to interrupt. Did someone park a white Mercedes in front of the store?"

My grandmother nearly upsets her tea. "Yes. I did. Why? My driver is off today. I put my hazard lights on."

Seamus winces. "It's been towed, ma'am. Sorry. There was nothing I could do."

I don't miss the wink the custodian sends Jordyn. Or the look of promise she gives him in return, following him out of the office.

But I'm a gentleman, so I choose to pretend I see nothing.

"Heading back upstairs, boss," Leland singsongs, still waving the lighter on his way out.

I start to offer the use of my car and driver to my grandmother and Brad, but Shirley is already on the phone with someone named Gregory, offering him double his daily wage to come pick them up and drive them home. They cast twin glares at me on their way out, and yes, it still stings. Maybe it always will. But I feel lighter having let go of their expectations of me.

Simply meeting my own.

And finally, finally, I turn and give my full attention to Stella.

She looks like she's caught mid-swallow and there's a layer of moisture in her eyes. Without pausing in my attempt to re-memorize every feature of her face, I take out my pocket square, shake out the folds and hand it to her.

"Hi," I say.

"Hi," she whispers back.

"If it's all the same to you, Mr. Cook," Roxanne interrupts stiffly, "I'll work from home for the rest of the day."

"Actually, there's something you can do before you leave," Stella answers, catching me off guard. "Mrs. Bunting, do you have a love contract handy?"

My heart catapults upward and slaps against my brain. "What are you doing?"

"I'm signing it. We're signing it."

By the grace of God, I manage to keep from kneeling at her feet and weeping with gratitude. I can't, though. I can't accept what she's offering until it's right. Until it's good for her. "Not because of what I did here today, Stella. Not because you feel obligated—"

"No. No, it's not that at all. I don't feel obligated. I *didn't* take the earrings. And what you said, about the window. You were right. Maybe I haven't quite earned my right to be here yet, but I am. I'm *doing* it." She wets her lips, steps a little closer to me. Enough to make me lightheaded. "I want to sign the papers because . . . if you believe that much in me, enough to know I'm better than my past, then I can believe that much in us. I can try my best."

Oh boy. I'm heading down the hill in that wheelbarrow again, but this time there's no grassy field full of dandelions to land in. I just keep going and going until I'm free falling without an end in sight. For Stella. "You try for me and I'll do the rest," I manage, wrapping my arms around her, my damn heart knocking so loudly they can hear it in Staten Island.

"I just have to ask you one thing first," Stella says. And I look down to find her definitely gearing up for something. Almost steeling herself. "Aiden, this . . . wanting to be with me, isn't about . . . saving me, is it? You might not even realize what you're doing," she rushes to add. "You might truly believe you like me. But maybe your nature demands that you care for someone who needs it. And that's lovely, really lovely, but I don't think that's good for either of us."

It takes me a moment to get past my shock. Saving her? How long has she been worried about this? "Stella, you're going to succeed with or without me. If I didn't give you this job, you would have found another way in, here or somewhere else. I'm grateful I was the one who gave you a shot, because it's how we met, but you don't need saving. Support, yes. And I need it, too. But not saving." I pause, hoping my words are sinking in. "This isn't about me carrying you, it's about us walking together and deciding where to go, all right?"

She takes in a breath and lets it out slowly. "All right. Let's sign."

A moment later, the sound of the printer spitting out the paperwork makes me smile. I look down at Stella to see if she's smiling, too . . . and find her nose buried against my abominable snowman bow tie, instead. She inhales deeply and looks up at me, pupils dilating, her teeth sinking down into her bottom lip, her chest lifting up, shuddering down on a winded exhale.

And as soon as we get these papers signed, I have a pretty damn good idea how we'll be spending our lunch break.

Chapter 13
Stella

Well. I guess it's possible to want no one's help *and* be starved for someone to believe in me—all at the same time. And I had no idea. None. Not until Aiden stormed hell for leather into the human resources office. I was such an idiot to assume he would believe I'd stolen those earrings. Such. An. Idiot. Aiden Cook is not typical. He's a salmon swimming upstream. He's Sunday morning swooping in like a hero when you woke up thinking it was Monday.

So, hell yes.

I'm signing the paperwork.

I am given a document detailing my rights and the company's sexual harassment policy. Unlike with the employee handbook, I take my time to absorb and understand the words on the page. And once I do, my hand is moving, ink is coming out of the pen onto the dotted line and I'm consenting to a relationship of my own free will. Currently, I would probably sign a document agreeing to naked camping as long as I can be alone with Aiden sometime today. In the next fifteen minutes, preferably.

He strokes a big hand down my hair, picks up a pen and signs his own name, forgoing his right to make direct decisions about my employment going forward—a task that will be assigned to another manager—and he does it without taking his eyes off me once. Eyes that hold sensual promises and a guarantee that he'll deliver.

Be alone with him in the next fifteen minutes?

Make that five.

With the formalities out of the way, he stands in front of me, so tall I have to tilt my head back, and he presses a kiss to the center of my forehead, exhaling deeply. Then he takes my hand and guides me out of HR toward the elevator bank. There are two other offices located just off this hallway and every single employee has stopped to watch us walk past, hand in hand. The heroic paragon of ethics and his ex-convict girlfriend.

What the hell am I doing?

I seriously don't know, but I'm doing it. I'm allowing myself to grow from the lesson I've just learned. I'm not turning away from it. There are amazing people, like Aiden and Jordyn, who have spent time with me and made a positive judgment. One they didn't even question when push came to shove—and I want to believe them. Badly. I want to believe that I'm the kind of person worth standing up for. I'm still the girl who let down her parents. I'm still the girl who can't seem to withstand peer pressure from her childhood friend. But maybe it's all right to test-drive some trust in myself. My character. To see what I'm capable of. Just a little.

As I step into the elevator next to Aiden, our hands joined tightly, it's impossible to ignore that he is not doing anything in half measures. There's no pretending here. His all-or-nothing personality is another huge reason I hesitated to dive into a relationship.

I am . . . not all here yet.

Part of me is still mentally locked up. I woke up from a coma after four years to find that the world took giant leaps forward without me. When I walked out of Bedford Hills, my online courses, my secondhand car and my future were all gone, along with my makeup bag, clothes, phone and social acquaintances. All a thing of the past. Being here in New York, decorating windows for Vivant, still seems like an elaborate dream. I'm not used to it. Yet here I am, taking another wild leap into the unknown. And what it really all comes down to is . . .

I worry that I'm just *pretending* to be someone else. Someone new.

I worry that if I peeled back a single layer of skin, I'd find the girl who vandalized cars and blew off school and treated her parents with a lack of respect, all so she'd fit in. All so she could fulfill some bad-girl persona. How could I have changed so much? From that troubled girl to this . . . woman who is proficient at her job and holds this *deeply* good man's hand?

I don't know. Maybe I haven't.

But I'm going to explore this and hope that eventually the universe will send me a sign that I'm living right. That I've changed. That I can sustain that change permanently.

For now, I'm going to let myself have Aiden and this moment.

Maybe if I jump in with both feet, it'll start to feel real.

Most of the employees in Aiden's front office are gathered in the break room having their lunch. He nods at them as we pass, leaving their jaws unhinged. When we enter his office, Leland is at the desk opposite Aiden's, merrily typing away, "Blue Christmas" by Elvis playing at a high volume. "BRB, boss, while I write literal fan fiction about you. I mean, that was just . . ." Leland trails off, making an explosion sound. "I think I'm going to join the gym. I'm just so *motivated* right now. I mean, this momentum will fade and I'll regret locking myself into a contract but I'm going to ride this steed of ambition until it bucks me off—"

"Leland," Aiden says, his thumb pressing into the center of my palm, moving in a slow circle and robbing the breath clean out of my lungs. "Your mother is looking for you outside."

"My *mother*?" The head of Aiden's assistant snaps up, his eyes appearing over the top of his Mac. When he sees us standing just inside the door, our fingers twined together, his eyebrows shoot up to his hairline. "Ohhh. My *mother*. That's right. We're going to lunch. So nice of her to drive in from Connecticut at the last second." He stands and swipes up his keys, checks for his wallet, and breezes past us with a thousand-watt smile. "The official word is that you're discussing the direction of the spring window designs."

"Thank you," Aiden says to his assistant's retreating back.

The door closes, leaving us alone in the office.

"People are totally going to know what we're doing in here," I murmur, "Carol of the Bells" starting to play. Aiden turns to face me, crowding me against the door, sending a wave of heavy heat careering into my belly. "What, um . . . what are we going to do in here?"

A shudder goes through his sturdy frame. "That's up to you, sweetheart. I just needed you to myself."

He reaches past my right shoulder and taps a switch on the wall. There's a mechanical whir and the room begins to darken. A thin black shade is coming down over the window, still allowing some light in but blocking most. In the space of seconds, the office goes from a professional setting to something else entirely. But when Aiden drops his mouth to mine and whispers my name, we could be on the N train during rush hour for all I care. I just want to kiss this man. My toes are curled up tight in my boots, anticipation making me dizzy.

God, he's so big. Did I notice that enough before? How his shoulders block out the world? How it feels so natural to rub our foreheads together, to treat my hands to a ride up and over his pecs. Touching this man is like second nature while being entirely new. Thrilling. Right.

"Stella," he says, tilting my chin up. "Are you sure you're okay after what happened?"

I start to lie, to say yes, but the words won't come out. Not to him. "It shook me up. But now . . . I don't know, I feel shaken up in a good way. Maybe that doesn't make sense. I just know I'm not scared anymore, but my adrenaline is still pumping. I haven't come down." I press up on my toes to meld our mouths together. "Don't let me come down."

Our kiss is a perfect assault. It's nothing like the other ones, because there's no holding back. There's no reason to temper the heat, except maybe the fact that we're in his office in the middle of the day. Our location is the furthest thought from my brain, however, when our lips open in tandem, the condensation from our labored breaths making the kiss slippery. Hot. Sexual. We're in the dark and there's nothing to stop this. Nothing to stop Aiden's tongue from pushing past my lips to stroke mine. Nothing to keep his hands from cupping the sides of my face, his thumbs tracing the curve of my jawline. With a groan, he tips my head back to kiss me more fully, taking the access I grant him with hunger growing more and more unchecked.

"Dammit, we should have gone back to my place," he rasps, drawing me onto my toes and crushing me to the door, dragging his hot, open mouth up the curve of my neck. "I just need to be alone with you so bad."

"I need to be alone with you, too," I breathe. "I missed you."

"Did you?" he says, pausing our kiss long enough to search my face—and I don't hide anything. For now, I'm an open book and the unspoken sentences he reads in my eyes make him huff a hard breath, our mouths crashing back together with more intention.

More urgency.

Our hips roll together, my stomach dragging sideways over his sizable erection—and I'm immediately pinned harder to the door. There's a short pause, neither of us moving, balanced on razor wire or maybe the point of no return. And then he slides his feet back to position his sex lower on my clothed body, pressing that ridge tight to my mound and grinding upward, bringing my boots momentarily off the ground, before they land again. We exhale shakily, his hands climbing up the sides of my hips, framing and squeezing them *hard*, humping me again.

"Oh my God," I whimper, wrapping my left leg around his hip, watching his mouth skate through the valley of my breasts, kissing each of them through my shirt, his hips shifting restlessly between my legs. "I've never been this turned on in my life."

"Is that what I am? Turned on?" He surges up, forward, pressing his bared teeth against my ear, his thickness pulsing at my inner thigh. "Stella, you've got my dick so hard, I'm going to pass out if I don't come."

Hearing the words *dick* and *come* from this man's normally squeaky-clean mouth hardens my nipples like pearls. His hair is in disarray, his mouth shiny and swollen, bow tie askew. Gorgeous, aching man. Desperate man. I love the change that comes over him when we're intimate. It's like watching the sun set, filling the sky with orange fire.

And his hands are magic. *Magic.* Massaging my bottom now, slowly, reverently, as if he's discovered buried treasure after years of searching. His confident touch strokes up and down my buns, heating my flesh through my skirt, our mouths in a state of madness now. There's no savoring, no going slow. Our mouths are open and we're taking. My upper half is flattened to the door. I'm a willing victim. I want to rub myself against his hard shaft, but despite the lust storm building inside of me, there is a modicum of awareness left.

I care about this man.

I pushed him once to do something out of character and I won't do it again.

If we're going to rein it in, now is the time. A few more seconds of his mouth punishing mine with such perfect sensuality and I'll forget my own name.

"Aid—" His tongue rakes up my neck and my breath stutters out. "Aiden."

Eyes glittering, he cages me in tight to the door. "Yes, Stella."

Wow. His voice is bottom-of-the-barrel deep. "We can stop," I whisper.

He stares at my mouth like a starving man. "Is that what you want?"

If I say yes, I'll be lying. So I remain silent. Breathing, breathing.

"Uh-huh," he drawls, in kind of a . . . cocky manner? "That's what I thought."

Yeah, wow. He looks kind of arrogant right now and *oh man*, it is really working for him—and me. Without untangling our gazes, he fists the hem of my shirt, untucks it from my skirt and peels it off over my head, making me gasp. Now I'm in a bra and a skirt, pinned between my boss and the door. Did I really think this man was a dork once upon a time? Because right now, the bow tie is my only reminder of my first judgment of Aiden Cook. Gone is the Tennessee gentleman and he's been replaced by an absolute panty-melter.

"Listen to me," he says against my ear, brushing his lips up and down the sensitive shell until my eyes start to glaze over. "I've stretched my patience as far as it will go when it comes to you, Stella. I'm *starved*. And there's no more paperwork for this. I've fulfilled that obligation. The only requirement I'm interested in now is the one between your legs." He turns and carries me across the office, settling my backside on the edge of his desk and yanking my hips to the very edge. "I need to fill it. As long as you want that, too, I'm done stopping."

"I want it, I want it," I whimper haltingly. "I want you."

No points for subtlety.

But at least I can say I gave him one final out before we corrupt the walls of his office.

My fingers go to work on his belt buckle, unfastening it in a hurry and letting the heavy silver sag, wasting no time unbuttoning his pants and lowering the zipper. Oh my God. Oh my *God*—he's huge. Thick and solid and long. Hard as nails. I rub my palm against the distended cotton of his briefs, watching his eyes grow dazed and molten at the same time. When I tug down the waistband of his underwear and stroke his bare flesh, his body gravitates closer as if compelled, his mouth slamming down over mine, our hands moving together in a vigorous motion, up and down the rigid stalk of his arousal.

"Keep that up while I get your panties off," he says hoarsely, clamping his teeth down on my bottom lip, growling low in his throat while he shoves up my skirt and drags my basic black underwear down my thighs. It happens so fast. I'm so mesmerized by the flex of his forearms, the heaving breadth of his chest, that my hands stop moving and he begins to thrust into my fist instead. And if I was entranced before, that was nothing compared to now, because his hips move in such smooth pumps that my pulse begins to leap everywhere.

Especially *there*. Right there, between my legs, where I'm so wet. So wet without knowing how or when it happened, only that this man inspired it and there's nothing like him. Nothing like the way we touch each other.

We converge like it was choreographed, his hips pressing in between my spread legs, his mouth on my neck, a big, male fist winding and winding in my hair.

"Are you going to scream?" he asks raggedly.

I shake my head rapidly. "No."

"Good girl," he grunts, slanting his mouth over mine. "Put me in. Put me all the way in."

Am I crazy to feel those words resonating everywhere? As I guide his stiff sex to my entrance and press the tip inside me, both of us holding our breaths while he sinks and sinks, me gasping over the full, stretching sensation, I feel his words in the dead center of my chest. *Put me all the way in.* This is more than a physical invasion; he's making himself known everywhere. In my bones. Into the organ leaping in my rib cage. When his shaft can't push any farther, there's a catch in my throat and I exhale in a rush, gathering him to me. It's involuntary. Wanting, needing him closer, closer, closer. "Aiden."

"*Stella*," he groans, wrapping his arms securely around me, smothering my face into his shoulder, our breath racing in and out, loudly to our ears, but drowned out by Christmas music to anyone outside of the door. And in that single use of my name, in the way he holds me like I'm priceless, I know he's experiencing it, too. This sense of joining more than our bodies. It's like there's something waiting, eager to be unlocked inside of me, reaching out for the corresponding key in him.

He's giving it. He holds me so tight and *gives* it.

Powerful hips rear back and drill forward—and I just barely manage to muffle my scream into his shoulder, my fingers this close to clawing the shirt right off his body.

Aiden laughs in my ear, sounding pained. "What happened to not screaming?"

"I didn't expect it to feel that amazing," I manage. Amazing is an understatement. He's touching every forgotten corner of me, pressing tight and deep, his body wrapped around me, anchoring me, making me feel safe, needed, lusted for. "It n-never has."

He looks at me with an unnamed emotion in his eyes. "Nothing in my life has felt as amazing as you, either. Nothing."

I have no time to process the weight and intensity of our exchange before he's drawing me off the desk, keeping himself planted inside of my body while striding across the room. Toward another door. A filing room, I realize, when he brings me inside.

A second later he kicks the door shut behind us and my bottom hits the surface of a low filing cabinet. And then he's bearing down on me. Hard. *Downright rough*. Positioning my legs open wide with his lower body and the occasional desperate hand, his hips punching back and slapping forward, my cries muffled by his shoulder, but in the closet we don't have to try as hard to be quiet and that's a good thing, because the filing cabinet is bumping against the wall, Aiden is chanting my name into my neck and I'm panting words like *harder, faster, deeper.*

"I know, sweetheart. I know you want that cock hard and dirty." He kisses me until my mind is spinning, then presses our foreheads together tightly, his pace picking up, verging on wild. "And now *you* know. I can eat your pussy gentle and fuck you rough. Not so nice now, am I?"

"No!" God oh God, I'm ripping off his shirt. I'm watching my hands do this thing and have no control over them. I just want to *see* him. I want every inch of him to be in my memory bank. I resent the fact that I haven't witnessed him naked, haven't slid my nudity all over him and reveled in it. All of it, all of it. Now. I can't stop touching and whimpering and I can't wait for this torture to be over, but I also never want it to end. *"Aiden, please."*

"It's a good orgasm. That's what's coming. That's what's making you crazy. I know—I'm hurting, too. Hurting and feeling so goddamn hot at the same time. Do you know how tight you are?" He slams deep with a growl. *"Jesus*, it's so fucking tight."

He's right about the buildup inside of me. It's like nothing I've ever known. There's no reservations between me and this man. Not right now. We're giving everything to each other, selfish and generous in equal measure, and we're giving it physically, emotionally, and the turmoil is beautiful. So beautiful.

The flesh between my legs is seizing up around his pounding thickness in ominous waves. And when I finally succeed in opening several buttons of his shirt and the hard slabs of his pecs flex in the muted light, his long, guttural moan hitting my ears, a rush of sensation so violently perfect I can barely fathom it goes crashing through me, my sex pulsing one final time and quickening around him, hitting me with a turbulent knockout blow of relief.

"Shit. *Shit.* Been dying to feel that pussy go off for me. Squeezes even harder than I thought it would." Aiden picks me up off the file cabinet mid-orgasm, wrapping me in a bear hug and grinding his hips up, up, *up* so deep into me that there really is no description of the sound I make into his hot, perspiring neck. A second climax follows the first, turning those tiny, intimate muscles instantly sore, but that doesn't stop me from riding his stiffness, jerking my hips up and back and inviting him to follow me into the storm—and he does.

He drops a hand to my backside, clutching, drawing me roughly to his lap and he breaks apart, stumbling back in the small filing room until his back hits the wall, his warmth filling me while he groans my name, plowing his lower body upward over and over again, his shaft pulsing inside of me, jerking with every ounce he releases. "Jesus, Stella, Jesus. How is it so good? How are you so goddamn good for me, sweetheart? Move. Move just a little more. *Ahhh, fuck.* That's it, right there. Take the last of it just like that."

We just sort of collapse at the same time.

My body loses any sort of tension, sagging into Aiden's arms, and he slides down the wall, cradling me in his lap on the floor. It takes us long, long minutes to get our breathing under control. And if he's in the same boat as me, he's trying to corral his heart, too. Though I'm not sure that's an option. It seems to be an unbroken horse that has escaped from its pen.

"Stella . . ." His palm smooths the length of my hair, letting out an incredulous breath. "God, I knew it would be like that. I just didn't know it would be like *that.*"

I nod against his chest, knowing exactly what he means.

We're ruined.

He lays a kiss on my temple. "Come home with me after work tonight. Stay."

Somehow I know going to Aiden's home, being among his things and experiencing his routines with him is going to ruin me even worse than what we just did. Despite the niggling doubts in the back of my mind, all of them in myself and my ability to be this new person . . . I am powerless to do anything but nod. To do anything but hand him as much of my heart as I have available. "Yes. I'll stay."

Chapter 14

Aiden

I guide Stella into my apartment by the hand. "Keep your eyes closed."

"I promised I would," she laughs, squeezing her lids tighter. "You're not going to reveal a giant Furby collection or something, are you?"

"I'm saving that for the third date," I call back to her while crossing the room, flipping the floor switch to turn on the Christmas tree lights, as well as the lit-up garland that runs the perimeter of my living room window. I'm probably going to lose all of the progress I've made in convincing her I'm nothing more than a huge cornball, but so be it. I want her to remember the first time she walked into my apartment. I'm sure as hell going to.

Just seeing her outlined in the common hallway light in her puffy jacket and boots, her bangs dusted with the snow that has started falling outside, is twisting me up in more directions than a funnel cake at the county fair. I've lived in this place for five years and other women have darkened my doorway in that time. Those others . . . they had my respect, but my heart was never involved. Not a single corner of it. Not like this.

I've never turned on my Christmas tree and matching garland for anyone, that's for damn sure. Never wanted to see her hair spread across my pillow so badly, I ache. And here I am, already making a list of things I've *only* experienced with Stella to make myself feel better for every encounter I've ever had with another woman. That's how bad I've got it. I'm guilty for everything I ever did before we met.

She's lit up in a soft, white Christmas glow as I approach her again, sending my heart off clunking in my chest. When I stop in front of her and unzip her jacket, her eyes are still closed. Slowly, I pull the nylon off her shoulders, watching color infuse her cheeks, the pace of her breath increasing slightly. As if I'm undressing her completely, making her naked, instead of just removing her jacket. But that's how I've felt all day, too. My lust is on a hair trigger ever since this afternoon, when we ruined each other in my filing room for anyone or anything else.

Here's another thing for my growing list of firsts with Stella. I've never come so hard that my life flashes in front of my eyes. No sir. Not until her. I can still feel the hot clench of her pussy around me, the way she clung, the smooth friction of her inner thighs on my hips, the way she begged for more, more, more with her whole body. Truth be told, I've caught myself staring into space with a semi-erection around nine times since this afternoon.

Good *lord*, the sex.

I'm a changed man. Hell, I'm a grateful man.

In more ways than one. Just having Stella here, in my home, is more than enough. It's something I spent the weekend thinking was never going to happen. Sleep was lost and an unhealthy amount of bourbon was consumed over it. That'll teach me to doubt when it comes to this girl. She's extraordinary. She's got a hundred little cogs turning in her head right this very second—I can see them chugging away. By some miracle, she decided I'm right enough for her to claim officially, on paper, and now I just have to make sure she never regrets it.

It'll be easy.

That lie is so hard to swallow, I have to tug on the front of my bow tie to get it down.

Being with Stella might be easy, but there is a perpetual tug in my subconscious telling me she's not all in. Yet. She's window-shopping, while I've already bought out the whole damn store.

Patience.

My rib cage expands on a deep breath. "You can open your eyes."

Watching her thick eyelashes blink open, I notice absently that she's wearing less makeup than the first time we met. Less of that black liner under her eyes. When did she make the change? I probably should have—*would* have commented on it if I wasn't too focused on the blue eyes themselves to notice how they're made up. I like her either way . . . but God, I *love* her like this. Sucking in a breath over the haphazard Christmas lights, pleasure and nostalgia and joy washing across her features. Damn. I've done something right in my life if I get to watch this happen up close.

"Wow." She exhales in a rush. "Your place. It's even better than I was picturing. It's . . . a vintage bachelor pad. Like Don Draper if he had a soul."

I laugh out loud at that description and she relaxes enough to set down her purse, toe off her boots and close the apartment door behind her, turning the lock.

"Consider me called out," I say, taking her hand and tugging her deeper into the apartment. So help me God, watching the toes of her tights sink into my living room rug makes the fly of my dress pants feel tight. My voice is significantly deeper when I say, "I tend to gravitate toward the old-fashioned."

"I noticed." She glances over at me. "I'm kind of the furthest thing from old-fashioned, though. Did you take a detour and get lost?" Her tone is light, but her eyes are vulnerable. "That's just like a man to drift off course and refuse to ask for directions."

"I know right where I am, Stella." I hold her attention as long as I can before it dances away, moving to the Christmas tree. Not only am I positive I'm going the right way, but I've thrown out the map altogether. How would she react if I told her that? Probably by running out the door—and I can't even say I would blame her. We signed paperwork with HR so we could date, not get married. *Slow your roll, Aiden.* "When you're ready to talk about where you are on the map, I'm here."

Her chest rises and falls a little quicker, but she tries to pass off her nerves as arousal, flashing me a wobbly smile. "If your plan was to seduce me with cartography talk, it's working." She pushes her hair back, shifts her focus back to the tree. As always, Christmas seems to be her—our—safe place. "Your tree is beautiful, but not too beautiful. It's got character, just like the way you did your office."

The corner of my mouth tugs. I'm more than willing to let her get away with the subject change for now. If she wanted to do aerobics on the roof, I'd find a way to make it happen. "See any room for improvements?"

She rolls her lips inward, wetting them. Slaying me where I stand. "When I was a kid, we'd make a popcorn garland and string it around the tree. My mother had all these old Victorian doll ornaments, heirlooms passed down through the generations. The popcorn garland was our one modern touch." Her gaze drifts around the living room, the kitchen space just over my shoulder. "My old-fashioned boss definitely has popcorn and a sewing kit."

Boss?

All right. Now she's pushing it.

Or rather, pushing me away. Trying to establish a boundary.

And that's fine. That's her right. But we're going to negotiate where it lies.

I close the distance between me and Stella, watching the color climb her neck and cheeks. When I slide my fingers up through the back of her hair and grip, her eyelids droop like twin weights and the pulse at the base of her neck starts to sprint. Magic. She has to feel that. "That's boyfriend, Stella. Not boss." I fuse our lips together and she stumbles into me, giving me full access to her mouth, even though she denies me the same with her thoughts and fears. I'll get there. We'll get there.

Her tongue flickers against mine, inviting me into her mouth, and I take. Just like earlier in my office, I sense she needs to be . . . insulated. Surrounded. So I wrap both arms around her, crush her close and kiss her until she's whimpering. Until her arms are wound up around my neck and she's rubbing her tits side to side against my chest.

"Boyfriend," I rasp, when we come up for air. "That work for you?"

"You're still my boss," she breathes.

Using my grip in her hair, I tilt her face up to mine, studying it closely. "On a scale from one to ten, how much does that bother you?"

Those cogs are turning. She's thinking about it. Processing and re-processing. Good. The last thing I want to do is leave an issue undiscussed where it could pop up and bite us later. "It doesn't bother me," she whispers, as though she's realizing it in real time and it's surprising her. "It . . . just doesn't. You've given me no choice but to have total faith in your actions and judgment." She frowns at my chin. "Sneaky. How did you do that?"

"Pure willpower. And the worst blue balls known to mankind." I'm trying not to project everything inside of me onto my face, but I'm pretty sure I'm losing the battle. "The pain of walking out of your apartment was worth it, Stella. You just said you have faith in me."

She hums. Keeps on frowning. "Apparently you have it in me, too." After a moment of lip chewing, she lifts curious eyes to mine. "How did you know I didn't take the earrings? Did you Google me? You did, didn't you?"

Her question throws me for a loop. It's not that I haven't considered Googling her to find out more about the night of the robbery that sent her to prison. I *have* thought about doing it. A lot. I suspect the finer details of what happened matter quite a bit. "No. I didn't. You're going to tell me what happened when you're ready."

"I told you what happened."

"Not all of it."

Lord, her heart is jackhammering against my chest. I want to lay her down and press my full weight down on top of her, just to make her feel grounded. But I appease myself by walking her backward to the couch, turning and sitting down, pulling her sideways into my lap.

When she tucks her head under my chin, I swear I've died and gone to heaven.

"You were right. I've got popcorn and a sewing kit. We're going to make a garland worthy of the Rockefeller Center tree just as soon as you get this off your chest."

"There's nothing on my chest," she grumbles, sniffing my bow tie. Snuggling in.

"Nothing but a forty-pound boulder," I manage through my tightening throat.

"Wow. Who's calling out who now?" Stella sighs and I wait, trying not to be obvious that I'm holding my breath. "I thought maybe you Googled me and found out, you know . . . that I didn't leave the night of the robbery. When the restaurant owner was shot, I called 911 and waited with him, holding my sweatshirt over his wound. I didn't leave with Nicole. I couldn't." Her voice grows a little shaky but she clears it. "And I thought maybe you read about that on the internet and assumed I would never steal earrings. Or hold up a restaurant with a *real* gun, having no idea it wasn't fake. Because you're a man who wants to believe *everyone* is redeemable and good deep down."

It takes me a minute to speak. I'm not even sure what's happening inside of me, I just know I want to go back in time and be in her corner that night. "I won't deny that. I do think everyone has some good inside them deep down, even my grandmother and father, but I'm also logical. I'm realistic enough to know some people might never locate that good or do anything with it. You're not one of them. I don't need a search engine to tell me that."

"Did you at least type my name into the Google search bar without hitting enter?"

"Sixty-three times, at least."

Her laughter is light. Lighter than I've ever heard it and it sends my heart climbing up into my throat. When the musical sound fades, she's silent for a moment. Then, "Nicole is getting out of prison earlier than expected. I found out over the weekend. I ran into you right after I spoke to her on the phone—"

"That's why you were upset," I say on an exhale, relieved by all of the puzzle pieces fitting into place. "You're not on good terms with her."

A beat passes. "I'm not sure our terms have ever been good. We've been best friends for a long time. But it's a relationship that . . . I don't know, it got twisted up somewhere along the line and I couldn't . . . I *can't* untangle it." Her curled hand settles on my chest almost hesitantly, relaxing slowly. "I'd never put the blame on Nicole for anything I did. I'm responsible for my own actions. I can't pretend I didn't go along with her ideas so she'd be happy, though. She had it so much harder than me growing up. Why couldn't I just do these things that bonded us, made us a team, so she'd feel a . . . connection? I had one. I had a *great* one. But time passed. Our antics escalated. And one day, I realized I *didn't* have my family connection anymore. We'd drifted apart. I'd gotten closer and closer to Nicole. By then, I was in too deep to climb out. I'd gone along with these plans that made me uncomfortable for so long that I'd gotten comfortable. Until the night of the robbery. It all just came into focus. I didn't want to be there. I wanted to go home. But the home I remembered wasn't there anymore. I'd ruined it. I'd lost the respect of my parents and I'd lost myself." She looks up at me. "I'm still trying to locate her again. But today . . . it went a long way. What Jordyn did. What you did, standing up for me to your family like that."

"Well." Ah, Jesus, I can barely speak around the rawness in my throat. "A wise woman once told me it's not my job to teach people to be happy."

She rubs her cheek against my shoulder. "Who?"

"*You*, Stella." I laugh, tipping her chin up with my finger. "You did. I've been bending over backward trying to make them happy for years. You were right. They don't want to be. Not right now. I wouldn't have loosened my grip on that responsibility if you didn't give me that to think about. All right? You're as responsible for what happened today as I am."

"That's a stretch," she whispers, visibly processing my words. Taking them to heart despite her obvious hesitation to do so. "But if you insist."

More than life itself, I want to pin her down on this couch, ruck her up skirt and make love to her in front of the Christmas tree, but my heart might as well be on the outside of my body right now, after the way she opened up to me. After the trust that took on her part. And if I get inside of her when I'm feeling like this, I'm worried I'll try to push our tenuous boundary even further and scare the bejesus out of her. It takes an enormous effort to tamp down my hunger for Stella. For *more*. More physical and emotional connection—all of it, everything she's got—but I force myself to have patience. "What I insist on . . ." I clear the growl from my voice. ". . . is making a popcorn garland and eating so much of the materials that we have to pop the whole box."

A smile blooms across her beautiful face. "You make it on the stove, don't you? Like an old-timey gentleman."

"Is there any other way?" I lunge to my feet without warning her, lifting her in my arms and drawing a squeak from her mouth. "Come on. Let's Stella-fy my Christmas tree."

* * *

Stella

I wake up in a mountain of bedding. Early morning light. Soft sheets that smell like peppermint.

Aiden. I'm at Aiden's apartment.

Sitting up in the bed, I glance to my right. The indent of his head is there on the pillow, but he's not asleep beside me. I remember him being there, sort of unconsciously. Holding me in his arms in the darkness. He snores. Why am I pressing my knuckles to my mouth and smiling over that little nugget of information?

Then the night comes back to me in a flood and I clap both hands over my face.

I fell asleep. Curled up at the foot of his one-of-a-kind Christmas tree, head in his warm lap, listening to stories about Aunt Edna, surrounded by foot after foot of popcorn on string. We'd been talking for hours. Favorites. Likes and dislikes. His honey company. Growing up in Tennessee versus Pennsylvania. How I sketched store window designs in Bedford Hills to pass the time. His favorite spy movies. We even speculated on the state of Jordyn and Seamus's romance, which Aiden has been pretending not to notice—as if I could like him any more than I already do. I've never been so relaxed in my life as I was last night. Not that I can remember. And I just kind of . . . drifted off.

But not before I asked Aiden about his perfect Christmas.

"What would be your perfect Christmas?"

He takes a moment to think about it and I use the opportunity to study the strong line of his jaw from below, growing drowsier by the second as his fingers thread through my hair, stroking it from the roots to the very—probably split—ends. "You promise not to laugh?"

"I promise," I sigh, half asleep.

So close to giving up the fight and letting oblivion claim me.

"Matching robes," he says, shaking his head at himself. "I think of having a family around the tree in matching robes."

"That's nice." I yawn. "I like that."

Waking up a minute ago is the next thing I remember. Did he carry me in here?

Undress me?

I'm already shaking my head. Not Aiden.

I don't even have to feel for my tights to know they're still on.

Wiggling my way out from under the mound of covers, I stand up and stretch my fingers toward the ceiling, frowning when my back and shoulders feel completely different. Relaxed. Free of knots I didn't realize I had. Have I been waking up sore every morning from sleeping on the old mattress in my own apartment? I might as well have slept on a cloud last night. There is some definite tenderness between my legs, but that ache has been there since our office sex adventure yesterday afternoon. The memory of that—and perhaps the fading feeling of Aiden's hard body against mine throughout the night—sinks a ticklish weight low in my belly.

I walk to the window and take a moment to marvel at the glow of orange and gray rising behind the buildings of midtown. Waking up like this is so far outside of what I consider ordinary that I might as well be flying through the rainforest on a zip line. Spokes poke upward from beneath my skin, trying to dissipate the warmth and safety cocooning me. There's a sense that I'm in the wrong place. I don't belong here in this luxury high-rise with a man who obviously has a lot of money. *You always did think you were better.* Ironically, it's that taunt, that sneer straight out of the past that makes me determined . . . to stay.

Makes me determined not to finger comb my hair, run out the door with a brief goodbye and return to my dark apartment that, truthfully, has always just felt like a holding cell between prison and real life.

I'm going to allow myself this morning with him.

I'll take on tomorrow when it gets here.

With a deep breath, I shed my clothes. Dress, underwear and tights. I trade them for one of Aiden's T-shirts, a white cotton one with a little bumble bee over the pocket above some script reading *Aiden and Hank's Honey Bank*. Breathing through the tug in my middle, I make a pit stop in the en suite bathroom to pee, wash my hands and finger brush my teeth. After making some kind of sense out of my hair, I follow the scent of coffee toward the kitchen.

Where I find a shirtless Aiden cracking eggs into a bowl, his hair wet from a shower.

Who knew so many muscles were required to flex to perform that domestic activity?

His back is wide up top. Thick with muscle, along with his upper arms. Smooth. There's a scattering of freckles down his spine that makes my mouth water even more than the coffee. From my vantage point, the breakfast bar is blocking him from the waist down, so I take several steps to the right until, dear sweet Jesus, his derriere comes into view in a seriously thin pair of pajama pants and heat coils up inside of me like a spring.

"Wow," I whisper.

Aiden does, indeed, have a bubble butt and that fact is so much more obvious without the advantage of dress pants and a jacket to hide it. Until meeting this man, I never fully understood the human fascination with butts, but I get it now. I'm a believer. At least in this particular set of taut, brawny buns. He should enter it into some kind of booty pageant.

A twinge of jealousy catches me off guard.

Oh great, now I'm jealous of the imaginary judging panel of a butt contest.

My life has taken a serious turn.

And when I walk into the kitchen and Aiden greets me with that gigantic heart in his eyes, I decide I don't hate the turn it has taken. Not one bit.

I'm deciding whether or not to kiss him good morning—is that too much too soon?—when he sucks in a breath and drops an egg on the floor. *Splat.* Yolk and egg whites everywhere. "Shoot. Sorry." He turns in a circle, eventually locating a roll of paper towels. "I just . . . you did something to your hair. Your bangs are pinned up."

My stupid heart is clunking like a car with cinder blocks for wheels. "Oh, um . . . yeah. They're messy in the morning, so I twisted them back."

He seems to have forgotten about the broken egg on the floor. "Your eyes look bigger. You look . . . oh boy. Wow." He comes toward me in a daze, stepping right in the egg, seemingly without realizing it. "Ahh, sweetheart. You're wearing my shirt, too."

Tingles run the entire length of my body when he just keeps coming, closer and closer until our mouths are locked. Peppermint and spicy deodorant envelop me, his full lips slanting over mine, those big hands settling on my hips, tugging me close, my head tipping back to maintain the kiss—a kiss that immediately grows desperate. Eager. We break apart to draw in shuddering lungfuls of air and dive back toward each other with a groan, tongues twining together, his fingers gathering the hem of my shirt, stripping it off and tossing it away.

His hands run over every inch of my naked body, memorizing every swell and valley, every spot that makes me whimper. And when they find my backside with a rough squeeze, jerking me up onto my toes, it occurs to me that *my* hands have carte blanche, as well, and I should definitely be taking advantage of that.

Head swimming with anticipation, I rake my palms down his heaving sides, traveling around to his hotly muscled back and down. Oh yes. *Down.* I plunge all ten of my digits into the waistband of the pajama pants and grab hold of that glorious bare butt—and oh my God, if possible, it's even better than I imagined. To the naked eye, his buns look hard as boulders, but not so. Not so. There is some definite give. Some extra flesh that makes it even hotter.

I moan into his mouth and knead him hard.

But my eyes pop open when Aiden breathes a laugh into our kiss. "You enjoying that, Stella?"

"Yes," I say honestly, trailing my middle finger down the split of his cheeks. On the way back up, I press a little deeper and Aiden's eyes darken, his Adam's apple bobbing up and down. Between us, his sex turns noticeably bigger. More erect. "Am . . . I *supposed* to be enjoying this?" I whisper.

"Believe it or not," he rasps, "I was just asking myself the same question."

What exactly we're doing isn't clear, I just know neither one of us has been here before and the shared unknown drops an anchor of lust in my stomach. I'm confident with Aiden, missing my usual self-consciousness. And it feels ten kinds of right to go down on my knees in front of him. To untie the drawstring beneath his navel and tug down the garment to midthigh, revealing his arousal to the morning light. Feeling his fingers sink into my hair and grip. I've never done this. I don't know what I'm doing. But the light being cast on Aiden somehow makes me braver, because it hides nothing. There are springy hairs and ruddiness and moisture pearling on the tip. Human. We're both human in the daylight. Two people who want to give each other satisfaction, and I will figure out how to do that for him because, right now, it's the only thing I want in life.

"Stella," he begins thickly. One second he's guiding my mouth toward his hard flesh, the next he's using my fisted hair to hold me away. "No. You can't. I'm . . . we didn't, ah . . . relieve each other last night. And that's totally okay, sweetheart. But I'm so sensitive now. You understand? I almost came when you walked into the kitchen with your bangs off your forehead."

If I didn't know Aiden, if I wasn't positive he doesn't play mind games, I would think he's using reverse psychology on me. Because him telling me his erection is extra sensitive is making a blow job nine times more appealing. "Just a little," I whisper, scooting forward on my knees, rolling my forehead side to side on his abdomen and wrapping both hands around his long, heavy manhood, reveling in his hissing intake of breath.

"God help me," he says through his teeth. "You're so fucking beautiful."

My heart skips and lands, going faster than before. There's a whisper of some important truth in the back of my mind, but I don't want to acknowledge that I'm in love with this man while I'm about to service him on my knees—at least not the first time—so I shoo it away for further examination later. This is about pleasure. His. Ours.

Not wanting to miss a single reaction, I look up at Aiden from below, bringing him to my mouth and pushing his salty abundance of flesh past my lips. Closing them tight around the pulsing trunk of him, sliding them up and down. When he's wet, it's easier to glide, so I'm able to take another inch of him on the next bob of my head—and now I add suction, my hands beginning to stroke the part of him I can't reach without choking.

Aiden slaps a hand down on the edge of the counter and curses. "Stella. Stella, *please*."

Is he asking me to stop or keep going? I don't even think he knows. But I'm enjoying myself too much to end this so soon. I have a front-row seat to watch his straining stomach muscles. And when I look up, I see him bite his bottom lip, eyes squeezed shut, his stifled moans filling the kitchen, and the combination is such a powerful turn-on that my mouth becomes hungrier, eager for his reactions.

"Felt so guilty thinking about this. For weeks," he slurs. "Especially this. Fucking your mouth. Hated myself for thinking of you kneeling. Licking it. Loving it. God help me."

His words incite a fervor. I can't stop thinking about how his eyes glazed over when I had my fingers *back there*. I want that again. *Again*. Before I can question myself, I leave my left hand to steady his erection and bring my right hand up between his splayed legs, palming his backside from below, massaging him with my palm, feeling the way his buttocks flex every time I tunnel him toward the back of my throat.

"Ohhh fuck. Stella. I'm going to come. Don't do this to me." Even as he begs me to quit, he's beginning to pump his hips. My God, it's the hottest contradiction. This man, the master of doing what's right and morally sound, is captive to his lust. He can't stop pushing his thickness into my mouth, over and over again, his groans getting louder. And he likes when I squeeze his ass, likes me touching the crevice between. I know because his pumps grow more desperate. "I'm serious." He's growling at me now. He's losing his grip on willpower, on control, and it's only serving to excite me more. Makes me want to watch it happen. "That sucking little mouth is about to blast me off."

I moan around his erection, my throat opening with the sound to bring him deeper, and I just want to touch, touch him everywhere, feel him all over. And with that goal in mind, I press my fingers between the cheeks of his backside, feeling for the puckered opening and I rub him there, my sex clenching when he lets out a shocked sound, beginning to pant.

"Stella . . . I . . ." The edge of the counter creaks in his grip. "Christ. Don't stop."

A shudder goes through his powerful thighs and there's a corresponding pulsation between my legs. Like I could have an orgasm just like this. From watching this man come apart for my mouth, my touch. He's so heavy and stiff in my mouth now, I know instinctively that he's not lying. He won't be able to last much longer. And I'm more than okay with that. I'm craving that moment he loses the fight. Because of me. The anticipation is making me bolder, braver, my middle finger pushing against his rear entrance until it allows me in—and then I take him as close to the back of my throat as I'm able.

Aiden's strangled roar is like a bomb going off in the apartment and I wait, muscles tense with expectation, to feel his liquid warmth in my mouth. I want it. I want that intimacy with him so terribly bad. But it never comes and suddenly, I'm being jerked to my feet. I'm gasping for air, gasping from the wild pull of lust in my belly being jostled—and I'm being turned by Aiden's strong grip toward the counter. I'm bent over face down, my cheek landing on the cool marble. Laboring to breathe, he takes a big handful of my backside, fondling it roughly, before his fingertips travel down. Around to my wet sex.

Without preamble, two fingers are thrust inside me.

"You like me coming in your sexy mouth, Stella, then we'll arrange it. Believe me. As often as you want." Tennessee flavors his tone more than usual. "But your first day as my girlfriend?" I look back over my shoulder to see him shaking his head, eyes glittering with need. "Nah. You're going to leave here with the memory of my cock between your thighs. You're going to spend the day missing it. Wanting to climb back on it as soon as nighttime hits." His fingers leave my flesh, moving in a tight drag through the valley of my bottom, stopping at my rear entrance and—using the wetness he gathered—he tucks his pinkie inside of me. "You like that, too, sweetheart?" I moan incoherently in response. "Yeah, you do. We're both a little dirty, aren't we?"

Behind me, I hear the tear of a condom wrapper. The sound of latex being applied.

Of course he's protecting me. Of course.

"I'm dirty just for you," I gasp, my fingers clawing at the marble counter.

I have no time to wonder if that admission was too revealing, because Aiden is pulling me upright again, spinning me around to face him. He captures my mouth with a low growl, hooks his elbow beneath my left knee, yanking it up to his hip—and slams his shaft home between my legs. My scream is unrecognizable, victorious. I don't know how to feel any other way with this full pressure stretching, seeking, *marauding* inside of me.

"Oh Jesus. Oh fuck yes, you hot-ass girl," he grunts. Pumping, pumping.

My backside is flattened against the cold edge of the counter, Aiden taking me hard, our gasping mouths attempting to kiss, to lick, to make any sort of contact, but what's happening below is too consuming. We're too primed for it. Wet, willing female. Hard, horny male. My face ends up buried in his neck, his hands boosting me higher until both feet are off the ground and he bucks into me wildly, slamming me repeatedly against the side of the counter.

His mouth finds my ear, laps at it. "You like getting rough dick, Stella?"

"Yes. *Yes.*"

"Did you think I'd be able to fuck you any other way after you let me stroke your throat?" he rasps into my neck. "So good to me on those knees."

His unfiltered words, the knowledge that this man is a coin with two very different, equally appealing sides, has me tightening up, my climax creeping in to twist muscles that were never used before yesterday. They know Aiden already, though. They choke up around his length and make him gasp my name, his hips sprinting into a wild pace. Now my right leg is being levered up by his hooked elbow, too, nearly bending me in half in our quest to get him deeper. Deeper. And yes, it's both of us. He's not just taking me, I'm heavily involved, opening my thighs for his pleasure and clawing at his shoulders, his hair.

It's the sound of our flesh smacking together, the digging of his fingers into my knees and that place, that incredible, elusive place inside of me that he *hits, hits, hits,* that causes me to seize up, my entire body shaking under the onslaught of pleasure.

"Aiden!"

"Got you. Got you so good, Stella." He grinds himself deep, his breath stuttering in my ear, his stomach hollowing against mine. "Ah shit, I'm coming, too. You're doing it to me with that hot squeeze. *Fuck!*"

Even in the midst of my orgasm, a storm of pressure and release taking place beneath my belly button, my jaw can't help but drop over the force of Aiden's finish. Being the focus of it is nothing short of magnificent. A rush like no other. He pins me to the counter and bellows my name into my shoulder, his huge frame shaking against mine, transferring his sweat to my skin, his grip bruising where he holds my legs up and open for his pleasure. I'm the focus of lust and the consumer of it at the same time. I'm both. I'm . . . part of a we.

That realization hits me hard on the heels of such a physical uproar and I find myself clinging to Aiden, arms and legs wrapped around him tight, it's anyone's guess if he can breathe. "Okay. We're doing this. Okay."

I don't realize I've said those words out loud until Aiden tightens his hold, cradling me against his still heaving chest and crossing to his bedroom. A moment later, he's lying down beside me in the mess of soft sheets, his arms banded around me like steel.

It's almost too much, too intimate, to be face-to-face with Aiden when my emotions are like leaves trapped in a gust of wind, but he holds my chin and doesn't let me look away. "You're right, Stella. We're doing this. *Our* way." He kisses my forehead. "There's no script. We get to decide what our way looks like. Okay? Help me figure out what that is."

Communicate.

I . . . can do that, right? I told him about Nicole last night. Shared things that I'm ashamed of and he still got up this morning to make me eggs. They ended up on the floor, but still. The thought was there. He kissed me, made love to me like he'd die without my touch. Our bond is real and it's not going to go anywhere. No matter what I say. That realization is so freeing, some extra space opens up in my lungs.

"I guess . . . I guess it's just taking a while for me to believe this is my life now. New York, the decorating job. You. It all happened so fast. It's this huge jump from who I was before Bedford Hills to who I am now. I don't know which one is the real me." Swallowing, I reach up and mold my palm to his stubbled jaw. "I just know I like this me a lot better. I like myself with you."

He must have been holding his breath, because it all sails out now in a peppermint rush against my forehead. "That's a damn good place to start," he says thickly, looking me hard in the eye until I nod. Then kissing my mouth, our lips opening wider, tongues eventually seeking friction until Aiden rolls me over onto my back with a groan, his weight pressing me down into the mattress. "We both feel real like this," he whispers, slowly giving me his shaft, inch by inch until he's buried deep and I'm gasping. "Everything about you, everything about us . . . is real." He rears back and pushes forward, his forehead dropping to mine. "Feel it, Stella."

His meaning isn't only physical, it's emotional, and I can't shy away from that. Not when he makes love to me again and I have nowhere to look but his eyes, reading the promises there. And coming close, so close, to making some of my own. There's something holding me back from diving in uninhibited to what Aiden is offering me that I can't quite name, but I bury the doubt in kisses and arches of my back until he stops looking too deeply and gives in to the bliss.

For now, we're . . . we're a we. We're real.

I'll take on tomorrow when it gets here.

Chapter 15
Aiden

I t's Christmas Eve. And while holiday music might be pumping through the speakers onto the main floor of Vivant, "I've Got You Under My Skin" by Frank Sinatra is the song I'm hearing in my head. The horn section goes for its big moment and I flash back to this morning, waking up next to Stella. Drinking coffee with our legs crisscrossed in the sheets, watching the sun come up over Manhattan. Coming out of the shower a while later and finding she'd made us breakfast. Toast and eggs and half a leftover donut. It was obvious she hadn't cooked in a while and was self-conscious about her efforts, so I ate it all without taking a single breath and the smile . . . I can't stop thinking about the bemused smile she gave me.

Now it's late afternoon and I'm collecting sales reports from each department. Normally this task wouldn't fall to me, but I let some of our managerial staff go early, despite the store being busier than I can ever remember seeing it.

On my way toward the back of the main floor, I have to weave through customers who are purchasing last-minute gifts for loved ones. They're harried and red-cheeked from the cold outside. Indecisive. Classic last-minute shoppers who were brought in off the street by our new eye-catching window displays. I'd bet anything on it.

Our social media following has quadrupled in the last week, according to Leland. We're getting tagged in pictures taken by passersby on the street. The new window, featuring makeup and skin-care items, has been a particular favorite, inspiring people to pose like the mannequin and call it the #VivantChallenge. I can't comprehend or predict that kind of thing, but I do know this: Stella's talent is the cause. The renewed interest in our store is not an accident. There's something special inside of her, she's sharing it with the public and they're responding.

Almost to the rear of the main floor now, I pass the jewelry case and an engagement ring twinkles up at me. Now, Lord knows it's way too soon for me to stop in my tracks and casually, very casually, lean down to look through the glass. But sue a man for dreaming.

And that's all I can do for now. Hell, Stella is still having a hard time committing to spending the *night* at my place. She has gone back and forth about it every night this week, right down until the last second when she finally lets me pull her into the backseat of my town car and buckle her seat belt. There are moments when I swear we're sharing a mind. That we're looking at our soul mate and both of us damn well knows it. But there are other moments when I can see her looking for the parachute tab, prepared to pull.

I pat the glass of the ring case twice and walk away. I'm getting way ahead of myself. Of course I am. Just because I know in my bones that she's mine doesn't necessarily mean I'm hers, does it? Like she told me, she's still finding her footing after the last four years. All I can do is be patient and support her . . . and hope that when she does get steadier on her feet, she still wants to stand beside me.

Massaging away the object in my throat, I take the elevator to the second floor, jolting a little when a dozen customers are waiting to board the elevator once I vacate. Younger clientele than we're used to browse the aisles. Sales associates don't have to pretend they're busy when they see me coming, because they are *actually* busy. "Silver Bells" plays over the loudspeaker, paper shopping bags crinkle . . . and there's a muffled sound of laughter coming from the dressing rooms. Glad the customers are enjoying themselves, I continue on my way—but I halt in the middle of the aisle when Stella's laugh reaches me.

What is she doing in the dressing room?

Granted, she's done working on holiday-themed windows for the year. This week has been spent sketching out ideas for spring designs and budgeting for materials. Historically, our window dressers have never had an office at Vivant, generally using the storeroom as their base and doing a lot of work from home. And I *know* it's special treatment, okay? But I had Seamus clear some boxes from the storeroom and bring in a desk, so she'd have a place to imagine what's next. Stella read me the riot act about favoritism, but hell if she didn't kiss me in the same breath, so I'm standing by the decision.

Even if I was just desperate to make her presence seem more . . . permanent.

Relax. She's not going to disappear.

Another round of female laughter kicks up from the dressing room and I reverse directions, walking backward a few steps. And that's when I see her. My Stella.

In a dress.

Not like one of her sweater ones.

Not at all.

It's emerald green. Shiny material—satin, I think. Tight on top where it hugs and plumps her tits, before coasting down over her hips. There's a high slit on the right thigh that makes my fingers twitch. Makes me ache to take two fistfuls of the dress's hem and slip it higher. The gold key chain necklace I gave her plunges down into her cleavage, visible for the first time while at work. I wonder if she's noticed. Normally it remains hidden during business hours. Is it too much to hope for that she's getting comfortable with everyone knowing she's seeing the boss?

Because everyone does know.

Monday was the first time I needed to be inside her during business hours, but it wasn't the last. People might not suspect that I've got her legs shaking around my waist in the filing cabinet room, but there's no way to deny we're spending our lunch hour together. Leaving together at the end of the day. And I don't want to deny what this is or hide. There is no reason to anymore, save Stella's hesitancy to be all in on our relationship. And I'm going to be patient about that. I am. I'll give her as long as she needs. But I can't pretend I don't love seeing my gift resting on her skin right out here in the open.

Jordyn hustles Stella onto a platform in front of the full-length mirror, hushing her protests. My girlfriend stills completely when she sees her reflection, her lips puffing open in surprise.

It's a wonder that my heart hasn't climbed out through my mouth and taken off running on little legs toward the dressing room. As the man who has been seeing Stella naked on a regular basis since Monday, I am not surprised that she looks so beautiful. Not a smidge. Whether she's moaning against the tile wall in my shower, drifting off to sleep to one of my Aunt Edna stories or staring out the window of my living room, brow wrinkled in thought, she's never not messing with my pulse. Clothed, unclothed, the damn thing is erratic twenty-four seven. At this point, I'm pretty sure I'd cause an EKG machine to start smoking, so no. I'm not shocked in the slightest that she looks like an angel in the dressing room mirror.

But damn, watching Stella notice her *own* beauty? Watching her turn a little and look over her shoulder to see things from the back? I feel like I'm being let into the place where she's afraid to let me go.

Our eyes meet in the mirror and just for a second, I am let in.

There's surprise at seeing me, but then . . . it fades to wonder. Like she's saying, "Can you believe this?" And I nod in response, because I can. I believe anything when it comes to her.

"Mr. Cook," Jordyn says, following Stella's line of vision and noticing me, where I stand spellbound in the middle of the women's fashion department. "We're the only ones in this fitting room. Come here and give us a male perspective."

A trio of older women walk by, glancing between me and Stella. Whispering to each other with knowing expressions. And I can't help but tug the side of my shirt collar anxiously. I'm standing out like a sore thumb in women's petites, aren't I?

But it looks like Stella is hesitating to buy the dress, even though she clearly loves it, so I swallow my qualms about approaching a customer dressing room and stride my way through the racks until I'm stopped just outside.

Ah Jesus, she looks even more incredible up close.

"Help me out, Mr. Cook." Jordyn sidles up to me, arms crossed. "Stella needs something to wear tonight to the Christmas party. Tell me this isn't the perfect dress. I'm wearing red sequins, so on top of making her extra stunning, she should offset me very nicely."

Stella's eyes catch mine in the mirror, her lips twitching. Mine do the same.

A couple sharing an inside joke.

I'm thinking about the diamond ring case again. God help me.

Jordyn elbows me in the side, surprising a chuckle out of me. We've gotten a lot more comfortable with each other since intervening on Stella's behalf on Monday. In fact, the morning after the showdown, damn near every Vivant employee said good morning to me on my way up to the tenth floor. On Wednesday, I was invited to happy hour, an invitation I would normally decline, not wanting to be the boss putting a damper on everyone's good time. But Stella was going to be there, so of course, I went. We sat next to each other without holding hands or touching and that might have felt unnatural, but what *didn't* feel unnatural? Just talking to folks. Stella encouraged me to tell a group of salespeople about Aunt Edna and they actually seemed to enjoy it. One of them even said he was excited to introduce me to his partner at the Christmas party. It seems I'm not as much of an outsider as before.

I've started working on putting less pressure on myself to make everyone happy at the cost of my own convictions. To appease my family so they'll treat me like one of their own. And I feel more like myself since letting go of that constant pressure. I can be positive. I can be a cornball until the cows come home. But I draw the line at pretending to be happy when something is wrong. I'm allowed to do that. I'm not letting anyone down by being less than upbeat. And I'm not sure I ever would have given myself that permission until her.

Until Stella.

"Do you like the dress?" I ask Stella now, sliding my hands into my pants pockets so I don't settle them on her hips instead.

She nods slowly, a smile spreading across her face. "I love it."

Take it.

I'll buy it for you in nine colors.

Knowing better, I swallow those words. Stella isn't uncomfortable taking gifts from me, thank God. But my gut tells me when she needs to achieve something by herself—and this is one of those times. "It's a great color on you," I say, my voice about ten octaves below normal.

My eyes find hers in the mirror.

We're not even going to make it to the bed later.

Her throat works with a swallow. "I'm going to put it on hold until my direct deposit hits." She leans down to check her phone where it rests on the dressing room bench. "Shouldn't be too much longer."

"Baby's first paycheck," Jordyn whoops. "It seems like such a hassle to hoof it back here before the party. Are you sure I can't put it on my credit card now? You can pay me back later."

"Positive," Stella says, turning away from the mirror to face us, her tits so touchable in satin that my hands ball into fists in my pockets. "Thanks for the offer, but it's really no hassle."

On her way down from the platform, the toe of her boot gets caught in the hem of the dress and she loses her balance. Her arms flail a little, trying to reestablish her center of gravity, but it's too late. She's already pitching forward. I lunge, ripping my hands out of my pockets, just in time to catch her as she falls.

"Jesus," I rasp, hauling her up against my chest. "That was a close one."

"Note to self: stick to knee length," she breathes, deflating, her cheek coming to a rest on my chest. "Nice save."

I will my heart to calm back down to its normal rate, whatever the heck normal is for my heart these days, and without thinking, I skim my palm down her hair. Her bare back.

God, I just want to be back in bed drinking coffee with her.

"Had a feeling your 'in a relationship' status was more than just a rumor," Jordyn says, bringing Stella's head up so fast, it bumps into my chin. "I guess me and Seamus have some competition for top spot as Vivant's reigning power couple."

"You and Seamus?" Stella asks—not pulling away from me. In fact, she straightens my pocket square and I forget what year it is. "When did that become official?"

"Any man who would send his boss's vehicle to the impound lot without setting down his broom deserves a shot." On her way out of the dressing room, she squints back at us over her shoulder. "You didn't hear that from me."

"Hear what?" Stella and I say at the same time.

Alone now, my girlfriend turns her smile up at me, as if that's going to help my heart slow down from a sprint. "Did Aunt Edna land yet?"

No way I'm taking my eyes off Stella to check the time. I estimate, instead. "She's got another twenty minutes or so till the wheels touch down."

"Are you still anxious about it?"

"She gets lost in Kroger's."

"Poor Aiden." She exhales. Goes up on her toes to kiss my chin. "You just want to be everyone's hero . . ." she murmurs, playing with the hair at the back of my neck. ". . . and you've got stubborn women coming out of your ears, don't you?"

Christ. My cock is thickening faster than whisked gravy over a high heat. "I'm not complaining." She's got her body pressed to mine, she's smiling—and I've got a great view of her ass in draped, emerald satin. Grievances are not on the agenda. And the sense that a new chapter has started between us is probably why I forget to be patient. "I'll complain a lot less if you walk into the party with me tonight."

The light in her eyes flickers.

Dread pitches in my stomach.

"I've just barely decided to *go* to the party, Aiden." She laughs haltingly, her arms dropping away from their position around my neck. She paces away in silence. "Please, just . . . try and understand that I went from occupying a tiny corner of space to having this . . . this giant world spread out in front of me. I have to inch forward, okay? At my own pace."

She's right. I keep forgetting how new every single experience is to her. Even the act of trying on a dress or getting a paycheck is unfamiliar. And I'm downstairs looking at rings like an idiot. I wish there was a way to make Stella believe in herself the way I do, but that kind of faith can't come from me. It's a process. A process I'm rushing.

And I'm probably going to push her away in the process.

That thought makes my spine feel like ice. I'm going to lose her if I don't slow the hell down—and I can't seem to remember to pace myself when she looks at me. My resolve just goes straight out the window and next time? Next time she could just walk. "Yeah, you've just blown me away so often, sometimes I forget you're inching forward," I manage past my numb lips. Why are my vocal cords aching? Probably because what I need to offer her, to keep her, is going to split me in half. "If you need more . . . space, Stella, I'll give you that."

The glow leaves her face. "What? I . . . no." She takes a step forward. "No, that's not what I meant—"

Her phone rings on the bench. A riotous series of notes.

That's not her usual ring tone. I've been with her when Jordyn called. I've called her phone to locate it when she lost it in my apartment. Normally it's just a light, repetitive chime. This is different. Judging by the way her face drops, it's not a welcome sound.

"What's wrong, Stella?" I reach out and cup her bare shoulder, brushing my thumb over the smoothness. "Who is that?"

She looks up at me, then away. Doesn't answer me.

Instead, she moves out of my reach, snatches up her ringing phone and closes herself in one of the changing rooms. It's a very scary thing, how fast everything has shifted in the space of one goddamn minute. I can't get my footing. Or think straight. But I'm pretty sure I just fucked up. Badly. I created a divide between us out of fear of that exact thing. What the hell is wrong with me? And now she's shut me out in a moment that I sense she could really use someone to talk to. "It's Nicole, isn't it? She's out."

"I think so. It's her old number," she whispers. "I'm afraid to answer."

"Let me in. We can do it together."

She laughs without humor—and I don't blame her. I just got finished offering to give her space when that is the last thing on this earth that I want. Jesus. Does she feel insecure with me now? "Look, Aiden . . . this is too complicated."

I watch the green silk pool on the floor of the dressing room. Her hand appears, picking it up, and the sound of a hanger clangs against the wall. I'm experiencing all of it in fast motion. Everything is getting away from me. Moving too fast for me to fix.

She opens the door of the changing room, dressed once again in the black turtleneck dress and tights she wore to work this morning. I watched her put them on over the rim of my coffee mug and now I think . . . are we breaking up? I just found her.

"Stella, slow down."

"*Now* you want to slow down," she says in a shaky burst, avoiding my eyes. Her movements are unnatural. Nervous. I'm realizing too late how serious this situation is with Nicole and somehow I've forfeited my right to help. She tries to go around me and I step into her path to block her without thinking. "I have to go. Let me go."

I can't. I'm in love with you.

It's the exact wrong time to tell her. To say those words out loud. So I keep them locked up tight even though they're fighting to get out. "I swear to God, Stella, if you're going to see her . . . and that puts you in some kind of danger, I'll go fucking ballistic." My vision starts to turn gray. "The thought of you hurt—"

"Stop." She closes her eyes momentarily. "Look, Aiden. You've been my hero since day one. We can pretend it's not true, but it is. I was trapped under all this . . . debris and you pulled me out. Gave me a place to heal. But if I'm going to stay here, if I'm going to feel like I earned this second chance, I have to be my own hero. Okay? And you need to have faith that I can do it. That I can do *anything*." She pauses. "Please? Because I don't even believe it right now."

"Of course I do," I rasp, heat searing the sides of my throat. "I believe in you every day of the week. Set your watch on it."

"Thank you." She hesitates on the threshold of the dressing room, then goes up on her toes and kisses me on the cheek. "Bye, Aiden."

My knees threaten to buckle.

Standing there while she walks away is the hardest thing I've ever had to do.

But I suspect wherever she's headed, she's about to face something even harder, so I suck it up and start praying like hell that she comes back to me.

Chapter 16
Stella

I'm outside your building.

When I didn't answer Nicole's phone call in the dressing room, that is the text she sent. She must have gotten the address from my parents. I don't know how else she would have known where I'm staying. Have my parents completely given up on me that they would send Nicole straight to my doorstep when they used to beg me to take a break from her? There's a possibility that Nicole tricked the address out of them, maybe by saying we had concrete plans to meet. That it was understood and I'd agreed to it. Or maybe Nicole told them that she's still in prison and just wanted to send me a letter.

However she found me, she's here now.

She's in New York.

After being away from Nicole for so long, the fact that she gives me a massive case of anxiety is a lot more obvious than it used to be when I saw her every day. Somehow this pulse-pounding, on-edge, twisted-stomach feeling became the norm. But it's not normal now. I don't want to feel like this. I don't want to be sweating under my clothes wondering what's going to happen. Or what she'll say to target my insecurities. Friends shouldn't do that. It's not okay and I know that now.

My legs are made of gelatin on the walk from the subway.

The shadows of evening are beginning to cast themselves on the sidewalk. The Christmas Eve buzz is alive on every block of the city, though the crowd is thin in my neighborhood, locals having traveled home for the holidays. Someone walks out of a coffee shop to my left and Nat King Cole's voice drifts out with them. Big red bells made of Styrofoam and tinsel hang from the streetlights, shifting in the cold wind.

Oh my God, I'm so cold.

Cold and hollow.

I miss Aiden, even though I only left him half an hour ago. I'm pretty sure I hurt him. Or pushed him away. Both. If that patient, understanding man is frustrated enough to suggest we add some space to our relationship, I have well and truly messed up. But I don't know how to make it any better. Not right in this moment. I can't just sever the past from the rest of me. It hangs from me like an errant limb. It's always there. *She's* always there.

I turn the corner at the end of my block and I see Nicole, huddled up against the side of the building, blowing warm air into her cupped palms. She must have gotten her hands on some bad hair dye in prison because her naturally light brown hair is almost orange, about two inches of her roots showing. She has it pulled up in a messy bun. Her jacket is thin, skin pale. She's cold with nowhere to go. Serious problems. Immediate ones that I didn't have to worry about—and that's when the guilt begins to prod me. Responsibility for her. Suddenly I'm walking with sandbags strapped to my shoulders and ankles whereas this morning, I woke up so light.

I woke up with him. Happy. Safe. In the light.

Now I'm leaving that light. I'm standing in the cold nighttime and honestly, this is so much more familiar than a high-rise with a view. But that familiarity makes the hair on my arms stand up straight, makes me shiver and pull my jacket tighter. There's a beep on my phone and I pull it out of my pocket to see the bank notification that my direct deposit is available.

In another timeline, I'm buying the green dress right now. I'm browsing for matching accessories and shoes. Nothing too expensive, even though a window dresser makes a healthy salary. I was looking forward to having four figures in my bank account for the first time in my life. Why does it feel like none of that is real or possible now? Why does it feel like I shed that new skin when I walked out of that dressing room?

Nicole's head turns sharply at my approach. Using the building for support as she comes to her feet, she smiles. And for a moment, she's just the girl I bought matching best friend bracelets with in seventh grade. The girl who whispered across the pillow to me during sleepovers about which sophomore boys we liked. Nostalgia spreads in my chest, warm like honey, and I walk into her arms. "Hey."

She embraces me, laughing and smacking me on the back. Once, twice, before squeezing. "Hey. I was starting to think you were going to let me freeze to death."

"Sorry. Come inside and warm up," I murmur, the warm honey already beginning to dilute. To water itself down. This apartment never really felt like home until this moment when I encounter a surge of protectiveness. This is where I landed. Where I chose to make a new start. I don't want to let go of that. I don't want to upset the delicate balance of work and life and personal connections I've created. All of it is still so fragile.

Releasing Nicole, I let us into the building. She follows me down the hallway, our boots heavy on the cracked linoleum. I unlock my apartment door and hold it open for her, trying not to let it show on my face how exposed I feel.

"Oh wow. This is pretty decent." She peels off her jacket, balling it up and holding it in front of her, instead of just setting it down. Sympathy prods me. I get that. I've only started leaving my things in various spots around the apartment this week, rather than corralled into one corner. One night at Aiden's place, he pointed out that I'd been placing all of my belongings in one spot by the front door, tucked beneath a console table. In that same breath, he picked up my messenger bag and plopped it in the middle of his dining room table. Then he carried my shoes into his bedroom and set them at the foot of the bed.

Longing sweeps into my chest with spokes attached, making it hard to catch a breath.

"Yeah, it's been a godsend, this place. I don't know what I would have done without it."

She eyes me as I remove my jacket, raising her eyebrows at the gold designer key chain around my neck. Normally I keep it underneath my clothes, but I dressed in a hurry earlier. Being discreet about my relationship with Aiden was the furthest thing from my mind. "Yeah, I don't know, Stella," she laughs, reaching out to finger the necklace. "Even if you didn't have this apartment, you would have figured out something, right? You've always been lucky like that." She takes her hand back, tucking it under her armpit. "A lot luckier than me, that's for sure."

A tire iron sinks in my middle. I can't remember when this started. When we went from children to adults who weighed their advantages. I just know that I came out on top and spent years and years trying to even the scales so we wouldn't lose this friendship. So she wouldn't feel lacking. So the differences between what we have or don't have wouldn't be noticeable and we could get back to that innocent place where we started. Where all that mattered was a five-dollar friendship bracelet and a couch on which to watch *America's Next Top Model* reruns. Somewhere along the line, I started to realize that wasn't possible, but by then I couldn't stop sacrificing what I wanted to keep us close.

And now. Because of all the advantages I tried to play off or ignore, I feel guilty for anything good that comes my way. The job at Vivant, this apartment. Even Aiden.

"Yeah, I am lucky," I say hoarsely. "You're right."

Me admitting that out loud surprises her, but she doesn't show it for long. "What have you been up to?" She paces to the window and looks out at the street. "Where are you working? Must be good money if you're buying gold necklaces."

I start to tell her about Vivant, but hesitate. Then I close my mouth altogether. If I thought I was protective of this apartment, it's nothing compared to the way I want to shield my beloved window boxes on Fifth Avenue. Jordyn and Seamus and the staff. Aiden. Oh my God, I would do anything to have my face pressed to his neck right now. Anything.

"You're not going to tell me? Where you're working is top-secret information?" Nicole laughs, growing visibly affronted by my silence. My withholding of information. "Wow, it must be a big fucking deal, Stella. You must be *super* important."

The years are stripping away and I'm nineteen again. I have something that's dear to me now—my new start. Back then it was my secret online courses. My parents. She doesn't even know where I'm working or what I'm doing yet and she's already stripped it down to trivial. Once upon a time, I would have laughed. I would have agreed that something I loved was insignificant so she wouldn't feel bad about not having found her passion yet. Or worse, not having the means to pursue it. But all I can do is stand here numb right now. The words won't come. My heart won't allow them.

"You don't even want me here, do you? It's obvious." She's rolling and rolling that jacket in her hands, the only giveaway that her tough-as-nails personality isn't quite as hard as she makes it seem. "You don't want me here interrupting your perfect life. All I've ever been to anyone is an interruption. I thought you were different, but I guess I was wrong. I guess this friendship isn't what I—"

"Stop."

She swallows, rocks back on her heels a little. That glittering in her eyes is vulnerability. I was too young to recognize it before, but I'm older now. And I see what drove me to protect Nicole and her feelings. I have the same drive now, but . . . the same solution won't work. Not for me and not for her.

"What?" she prompts me, chin firm.

What, indeed? I'm at a crossroads. I've been standing in the middle of it, not sure which path I'm supposed to be on. Being pulled in two directions. Past and present. Not sure if I was just pretending to be this new person. A woman with a career and a boyfriend and a paycheck. I can see now, though, as I'm looking at my best friend through an entirely new lens . . . that I *have* grown up. I'm different. There are things of value in my life that have nothing to do with advantages. I earned them by being me. I made friends. I fell in love with a man.

Oh wow.

Yeah, I love Aiden. The way-down-deep kind of love.

I can keep him. I can allow myself to accept the new good in my life. I will.

Can I do that without abandoning Nicole, though? Our friendship shaped me. Before it became toxic, it was important to me. She's someone I can't help but still love, too, no matter what has happened between us. Or the destruction our relationship caused. It's going to be a part of me forever, whether I like it or not.

"Nicole . . ." I twist my bangs back behind my ear, looking her in the eye. Dr. Skinner's words drift back to me through the distance, and for once, I don't struggle at all to recall them. They come out naturally. "You're my best friend. If you're going to be in my life, though, I need you to understand it's going to be separate from yours. I need you to understand that we're two different people with separate choices." Heat rushes in against the backs of my eyes. "I got my first paycheck today. And I'm proud of it. I'm proud of myself for starting over even though it was scary and I felt like a fake. Yes, I had help. I had *a lot* of help and you deserve the same. You always have." She looks away sharply, her lower lip trembling, and I take an unsteady breath, forcing out the rest. "You can stay here while we find you a place. While we get you a job. I'm *not* abandoning you. But I'm not abandoning myself for you, either. Stop feeling bad for yourself and putting it on me, Nicole. I'm not having that shit anymore, do you understand?"

Seconds pass that feel like hours.

There is a Christmas Eve party happening down the hall and the distant laughter and scent of burned poultry drifts between us, punctuating the silence. I'm holding my breath, adrenaline firing in my veins like tiny bullets, making me lightheaded. I can't believe I said that. I can't believe it, but I won't take it back, because I meant every word. I'm finally being truthful with her. With myself.

"Yeah," she says, blowing out a breath, her entire demeanor softened. Even relaxed. "I understand."

"Thank you," I respond, voice firm. I don't know where the bravery inside me is coming from. Maybe it's everything I've accomplished recently. Maybe it's newfound confidence. Or perhaps I'm in love with an optimist and he's rubbed off on me. I don't know, but I close the distance between me and Nicole, taking her by the shoulders. "You are strong. You can do this. You can be someone you're proud of. Tomorrow can be a great day."

She bursts into a tearful laugh. "God. When did you get so fucking corny?"

My answering laugh is real, genuine, and it comes easy. So easy. "Corny is underrated."

We back away, swiping at our eyes. With this lightness in my chest, I could float away. I've been walking around with a pile of bricks trapped in my body. They're gone now and there is only one person I want to share this weightlessness with. He'd already taken away some of those bricks, but I had to shed the rest of them myself. I wasn't able to give myself completely to my relationship with Aiden before, but I am now. And there's *nothing* I want more. I belong with him and he belongs with me. There's not a single doubt in my head any longer.

Please, please, don't let my fears have ruined everything.

"I have somewhere I need to be," I murmur.

Her immediate impulse is to complain about that, but she pulls back. Nods. "Sure."

I turn and find my jacket, zipping it back on. "There is food in the fridge." I wait for eye contact. "You can put your jacket down wherever you want."

A lump travels upward in her throat. "Thanks, Stella."

"You'll hear from me tomorrow."

I smile at her on my way out the door—and then I'm running. There is something I need to do before I go to the Vivant Christmas party. But it's no longer purchasing the green dress and the appropriate accessories. No, it's something else entirely.

*   *   *

Aiden

I'm standing in the middle of three hundred people, the din of conversation carrying above the straining strings of the band, which is in the middle of a Sinatra classic. The ballroom of the High Line Hotel has been decorated to the nines with white-and-blue lighting, frosted hurricane lamps flickering with candles on dozens of intricately decorated tables right down to the sprig of holly in every napkin holder. There is laughter and champagne and even the stodgiest member of the managerial staff is cutting loose on the dance floor, alongside my aunt Edna.

I'm watching it all through a periscope, my head and my heart a million miles from here.

Or wherever Stella happens to be at the moment. The fact that I don't even know where the hell that might be is a constant raking of knives through my gut.

Being in this tuxedo is wrong. Leland's peach habanero salsa, which I choked down earlier out of tradition, rather than hunger, is running laps around my belly. How is everyone carrying on with life as usual when the girl I love has left to find the friend who helped land her in prison?

The only thing—and I mean the *only* thing—that is keeping me right here, rooted to this spot where the bourbon is easy to reach, is my absolute faith in her. Whatever she's facing right now and with whom, she's going to do the right thing. She's going to do the *safe* thing. And even if she doesn't come to the party, which is more than halfway over at this point, I have to believe she'll continue to work at Vivant. She won't take herself away from me completely, will she? No matter how badly I've fucked this up, I'll have a chance to win her back.

I have to believe that.

I *do* believe that, because I believe in Stella. This thing between us can't just melt away and cease to exist like one of the ice sculptures sitting on the buffet table.

God, my chest hurts. I need to go sit down. Or bribe someone to knock me out. Maybe that would be better. I could stop replaying the way Stella's eyes filled with tears when I asked if she wanted some space.

You are a complete and total moron.

My aunt Edna materializes in front of me in a Santa hat that she didn't arrive wearing. "A watched kettle never boils, Aiden. Quit staring at the door."

My smile drops as soon as I attempt it. "Do you need another drink?"

She slaps me on the shoulder. "What kind of question is that? Of course I do."

Taking her empty glass and setting it on the bar, I signal the man filling drink orders. When he sees Edna, he doesn't even need me to tell him what she's drinking. He's been making extra-dirty martinis for her since six o'clock. "Are you having a good time?"

"Oh no. Don't you dare make small talk with me." She pokes me in the side. "You're standing over here looking like you're in the middle of a colonic."

"Compared to this? I'd prefer it."

Aunt Edna snorts. "You've obviously never had one."

"No," I sigh, staring into the depths of my bourbon, the ice cubes forming the shape of Stella's profile. "Maybe I'll schedule one. Sounds like sufficient punishment."

"For what?" She harrumphs. "You're not the type to mess anything up so badly that you need a tube up the—"

"Hello," Jordyn says smoothly, coming up beside Edna, her hand tucked inside Seamus's. He's holding a pint of beer in the opposite hand and he salutes me with it. I nod back, the movement making my head hammer all the more. "You've got the party buzzing, Aunt Edna," Jordyn continues, smiling. "I love a woman who knows how to lead a conga line."

Edna sips from her fresh martini. "What can I say? It's a calling."

With a laugh, Jordyn looks over at me. I think. I'm back to staring at the door. "Why don't you come out on the floor and try to dance, Aiden?" she suggests, tugging my elbow. "Good God, man. It's Christmas Eve, not Tax Day."

To my surprise, another one of the sales associates appears behind her. "Yeah, come on, Mr. Cook," he says, quickly joined by two other half-drunk employees. "Loosen the bow tie. We're about to teach your aunt how to Renegade."

"How to what?"

Jordyn continues to pull me toward the dance floor and with so many people on her side, I have no choice but to follow. Someone takes my jacket and the music changes, going from Sinatra to hip hop and everyone cheers. With a hard object lodged in my throat, I have no choice but to stand in the middle of the dance floor and nod along as someone from accounting tries to teach me dance moves that seem so easy in theory but are actually very complex when I try to execute them. Maybe because my arms currently weigh a thousand pounds each.

With what little of my brain is functioning, I notice employees smiling at me. They like me, they're addressing me by name. I've always been friendly with the employees in my immediate office, but now my network extends beyond that. To the electronics department whiz kid. To our children's footwear buyer. I didn't have those connections a few weeks ago. Before Stella. She's opened up the world around me and I just need her back in it.

I'm not sure what causes me to stop attempting the Renegade and glance up.

Maybe it's the increased thudding of my heart. That internal metal detector that beeps whenever Stella is nearby. X marks the spot. But I look up and there she is at the edge of the dance floor. She's smiling at me with tears in her eyes, so beautiful I have to suck in a breath.

And she's wearing a robe.

A red-and-black-plaid robe that goes all the way down to her toes.

There's a matching one draped over her arm.

Before I register the movement of my feet, I'm weaving through people on the dance floor, love and relief cutting through me like a buzz saw. *She's okay. She's okay. She's here and she's okay. Thank God.* My brain tells me to stop when I'm close and ask how she's doing, where she's been, if she's sad or happy or both. But I just keep right on walking, plowing into her with a bear hug big enough to set her off laughing—and it's the best sound I've ever heard in my entire life.

"I don't want space," I growl without preamble.

"Me either," she whispers unevenly. "I don't want it or need it."

Another current of relief flows through me. "Thank God," I rasp into her neck. Her sweet, perfect neck. "Is that robe for me?"

"Of course it is." She lets me pick her up off the floor and squeeze her tighter, as if I have any choice when she's just shown up with matching robes. "I wasn't free to wear one with you. Not yet. I had to fix something first, okay? But I'm here now." Her arms wrap more securely around my neck. "I'm one hundred percent here and I love you."

God help me, my heart starts slamming up, down and sideways with such a vengeance, I almost lose my balance. The declaration is unexpected. It's also the best gift I've ever received. The only one I'll ever need. "I love you, too, Stella." I kiss her forehead, her cheeks, her nose, everywhere I can reach until she gives me that incredible laugh again. "You're home now." But that's not quite right, so I amend it. "*We're* home now."

I'm forced to set her down so I can wipe the tears off her face. I perform the task with a sweep of my thumbs. Then, without taking my eyes off her for a single second, I bend down and pick up the robe that had fallen while I hugged her half to death. I put it on, belt it, take her by the hand. We smile at each other on my way to introduce her to Aunt Edna.

It's our first best Christmas together. First of many over the decades.

And with her, each one is better than the last.

Epilogue
Stella

One Year Later

Fingers digging into the edge of my passenger seat, I turn to study Aiden's profile. "I'm no longer sure this is a good idea."

He takes one look at my face, frowns with concern and pulls our rental Jeep over to the side of the road, cutting off the engine. Without the wipers to clear the falling snow, white stuff immediately starts to block our view of the road. A familiar road. The one leading to my parents' house.

Aiden reaches over, brushing a hand down the back of my hair. "It's normal to be nervous, Stella. But everything is going to be fine." He dips his head until he makes eye contact, giving me a lopsided smile. "Miracles happen on Christmas, don't they? And really, we only need a quarter of a miracle here. We're just opening the door with your parents. There's no pressure on any of you to walk through it on the first try."

Borrowing some calm from my steadfast boyfriend of one year, I take a deep breath and nod. I look out at the curving road, remembering the last time I was on it. My father had just picked me up outside of Bedford Hills and the air was tense. Temporary.

He was bringing me home long enough to turn me around and send me in another direction. I understood. And not wanting to deal with their anger and disappointment, I'd remained silent. Distant. Closed off in my old room until it was time to go.

Has that lonely, directionless girl changed so much in a year?

Yeah.

I have.

Last Christmas Eve was the start of Stella Schmidt giving her whole self to life and love. I stayed with Aiden while helping Nicole find employment at a catering company. She lived in my uncle's place for about two months before he broke up with his current girlfriend and decided to return, so we found Nicole a room to rent in a three-bedroom apartment in Astoria. She shares it with two other girls our age and they've become good friends. We still meet for dinner once a month and talk on the phone, but we're individuals. She has her own life now and I have mine. Our relationship is a lot healthier and stronger because of it.

As far as my living situation . . . once I moved in with Aiden so Nicole could make use of my uncle's apartment, I sort of never left.

He made it way too difficult.

For one, he redecorated little by little. *Stella touches*, he called them. He kept the throwback *Mad Men* vibe of his apartment, but it slowly became a bachelor *and* bachelorette pad. His coffee table was replaced by an ornate vintage trunk. He had an accent wall painted a black metallic color. He brought home the retro dress cage from my first Vivant window and positioned it in the corner of our bedroom . . . and that's when I realized I'd started calling it our bedroom. Our apartment. He'd bamboozled me. Redecorated without actually mentioning he was making any changes. But one day I looked around and realized what he'd done.

"What are you thinking about?" Aiden asks me now, the pad of his thumb coasting across my bottom lip.

"I'm thinking about home." I turn my head and kiss his wrist. "Our home in New York."

His eyes go soft, searching, the way they do when he's feeling romantic. So pretty much constantly. "What about it, sweetheart?"

I narrow my eyes at him, but I'm smiling. "How you Stella-fied it."

The muscles shift in his throat. "Once I got you, I couldn't let you leave."

My heart starts to chug. "I was never going to leave."

We reach for the collar of each other's winter coat at the same time, pulling eagerly, our mouths locking over the center console. I can taste the hot chocolate we drank before entering Pennsylvania on his tongue, as if he needs any additional help being delicious. His big fingers spear into my hair and I unhook my seat belt with trembling fingers, no idea what I'm intending, only knowing I need to get closer to him. Always closer.

"There was a motel a mile back—"

"I saw it," he growls. We dive back into the kiss, my upper half leaning over the console now, his left hand leaving my hair to tease my nipples into points through my sweater, pinching them lightly and tugging. "*God*, Stella . . . I need you."

Here's the thing. Christmas season at Vivant was extra-spectacularly busy this year. We worked without cease from Thanksgiving through Christmas Eve—which was yesterday—

and had very little *couple time* in the home stretch. Last night was the annual staff party, we passed out on the couch afterward. Then this morning we had to wake up bright and early to drive to Pennsylvania to my parents' house for brunch.

To put it mildly, we're hornier than jackrabbits.

I'm strongly considering climbing onto his lap on this public road to get some relief.

Breaking the kiss, I raise an eyebrow at him. "Should we . . ."

Simultaneously, we glance at the dashboard clock. Eleven forty-nine.

"We told them we'd be there at noon," Aiden groans, his head falling back against the driver's seat. "And we've got another ten minutes to drive."

With a whiny sound I'm not proud of, I drop back into my seat and reconnect the seat belt. "Motel on the way back?"

"We might need to keep the room for a few days." Bravely, Aiden squares his shoulders and starts the car engine again. "I guess we should be happy the store broke sales records this year. Your windows, Stella . . ." A breath puffs out of him as he pulls back onto the road. "You outdid yourself and I didn't think that was possible after the summer designs."

Spinning pastel pinwheels and glowing Chinese lanterns dance through my mind, but when I see the turnoff for my childhood street up ahead, the rush of good memories ends abruptly and my belly flops over. "Aiden, I'm really not sure about this."

He reaches over and takes my hand, bringing it to his mouth. "I am." He kisses my knuckles, brushing his lips sideways over my diamond engagement ring. "I'm damn sure. You've spent the last year learning how to be proud of yourself, Stella. Now they get a turn. They get to see who you've been all along. The woman I'd crawl across the Sahara to marry in March." He squeezes my hand, saying in a softer tone, "We want them there when you walk down the aisle. Let's start working toward that now, okay?"

"Yes," I say on an exhale, giving Aiden a grateful look. "It's going to be a good day."

"It's going to be a good day," he repeats back to me with a lopsided grin.

I reach over to adjust his *How the Grinch Stole Christmas* bow tie, then climb out of the car, my boots crunching down on the snowy driveway. I belt my winter coat tighter, checking to make sure none of my grown-out bangs have escaped their pins. Aiden takes my hand and we walk to the front door together.

Before we reach the porch, the entrance swings open and my parents stand there, framed in artificial green garland, watching our approach dubiously.

My steps slow and I have the urge to run back to the car.

Aiden's grip tightens on my hand and he pulls me forward. "Merry Christmas, Dale and Kendra, it's a real honor to be here. We meant to arrive a little earlier, but we stopped for hot chocolate. Can't get enough of the stuff this time of year, can you? My aunt Edna used to break up a salted pretzel on top of her whipped cream. Just like that. I'll be polite and not mention the spiced rum she threw in there, too. Accidentally drank from her cup when I was eleven and spent Christmas passed out under the tree in footy pajamas. If you ask me, that's how it *should* be spent, rum drunk or not. How's brunch coming along? Need any help in there?"

I'm staring at my fiancé in disbelief.

Not because I didn't expect him to open with an Aunt Edna story.

No, that's pretty much a given.

I'm in disbelief at myself. For not believing this would be okay. In under a minute, Aiden has not only broken the tension, he's shattered it like it never existed. My stomach knots are untying themselves and . . . I'm even exchanging a bemused smile with my mother.

"Hi," I breathe into the cold Christmas morning air. "Yes, he's always like this. Isn't it wonderful?" I give Aiden a grateful look, squeeze his hand once and let it go, climbing the familiar steps and stopping in front of my parents. "Merry—"

They throw their arms around me at the same time.

I make a choked sound, reeling in shock for several beats before returning their embrace, a warmth I didn't realize I was missing spilling back into my limbs. Over their shoulders, I can see into the house. Framed on their entry table is a picture of my first Vivant window. My second one is right behind it at an angle. Same frame on each one.

I recognize the hammered bronze design from the housewares department at Vivant.

Aiden has been sending them pictures of my windows.

"Come on," my mother says, dusting some snow off the shoulder of my jacket, my father discreetly drying his eyes before stepping past me to shake Aiden's hand. "Brunch is almost ready."

On the way into the house, I look back at Aiden over my shoulder.

Snow falls around him, this man who can be both my hero and stand back and let me be my own. This one-of-a-kind man I can't wait to marry in the spring.

I pack every ounce of love for him into a smile. "I matching robes love you."

"I matching robes love you back," he rasps, emotion weighing down every word. Then he climbs the stairs, wraps an arm around the small of my back and walks side by side with me into the house.

Acknowledgments

In case you can't tell, this hero was inspired by the relentless optimism of the one and only Ted Lasso, a character that got us all through a collectively difficult time. I was in the middle of writing a book about a brooding piano prodigy when I was met with the magic of Ted and I immediately threw out that work in progress, wanting to write someone who was authentically kind and inspires strangers to become a supportive family, even while being beautifully flawed like the rest of us. Thank you to all the readers who have already read this story and everyone yet to develop a bow tie fetish. I'm right there with you.

About the Author

#1 *New York Times* bestselling author **TESSA BAILEY** can solve all problems except for her own, so she focuses those efforts on stubborn, fictional blue-collar men and loyal, lovable heroines. She lives on Long Island, avoiding the sun and social interactions, then wonders why no one has called. Dubbed the "Michelangelo of dirty talk" by *Entertainment Weekly*, Tessa writes with spice, spirit, swoon, and a guaranteed happily ever after.

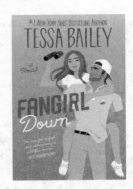